Sandra Dosdall is a proud mother of three, a dedicated wife and an established business figure. Producing a published work has always been an aspiration and she is elated to be on this path. Mentored by some of the best literary minds, Sandra invites you to join her on *Her* dramatic journey.

HER

Sandra Dosdall

HER

Vanguard Press

A CIP catalogue record for this title is
available from the British Library.

ISBN 978 178 465 211 1

Vanguard Press is an imprint of
Pegasus Elliot MacKenzie Publishers Ltd.
www.pegasuspublishers.com

First Published in 2017

Vanguard Press
Sheraton House Castle Park
Cambridge England

Printed & Bound in Great Britain

For the three of whom
I wake each morning,
tiny fingers of each hand
of which I have held,
who have captivated my mind,
and entrenched me in love,
for the only three people
who have ever shared
in my heart beat;
to each of you;
I dedicate my work.

ACKNOWLEDGMENTS

As a new Author, I feel an immense sense of pride in my work, and an enormous feeling of gratitude to many who have supported and inspired me. The journey has not been one that happened overnight, this wasn't a book that was written in a day or even a month. I always knew that I was meant to craft books, stories have continually unravelled in my mind for as long as I can remember. It wasn't until now that this path was meant to be. For everything has a perfect time, and now is the time for *Her*.

Father Alfredo Pereira, for your immense knowledge, your guidance, your direction, your prayers and support, I thank you. You are a true leader of men. Your appointment is divine, your smile and your dialogue genuine, I am honoured to be able to call you my friend.

James Patterson, my Professor and a *pretty good author*, I could not have achieved this without your input and fine tuning of the trade. Your teachings resonated with me from the very first day, I understood, I was inspired, I was excited, and learned. For that I am grateful, sir.

Suzanne Mulvey, my Editor at Pegasus Elliot Mackenzie Publishers, for finding the same passion in my work that I have, and seeing the potential in *Her*, merci.

Chad Loch, my dear friend, I adore you. For sharing your

passion, for supporting mine, I love you. Richelle Mead said, "Only a true best friend can protect you from your immortal enemies." Where and when we have been is a mystery, where we shall go is to be determined.

Lisa Heid, Candice Cain, Suzana Dimitrijevic-Dawe, Sabrina Rhodes, my girls, I trust you know why you are here. I love you all, to the end of time my heart is grateful for your support, generosity and the love you have given to me.

My Mom, a friend, a supporter, a confidant. You have always been my greatest fan. I hope that I can make you proud. I love you.

My husband, Cory, our path has been windy, often riddled with steep uphill grades. We have at times walked dead straight into the wind, with sleet pounding in our faces. But the climb has been done together, holding each other. Together we are stronger. And a pair of Aces plays better than a single. I love you more every day. Forever we are one.

For my maker, my God, I am grateful for each day that I get. Thank you.

Prologue

Her thoughts often drifted to Her birth, the difficulty, the strain and the delays. The pure anguish of waiting, wondering if She would survive this leg of Her journey. In the minutes after She was born, She lay in the bassinet brown eyes open, alert and making eye contact with the nurses, the doctors and Her loved ones. She knew their voices, She recognized those who had spoken to Her while She was in the womb, of that there was no question. She lay naked and watched people move around Her, Her tiny head turning from side to side, Her eyes following each person as it became busier in the room. Her hands reached up towards Her face and She placed her fingers into her mouth, Her tiny nails catching on Her lip. She surprised Herself with their sharp edges.

She listened as those who had come spoke in wonder and awe. About Her remarkable arrival, and the fact that Her eyes were the deepest chocolate brown, not blue as most babies' eyes were. She didn't see the point in selecting blue for an eye colour.

The iris is the coloured part of the eye that controls the amount of light that is allowed to enter. Melanin, the brown pigment molecule that colours your skin, hair, and eyes, isn't fully deposited in the irises of your eyes in the womb, and hasn't yet been darkened by exposure to ultraviolet light. Irises containing a large amount of melanin appear black or brown. Less melanin produces green, gray, or light brown eyes. If the eyes contain very small amounts of melanin, they will appear blue or light gray. Melanin production generally increases during the first year of a baby's life, leading to a deepening of eye colour. As She was in control of certain things, She decided just to come back into this world with brown eyes this time. It saved time and it saved hassle for Her. Brown eyes were less sensitive to light than a blue would be. And they provoked shock in some people, a reaction that never bored her.

She saw the lady who was with Her on many landings, the one with the kind voice. She heard her voice quite regularly, it was soothing, smooth like soft water pouring over your soul. She was quite pleasant-looking, beautiful smile and her eyes were green, She was pleased to see that the lady had come for Her arrival. But She was curious about her choice of eye colour, she made a mental note to remember to ask her about it at another time.

She had known that some of them would come today, She just hadn't been certain who.

This journey to here had been difficult, but She had welcomed it. She was glad to have returned and was excited at the prospects that this landing promised. Her plan was clearly determined, laid out carefully, and concisely. She recognized some of the individuals that She saw in Her first moments. She knew by feeling that She had memories with them. It would be some time, however, before She knew the extent and breadth of that history. She would need to wait for the great reveal. As everyone does, they wait, or dread, their finale.

CHAPTER 1

On Monday she climbed the wall, clinging to the shelving hung by my father. Her little fingers grasping each floating shelf as she looked over her shoulder at the floor below Her. Her red hair matting from sweat, she moved higher along the wall. Like a mountain climber, She pulled herself with Her upper body, using her little fingers to grip the shelves as tight as she could. She looked back at the low dresser that had been her starting point, the drawers had acted as a step ladder, the bottom one pulled out the farthest, staggered to the top, that had been the easiest part of this journey. Each shelf introduced new and different obstacles and obstructions, this next shelf was covered with reading materials. She pushed the books out of her way and watched them as they fell to the floor below. Crashing one on top of the other, sliding and smashing as they hit the ground, making her potential landing pad treacherous. She quietly hoped that she wouldn't need to rely on the floor below to break her fall.

Her toes now grabbing the lower shelves she hoisted herself higher until she could almost reach the top shelf and then grab hold of the object of her desire. The coveted Birthday Train Set. The one that she was not permitted to play with, the one that "Her mother" had placed up so high. Where it was safe from harm. Where it would last forever. It was unclear to Her at this time why someone would gift a gift that could not be touched or enjoyed. Why someone would gift a gift that could torment and agonize Her with crazy clown smirks, twisted smiles, their big lips and funky hair. They tortured Her, the Clowns teased Her and chattered at Her, and hollered and screeched at Her and made all that racket while She was trying to sleep. Stupid noisy train, She thought, She was pleased with Herself. Pleased that Her plan had worked and She had been able to climb the full height of the wall, and pleased that She had reached her goal.

She caught sight of the backyard through Her window. The light filtered through the blinds in such a way, that it looked like a rainbow shone on the wall opposite. She was surprised at how large the garden appeared from this angle. How large the trees looked, and how many leaves were on the trees. She saw Her swing set, and thought about playing outside later. She wondered if Her brother would like to play in the sandbox. She enjoyed the sandbox immensely. Mushing and gushing the sand in Her fingers, and between Her toes, filling Her bucket and creating piles and cones of sand, gave Her great pleasure. It felt cool and it calmed Her, it was a peaceful play place. She liked it very much.

She leaned forward and grabbed hold of the upper most shelf, She was relieved that it held her weight. Then She grabbed the head of the train set, the Clown Engine in Her left hand and with one over hand sweeping motion, threw it into the corner. The sound of the porcelain smashing startled Her. It was louder than She had anticipated; the sound was shriller, sharper and more exciting. The delight of smashing something, released in Her an adrenaline rush that She had never yet experienced. She peed her pants. She could feel the warmth of urine running down Her leg, She didn't care.

She could hear Her mother running up the stairs, moving towards the doorway of the bedroom. She looked out again towards the sandbox and wondered if that would be the consequence. Perhaps her love of sand would be taken away for a period of time. She might be forced to watch as Her brother enjoyed playing and She would not be allowed to join him, maybe she would just have to sit and watch as he built sand castles and roadways within the box. She hated exclusion. Despised the idea of being left out or omitted from the group. Banishment should be banished, when she could, She would bring that up.

She knew that there was going to be consequences for these actions. These actions were a direct violation of the rules. She was aware that Her mother was going to be very upset. She quickly grabbed the second piece of the train and threw it into the pile of rubble with the first smashed piece. She had gone this far, there was no point in turning back now, the punishment would likely be the same regardless of the size of the disaster. The satisfaction that came from smashing them was fulfilling. Quickly she grabbed the third and threw it, and the fourth and the fifth and just as She heard Her mother hit the landing of the stairs, she threw the caboose. She grinned at Her accomplishment. Her urine-soaked panties felt cold. Her sweat-matted hair was sticking to Her neck and forehead. She couldn't suppress the happiness, She grinned enormously. She felt ready to face her maker.

The door of Her bedroom flew open. Her mother's face was ashen. She had heard the crashing sounds from below, the smashing of porcelain. She saw her toddler near the ceiling on the wall, in nothing but pink lacey panties and T-shirt that said "Princess' Rule", Her red hair soaked with sweat. Her bottom wet with urine.

Her toes wrapped around the edges of the shelving in the way a monkey would use its fingers, holding onto the floating shelving apparatus for dear life. Below her a pile of books, and rubble impeded a safe landing. Her left hand was free, and held above Her head as if in triumph. The hand that had just released the last piece of the train to the pile of rubble was now held in a fist, as if victorious.

"No more, Mommy. No train."

"Oh, my God, how did you get up there? What have you done?" Concern, not anger, controlled the voice and movements of Her mother. She moved towards her child and reached for Her. She grasped Her under the arms and lowered Her from the wall. Her own feet unsteady on the floor below her. Books were piled high, stuffed animals and dolls lay strewn across the floor.

"No Train. No clown. No clowns. No. No more Train, Mommy." She began to sob at that moment.

"Okay, shhshh, come here, sweetheart. Shhh," she reached for her child and pulled her from the wall. She held her tight, stroking her hair. Kissing her rosy cheeks. She sat herself and her child into the chair in the corner, pulled a blanket from the back of the chair and wrapped her youngster in it. She held her tight.

"That is quite a mess that you have made. I wonder how long it's going to take us to clean up?" She looked down at her little girl. "What provoked you to destroy something that was a beautiful gift from your grandmother? Why would you want to break it?"

"No train. No clown, Mommy." She shook her head.

"Okay, well, you could have seriously hurt yourself. Where did you get the idea to climb like that?" She looked at the dresser, and the shelves on the wall that she had used to climb her way to the top where the train had been on display. She held her tiny foot in her hand and looked at her toes, and then at her hands. Holding each finger.

This youngster at only eighteen months of age, was not only vocally and verbally advanced for her age, but physically and intellectually as well. She had been potty-trained by fourteen months, completely. Diapers were not a necessity, not even for use at night. She began talking at nine months and was now making three and four-word sentences. She didn't bother with crawling, not because She wasn't capable, but because it wasn't fast enough. She was carried, and then She got up and walked. And once She walked, She wanted to do it all the time. As soon as Her feet figured it out, She was running, running to the table for meals, running to the bathroom when She had to go, running to the park, running in the yard. She wasn't particularly fast, but She was solid, steady and consistently running. She ran to the swing set and to the sandbox to play.

She marvelled at the amount of strength and courage that her daughter had managed today. The climb would not have been easy for any child, not even a five-year-old, let alone one of less than two years old. The planning that had been involved to accomplish this, and the sheer determination to carry out this destruction, the will of her... but whatever for?

They cleaned up the mess together, she got a garbage bag for the pieces of debris, together they picked them up and placed all of them into the bag. She watched Her, as her little hands carefully picked up pieces, a smile across Her face the entire time, no look of remorse, not a trace of shame.

"Are you ready to talk about why you did this?" She looked into the smiling face of her daughter, who continued to clean. Picking up the tiny pieces, placing them into the black plastic garbage bag one by one. Her face seemed relaxed, She seemed peaceful, and quiet. She continued to work, but looked up at

Her mother.

"No clowns, Mommy."

"Yep, I get that part, apparently, you are not a fan of clowns, however, you still destroyed something that a loved one bought for you as a gift. I would like to understand why you would choose to break all of this into a gazillion little pieces."

"No clowns. I don't like it, not the clowns."

"So, we don't like clowns, I've never really been a huge fan myself. Some of them are a wee bit terrifying. Were you scared of the clowns? Did they frighten you?" She thought of how many children are actually scared of them, and reasoned that perhaps that was why She had made the decision to obliterate them.

"Clowns not nice, Mommy, clowns make yelling at me. Clown very bad inside, Mommy, mean clowns, clowns make it very dark scary faces and grrrr noise."

"The clowns were yelling at you?" It seemed ridiculous, and yet nothing would surprise her. She wondered if it was imagination, or if it was a type of night terror? Some kind of strange dream that was manifesting as she fell into her sleep. She was supposed to be having a nap during the time that all of this tragedy had occurred after all.

She nods and climbs onto her mother's lap again and rubs her head on her mother's breast. She sat for a moment and then looked up into her mother's brown eyes.

"Mommy, inside clowns is bad. The bad yells at me, clowns not all bad, just inside clown bad. Clown just broken now." She held both of Her hands up signing to Her mother that there was nothing left, that She was sorry and that She loved her.

Where did she learn sign language? When did she learn

sign language? What did She mean inside clown bad? Sign Language? Her mother stopped to think about that for a moment. She didn't even sign herself, how would her child of less than two years accomplish learning a language without direction or instruction? The toddler spoke English better than most four-year-olds, but to be honest learning to self-sign? Really? Is it even possible?

Her mother took a deep breath and kissed her daughter on the top of her head. "Okay, Sweetie, Okay…" She wondered what the early signs of Schizophrenia were. Was this perfect little thing seeing and hearing from "others". Voices inside her head? Could her little mind be frazzled, scrambled, mixed up and less than flawless? She stroked Her hair and held Her tiny hand in her own. They sat together until sleep finally came for Her. Her soft sighs as She slept comforted a worried mother, the ease of having Her in her arms made it simple to disregard the episode that had just elapsed, Her warm body reminded her of just how real this afternoon had been.

CHAPTER 2

Together they cleaned up the mess from the clown disaster and removed the shelving from the walls. She didn't see any point in leaving temptation in the way of her little monkey. The holes would need to be repaired and the walls would need to be repainted, but at least the issue of safety or lack thereof had been removed from the forefront.

She made an appointment for the following week with their family doctor. She wasn't exactly sure what they were looking for, but she knew that something was different about Her. She didn't play the same games as the other little girls. Her thoughts seemed to be more abstract, and were often muddied with riddles. She would choose to play with dolls, but often was acting out dialogue. Not only dressing them, and interacting on a playful level.

The doctor entered the room and welcomed them, as he always did, asked the standard questions that one should ask of a young mother with a toddler. "How is She sleeping? Gosh She's grown!"

She didn't need to think about answers to the standard questions, "Well, good, She's a great sleeper, always has been. She goes down at seven, maybe seven-thirty and sleeps right through until seven-thirty every day, like clockwork. She always has."

The doctor made notes. "Is She still napping in the afternoon?"

"Yes, but only for about an hour."

"Lucky you, if every mother had a toddler with such a regimented sleep pattern we wouldn't have a need for social workers or psychologists."

His comment resonated with her, she understood his "joke", if you could call it that. "Ha, yeah I guess, sleep isn't Her problem, nor is eating, She's a great eater, well balanced. All food groups accounted for."

"Her bowel movements good?" The doctor looked in Her ears, and touched Her throat. He used his stethoscope to listen to Her heart beating.

"Fine, yeah, I think we fixed all of that with Her eating an avocado a day, Her bowels work just fine." She had had some difficulty with regular bowel movements, and had been referred to a specialist at the local Children's Hospital. A diary of her monthly intake of food and beverage had been used to determine that she in fact was not malnourished nor lacking in fibre or water. She was thought to be one of the best cared for children that they had encountered in years. In an effort to move Her bowels more regularly it was suggested that She be given two tablespoons full of Caster Oil each night at bedtime. This should work well to move things along... it was only effective in making her throw up. Her mother had researched on her own, and with the help of her family doctor had decided that perhaps using avocado would be more palatable and just as effective. It had worked, and She loved it.

"Look, Doc, She talks to herself, but it's not like other kids talking to themselves. It's like She's actually talking to someone... and She climbs the walls. Well, She did once, like literally." She looked up at the doctor, who was now looking at her, mouth slightly ajar, quite clearly surprised by what he had just heard.

"Climbs the walls how? Like Spiderman? Or how do you mean exactly?"

Laughing she said, "Not exactly like Spiderman, but sort of… She doesn't spin webs out of Her wrists like Spiderman, but She climbs shelves and book cases, railings, always wanting to get higher. And She always has a mission, to get hold of something. Like a sculpture, or a keepsake; and the one time specifically clowns."

"She what? She climbs to get at clowns? Like to play with? I think that's probably fairly normal, clowns are exciting for kids… what makes you think otherwise?"

She thought for a brief moment. Being careful of her choice of words, she knew that her selection would determine the outcome of this appointment. Either she, or her daughter could potentially end up in the psych ward, and neither was her intent, neither choice was optimal, and neither was an outcome that anyone, especially her wanted to unravel.

"She climbs the walls, utilizing shelving, bookshelves, chair rails, drawers of dressers that She has placed in a stair pattern, anything She can use to create height, to climb. She climbs with the sole purpose of destroying clowns. She believes that inside the clown is bad. Not the clown itself, but inside."

"Uh huh…" The doctor paused for a moment, he was tall, and had an athletic build, they had known each other for only a few years. His hair was dark, curly, and cut short. He knew he was handsome, but he wasn't particularly comfortable with it. He believed her to be a solid individual, honest, not one to make things up or manifest stories for attention. "And so you think what? That She's right?"

"Well, first of all, She is not even two. She has the vocabulary of a four-year-old. She communicates. She doesn't grunt, or point, or talk gobbledygook. She forms sentences. That is bizarre in itself."

"Didn't Her brother also speak very young?" the doctor asked her.

" Yes, he did." She nodded while answering him.

"And so you think it's odd that She is speaking because? What? Now other kids don't? Or what? I don't get it. You thought it was normal, and I remember you actually being thrilled about him being so advanced. Why the change with Her?"

"She's different. He didn't speak about clowns being bad on the inside, and he didn't do everything in his power to destroy every clown he set his eyes on. I just think that it's abnormal... She has somehow learned Sign Language. How does that happen? How does a toddler learn a language that I don't communicate in? She hasn't been exposed to it in anyway. It's weird. I'm not saying that She is weird, I'm suggesting that Her behaviour is abnormal for a child of eighteen months of age, if I am wrong then I am wrong, and I will just make sure that we never encounter another clown of any kind."

"Well, that might be difficult, what will you do at birthday parties? And what if you ever take her to the fair, or the amusement park? There are bound to be clowns around. I am not arguing with you, I think the behaviour is a little weird too. Actually flipping-off-the-grid kind of weird. Sign Language? Come on? How do you even know that she knows it? But what exactly would we do? I can't refer you to a psychiatrist. That type of referral would stay in her medical file for Her entire life. It could prove to be damaging later. And the fact of the matter is that She might just not like clowns. I don't like them either. They're Freaky, you can't trust them." The doctor shrugged his shoulders. "Look, let's keep an eye on things. Let's do this, why don't you plan to have Her see me every three months instead of the standard annual visits. We will watch Her together. I really don't think that there is anything wrong. Not medically. Nothing that we can do anything about."

She processed all that he was saying and presenting, she understood his reservations about Her medical file. She respected his intent to protect Her, and for some reason she jumped on board with his plan. She wasn't thoroughly certain that he was accurate in his findings, as there had been none. But she knew instinctually that he was right, and she didn't want to do anything that would be detrimental to Her well-being long term.

"Sure, okay, so what do I do just call in every three months for an appointment?"

"Exactly. I can have the nursing staff call to remind you if you like."

She looked at him in disbelief. It was out of her scope of understanding that someone would forget or need reminding about something of such magnitude. "That should be fine, I think I can probably handle the call in myself. Thanks though."

She picked up her small child, kissed Her on the forehead and moved towards the door. "Thank you, Doctor."

"I wish I could offer something to you, but She's just incredibly healthy. Tiny; but healthy."

"Yes, thanks again. Have a great week." They moved into the hallway and towards the reception area. Passed the nursing staff and out the door. She wondered if she was nuts. She wondered if her child was. She placed Her into the car seat, closed the door, and sat herself into the front seat of the car. The engine started easily. With her hands on the wheel she considered all of her options. She looked at her daughter in the rear view mirror, and smiled at Her.

"Mad at me, Mommy?"

"No, Pumpkin, not even a little bit, you okay?" She hated taking Her to the doctor and having Her hear all that they had to talk about.

"Yes, Mommy. We play Big Word Game?" The children liked to play a game while driving in the car, it was one that she had concocted for them to enhance their vocabularies. She would say a word, a big word, they on their turn would repeat the word. Then she would use it in a sentence, and spell the word. Then they would spell it back and use it in a sentence. She enjoyed it because it kept her on her toes. And the children enjoyed playing it. And they were good at it.

"Okay, honey, how about, circumference."

"Sir-Come-Fer-Ance," whispered the wee toddler from the back seat.

"Yes exactly, circumference, it is the distance around something, or the boundary or line around a circle or area. ... so I could say 'He walked the circumference of his land.' C.i.r.c.u.m.f.e.r.e.n.c.e."

She took a moment, looked at Her own little fingers. Pushed Her head back into the car seat, took a breath and repeated to Her mother "c.i.r.c.u.m.f.e.r.e.n.c.e, sir-cum-fer-ance, the round circle had a big circumference."

"Excellent!" Great Job, Sweetie! Second word, Consequence, a consequence is a reaction to an action. 'His decided to withdraw from the race, and suffer the consequence. C.o.n.s.e.q.u.e.n.c.e'"

She took a deep breath, "Consequence, C.o.n.s.e.q.u.e.n.c.e, cross me and pay the consequence."

Her Mother looked at Her in the rear view mirror, slightly

alarmed by her answer, "Would you like to go again?"

"No, I'm tired, Mommy." She lay her head back and closed her eyes. Exhaustion overcame Her. Her breathing soon slowed and She fell into a deep, needed sleep.

CHAPTER 3

After some time, and some additional strain on Her, she seemed to become better at managing the daily activity that occurred around Her. With the clowns gone, She was free of the disturbing chatter, and was able to sleep as She should.

Summer came and She knew she was nearing Her second celebration of life. She always did love a good Birthday Celebration, especially when it was in Her own honour. As always Her mother prepared the guests and baked a cake. There would be balloons and most hopefully a piñata, and She adored the little goody bags that the wee ones like Her would get to take home. Her mother dressed her in Her prettiest dress with beautiful colours and a poufy skirt. She donned an adorable hat that accentuated Her cherub face, and ballerina flats that made Her feel like a princess.

She was elated. The children started to arrive and everyone seemed so pleased to see Her. All of them that arrived through the door came with a brightly wrapped present. She thought this unique and wonderful. There was laughing and joyful noises coming from all of them. The room filled with unruliness quickly. She loved the attention she was getting, she felt full and contented.

Her mother gathered everyone in one room and announced that it was time to light the candles and have cake. Everyone gathered, giggling and smiling. She sat in Her highchair, in the midst of them.

"Happy Birthday to you, Happy Birthday to you, Happy Birthday Dear Her, Happy birthday to you."

"Now, Sweetheart, make a wish and blow out your candles!" The cake was shaped like a cluster of balloons, in pretty colours; pink, blue, purple, green and yellow. Happy Birthday Her was written across the centre of the cake.

She looked at their faces, and smiled at them as She inhaled. She used all of the air She had managed to suck in and She blew as hard as She could. The candles flickered and then the flame extinguished, on both the pink candle and the white one. She giggled on the inside. She knew that She had done this before. There were memories that were deeply rooted and yet seemed to resurface. Memories that were triggered by activities, people, or places; sometimes even the smell of dinner cooking, a fresh flower or the taste of a fruit, would generate a rush of visions that flowed through Her mind as though they were playing on an old-style movie reel... *click click click... she would see faces and feel the presence of individuals that she knew that she had known once, as the film clicked on, maybe in another lifetime.*

The room was filled with faces. She watched them all smiling at Her, there were so many here; some that She knew and others that She didn't remember just yet. Old and young, they were all pleased to share in Her day.

Her mother began to cut the cake and place it onto plates with ice cream on the side. On each plate she placed a fork, then passed it to each person in the room. She sat in her high chair watching as they received their cake and ice cream, on the plates that were passed around. They seemed to be enjoying it, but what She found most odd was that more than half of the party attendees had not received a plate, yet they said nothing to Her mother. Her mother seemed not to notice that she had missed more than half of the people who were here to celebrate. She wondered if one of them would speak up. Perhaps there was a shortage of dessert. Maybe there wasn't enough of the luscious vanilla ice cream.

She looked down at Her own cake and placed Her hand on Her fork. Her ice cream was starting to melt slightly. Everyone was laughing and having a wonderful time, even those without a plate of cake. Concern came over Her. Empathy began to fill her chest and worry filled Her thoughts. What if they felt left out, their feelings would be hurt and they would feel unloved. How could She let this happen? They would leave the party feeling as though She had done them wrong. All of these wonderful people had gone out of their way to be here for Her, and they couldn't even get a piece of cake?

Her fork made its way to the slab of chocolate cake that Her mother had baked, and She scraped the icing from the top. She took the fork full of icing and held it out to one of the visitors who was not given a helping. He shook his head no, but smiled at her. He said nothing. She noticed that he looked a little different than the rest. He was brighter; shinier, like a bright penny, glossy and fine looking.

She returned the favour and smiled back at him. He was handsome and tall with very chic clothing. His pants were dark and his shirt had short sleeves, but was light in colour. She thought She would call that colour butter. He had on black wing tipped shoes which were beautifully polished and a matching belt. She realized that She wasn't sure of his name, but there was a very familiar feeling to him.

This however was not unusual for Her. She nodded at him and played coy. She was just two after all. How could anyone even begin to imagine that She could remember everyone's names? Half the time She was nearly asleep when people came to visit. She loved a good nap and was often put to bed by seven in the evening. Now that the clowns had been effectively destroyed She was free to sleep at will. She enjoyed it, She loved resting and Her bed was incredibly comfortable. Her mother was quite adequate at making the environment restful, and inviting. She thought that she must have some very developed skills.

Her hand made its way to the plate, almost involuntarily. She touched the cold and melting ice cream with Her index finger then placed the finger on Her tongue. It was sweet, and icy, and rich tasting. She liked it. She did the same with the icing, which was too sweet and made Her squint. Her throat felt tight from the sugary taste.

Another plate-less lady approached her, smiled and then stroked Her head. Her auburn hair was soft and shiny. A lot of people liked to touch it, so this didn't surprise Her. The lady had a smoking thing in her hand, She couldn't remember what they were called, but it smelled odd. Her mother didn't use them any more, but She remembered seeing them in the past. Sometimes when her mother and her dad had fights her mother would use them. Just a little bit. Sometimes she would have them with coffee, and sometimes when her friends would come around, she would have the white sticks with wine. It was white and slim, and the lady kept bringing it up to her lips to suck on it. How strange grown-ups were...

The lady stayed beside her high chair for quite some time, touching her head and stroking her shoulder and back. She was enjoying it immensely. Her fingers were gentle and soft; her caress' were velvety, like cashmere on her skin. She adored being touched in an affectionate way. These sorts of touches made her heart glow. She felt loved.

Her mother came near, bent forward and kissed her on the

forehead.

"Hello, my Sweet, not enjoying the cake?"

"Don't like it the cake, Mommy, it's too sweet." She pushed the plate forward to the edge of her high chair tray.

"Well, then okay, let's get that out of your way, shall we?" She moved the plate and fork with the melted ice cream and soppy cake to the counter next to the stove. She then moved to the sink and grabbed a fluffy white wash cloth and ran the warm water through it.

"Let's wash your face and hands then, and then you can open your gifts, how does that sound?" She used the warm cloth to softly wipe the face and hands of her child who was celebrating her second birthday that day. As she did so she pondered the idea of her child's distractions and inability to focus on what should be exciting things. There were balloons, cake, ice cream and presents, and all of her playmates from around the neighbourhood. And yet She seemed so introverted. She seemed to want to keep to Herself, preoccupied, often staring off into space, smiling and always easy to please; but never really engaging with the other children.

She unbuckled the straps on Her highchair and lifted Her out, hugging Her tight before setting Her down on Her feet. "There we go, all set for the gifts! Are you excited to be opening them?"

"No, Mommy, I like the peoples not the presents, why no cake for all of my friends?" She looked up at Her mother inquisitively.

"I'm not sure what you mean, Love, everyone had cake and ice cream."

She looked to the left at Her lady friend who had not yet left Her side, and She looked across the room and made eye contact with the shiny man in the nice pants and clean buttery colored shirt. She shrugged as they both smiled at Her. She shook Her head at Her mother and nodded. "Okay then, Mommy, but I think you forgot some of my special friends, but they don't mind, it's okay."

There were gifts exchanged, there were thank-you's and good-byes. And then She became very present for the next few months. She became more engaged with friends and played with Her brother. Her vocabulary developed even more as She grew into a pretty and thriving two-year-old. Her mother assumed that there was a level of maturity within Her that was appreciating with time. Her diction became more elaborate and Her annunciation better developed; Her fine motor skills were acutely refined for a toddler. By the time She had reached twenty-eight months of age, She was becoming more of what one would expect a little girl to be.

She was soft and pink, She loved to cuddle and blow kisses. Her hair was billowy and radiant auburn, Her cheeks glowed when She ran in the fields chasing soccer balls and dandelions.

She delighted in playing with Barbies and Lego, She liked to watch Barney on television and like any little girl, She relished in Disney Princess movies. Life was evolving at a pace that everyone was comfortable with and that should be considered to be normal. Except of course for Her insane vocabulary, and Her ability with languages and communication, one might look at Her and think that She was just any other two-year-old.

CHAPTER 4

There was a woman, and she lived in the basement. No one really saw the woman; she was angry and she was rebellious. No one really knew why she was there, and no one was able to confirm how she had gotten there. The woman didn't always have a lot to say, but there were certain things that set her off. Her temper would flare, and the entire house would rattle and shake. The wrath of the angry woman was sometimes relentless and unforgiving. The woman was frightening.

The door to the basement was always to be left closed. It was a rule She had made to protect the family. It was necessary.

She had made the rule one day after an odd and frightening incident had occurred. Strangely enough, She had seen the woman herself; She wasn't certain if the others had actually seen her themselves, but as a precautionary measure- She had formulated the rule and had been successful in enforcing it.

The stairs to the basement were not a straight staircase, but turned one hundred and eighty degrees at a landing half way down. At the landing was a solid concrete wall, this wall completely obliterated any chance of seeing fully to the basement below from the upper doorway. This is why the rule about the door had been implemented.

One would be half way down before you knew that there was danger below. If you stumbled or if you weren't quick on your feet, the woman could catch you. It had happened to her once, and she had vowed to never let it happen again. Keeping the door closed also allowed you to turn on the light, by the switch at the top of the stairs, before descending into darkness. If one always followed the rules, and if one did things the same way every time, one could be certain of survival, certain of escape and safe passage. If one chose to not follow the rules… *well* risk taking really had no place here.

One day, when the rains came, after the snow had been for a while, someone forgot to close the door tightly. No one wanted to admit to leaving it open, no one was inclined to take the blame, but she knew who had done it. It had happened like this, it was terrible, it was awful, and the door had never again been left ajar.

She still came down the stairs backwards, She found it more efficient, and simply faster. As she rounded the corner from Her bedroom to the landing, She could see her brother playing in the landing area below. His trucks and Lego were strewn about the carpeted floor in a methodical manner. He had created a village or town, and was moving his trucks and cars through the streets, humming as they went.

"Vvrrrmmm, vrrrrmmmmm, vvvvrrrrmmm, errrrrrr, rroooommm, eeeech. Vvvvrrrrmmmm, vrrrrooom."

He looked up at Her from what he was doing, "Hey, do you wanna play cars with me?"

She stared at the open doorway to his right, Her mouth was locked open in disbelief. She raised Her hand and pointed at the stairwell to the basement, and at the door which was open about six inches.

"Why the door's open? What did you do to the door?"

He nodded. "Yup, it's open, but I didn't do it. Dad did it."

She was in disbelief. Complete disobedience of the rules should be punishable by death, or at the very least dealt with,

with the greatest severity. She was surely in shock. She was having trouble catching her breath.

"Why would he do that? Why would he open the door? When did he do it?" She was aghast!

"I dunno, while you were sleeping I guess. He came home for something that he needed for work I think, he went in the basement and then he left. But he told me to leave the door open. He said not to close it. So I didn't, I left it just like he left it, 'cause you know, I'm trying to be good. I don't want to make him mad at me."

He tried desperately at every opportunity to gain the approval of their father. Acceptance and the love that he so desperately wanted was often withheld from him with no explanation as to why. There was no reasoning, and no meaning, nor explanation offered to the boy. Their father did try, he attempted to connect, but his efforts always seemed to be so artificial. He was too commercialized and angered too quickly. He just wasn't good with children. Neither child understood why, but She was more willing to let their Dad go, to allow him the distance that he needed. She was more accepting of his inability to mould to the family unit.

She moved towards the open door, sweat beads developing on Her brow. She couldn't believe that someone would deliberately leave this door open, fully knowing of the dangers that were lurking below.

She pulled the door open just a few inches more, and She listened. She listened intently, for sounds, for breath, for voice, for indication of impending attack.

"How long?" She looked at Her brother, who was only three and a half years old himself, and raised Her voice an octave. "The door, how long has it been open? Do you think the woman could have escaped already?"

"Well, I didn't see anything, but I was outside with Mommy for a while. We were working in the garden, planting and stuff."

"Where is Mommy? She didn't go down there did she?" She nodded towards the open door?

"She's upstairs, ironing and putting away the clothes, but she did go down for a few minutes. She came up alone though. I think she was doing some laundry or something."

She took a deep breath and opened the door fully. It was dark, no light from below. The basement was void of sound, it seemed to be very still and almost empty. "We will have to go down, at least half way so that we can check that she's still there. If she has escaped, we will have to find her and try to get her back in the basement."

Her brother looked up from his Hot Wheels. "Look, Dad says there isn't no woman down there. He says you made the whole thing up. So I don't know if I want to help you. I want Dad to like me more. So I think I should do what he wants, I want to help, but I just don't want any trouble."

She was rattled. She was angry, and She was terrified that the woman from the basement was either already out, or she was planning to escape, while they were busy talking about keeping their Dad happy.

"You know how dangerous she is, you haven't forgotten have you? Have you?! Did you forget what happened the last time the door was left open? Do you remember what happened to me?! You were right there with me. How can you even suggest, or agree with Dad that I made it up? The idea of that is just preposterous."

He shrugged, tears welled in his eyes. "I know what I saw, but I also know that if Dad gets mad, he gets mad at *me*, and that isn't good for anybody. He wants the door open and he wants to be my buddy now. He says we can be friends, like we can do stuff together. He even called me that today. He said, "Listen, Buddy, leave the door open and we can hang out tonight, just me and you okay?" You know that I want to close the door just as bad as you do, but I want Dad to hang out with me too."

Aaaaghh! Her inside voice was screaming, "traitor!". She knew that she was going to have to do this alone now. She couldn't really be angry *at* him, but She could most definitely be disappointed; and that She most definitely was easily achieving.

She headed upstairs to Her bedroom to get Her gear. She opened Her closet doors and pulled out all of the items that She knew for sure would be necessary to complete the trip to the dreaded basement. She put on Her breastplate, and helmet, grabbed Her princess wand, and some pixie dust, the New Testament, and Her magic blanket, and of course some foil-covered Easter eggs. She put all of the loose bits into her backpack and strapped it on.

CHAPTER 5

She had travelled down from the upper most level of the home, on her belly. She slid down the stairs from the very top, feet first on her abdomen; it was a safety precaution for Her and it was faster. She had the ability to walk down the stairs as grown-ups do, but it took far too much time. Today there was no time to lose. She had a woman to catch.

She reached the door to the basement, which was still ajar, quickly. She took a deep breath and forged onward. She turned herself around and headed down after turning on the light from the switch inside the doorway. She bumped Her way down the first set of stairs.

She hit the landing in a matter of seconds, stood and looked into the darkness below. She could see shadows and noises. She knew that she was here.

It was in that moment that She determined it was finally time to take care of business. She could no longer live in fear. She chose to no longer continue living with the door closed. She would take charge and overcome this.

She moved forward down the final set of stairs upright, in adult position. Her heart beating fast in Her chest, the palms of Her hands sweating, Her knees shaking as She toddled on. Her hand touched Her silver breastplate, which had been a birthday gift, to ensure that it was safely attached. It was secured, and was protecting Her effectively, and therefore if danger prevailed, She would at least stand a fighting chance. She had the gear. She was prepared for nearly anything that might come Her way.

At the bottom of the stairs She sensed a presence, the light was illuminated only from the landing, so once all the way to the bottom of the stairs, She was once again in utter darkness. She saw almost nothing, a few shapes, and a light from the window across the basement on the other side.

She sat on the bottom stair and removed her backpack, Her heart still beating wildly. Her breath was rapid, and shallow.

She unwrapped an Easter egg and ate it. She then reached into her backpack and pulled out the New Testament. She placed it on her lap, and held onto Her princess wand.

She waved Her wand three times to the left, two to the right and then She began, "Ole Babba, Nica, Shabba, Ranna, banana, Ickenshan Cram."

The woman appeared in front of Her. With teeth grey and nasty with breath to match; her hair was badly tangled, grey and falling from an old bun at the nape of her neck. The woman's clothes were tattered and torn; her shoes were worn and out dated. She smelled of age, really old age. Not like a grandma's type of old, or a great aunt. This woman was at least three or four hundred years old. Rotten kind of smelling old.

"I told you never to bother me again, you little shit! Why did you come back, huh? I thought we had an understanding!"

"I didn't really ever want to come back, really I didn't, but this couldn't be helped today. I must say that you have really let yourself go. Since we last met I think you stink even worse."

"How dare you talk to me like that? Do you know who I am?"

She reached into Her bag and pulled out a second foil-covered Easter egg. She held it out towards the woman. "Would you like an egg? These were in my Easter basket, I would be quite pleased to share them with you."

The woman shoved Her hand back towards Her. "Easter? You get candy for Easter? What the hell is happening in this world now? Don't you know that Easter is about our Lord, and His great descent from the Cross to hell and his final ascent to the Throne next our Lord Himself? It's not about candy, and eggs."

"Yes I do know that, that's why I brought you this." She lifted up the New Testament, which was red and small enough that She could easily hold it. "I thought we could talk about this if you think it might help? For how long do you think that you might stay here? In the basement? Don't you want to move on? To somewhere else, someplace with lights and food?"

The woman grimaced at Her. "It's not so bad here, in this basement. I can hear you play, I don't really need to eat and I do get out once in a while."

"Yes, well, you scare me. Just the thought of you being here is scary to me. I think I would like it well enough if you moved on. See here, let's look at this in the Bible, where it says..." Her voice trailed off.

The woman brushed the New Testament away. "I don't care what it says in there, little missy. I get to do whatever I want. I'm staying. You can't make me go, and besides I like it that you're scared. I enjoy that you and your brother are afraid to come down to the basement, means I'm doing my job! I really liked that business that the clowns did on you." She laughed out loud. "I loved it that your mother thinks you're a little coocoonut. Oh but you showed them all didn't ya? Hey, little missy? Smashed those clowns to bits you did. You're tougher than they think. They think you're soft and pink, like a princess. They don't know who you are. They don't know what's waiting. They don't know what they're dealing with. They don't have any idea why you're here. Well, when they finally figure it all out I hope that they have behaved themselves. I hope that when they finally get to it they can live with their choices. I know why I'm here, and I ain't leavin'."

Again She reached into Her backpack, but this time She removed Her magic blanket and some silver pixie dust that Her mother had gotten for Her at the dollar store. She took a pinch and then a pinch more for safety's sake.

"Um, Scrum, Drum, Bora, Bora, Rattat, Tum, Icka, Bica, Bora, Rum, Ramma, Drama, Tat, Tat, Tum!" She blew a handful of pixie dust in the general direction of the woman as She placed the magic blanket over Her head. "When I remove this blanket, you will be gone from here, and I won't be scared of you any more!"

She sat still, with the blanket over Her head, breathing softly, waiting. She felt the need to pee. She held it. She would not pee Her pants. She wasn't a baby. She was a big girl. She waited longer. She peeked out from beneath the blanket and the scary woman was gone, her grey nasty teeth were now clean and shiny, her clothes were clean and her hair neat and tidy. Her smell was gone.

"So you're staying then?"

"Yes, dear, I am staying, but I would never harm you. I am here to protect you."

She began to pick up Her things before starting up the stairs. "Fine, but I like you better like this, you smell better." She took her first step towards the landing. Her first step beyond fear, Her first step towards facing fear. She was stronger now than She had been in the morning. She was a force to be reckoned with.

She looked back at the woman as She climbed the stairs, the woman was smiling at Her, and eating the Easter Egg.

CHAPTER 6

The Children's Hospital is not a place that any child aspires to be going. They don't lay in waiting hoping to visit as they would for the circus or to the movies. The Children's Hospital is a venue used specifically for treating sick and dying children. It is used to house those children who are chronically ill, injured and those being treated for serious illnesses. It is not a playground, nor a zoo: it is not a place to hang out or a place to hope to someday go to.

Her body was physically small. Her mind was large, her spirit enormous. Her physical size gave reason for concern to medical professionals; She didn't seem to be growing at the same rate as "other" children Her age. According to the doctors' charts and graphs, She was in the fifth percentile of Canadian standards, -meaning that in a group of one-hundred children of the same age, ninety-five of them would be taller and heavier than She.

She didn't see this as cause for concern. She understood the reason for Her slight build and She was pleased to adorn it. She was proud to be tiny, She knew that She would not always be small, and that She would one day be of average size. Her mother, however, was alerted by the doctor and his own concerns for Her well-being.

Was She eating enough? Did She eat the right things? Why did She refuse to eat certain things? Why did some foods give her diarrhea? The doctor determined that the very best thing for Her was to complete a dietary physical assessment through the Children's Hospital. She would see specialists there who would assist in establishing a reason or source for Her very slight build and for Her dietary limitations.

Certain foods seemed to aggravate Her digestive system and cause a negative reaction in Her. For thirty days She was on a strict watch by Her medical team. Every item that She ingested during the time period was diarized by Her mother; solids and liquids. After the one-month control period; all of the information collected was forwarded to the doctors at the Children's hospital in Calgary; where a small team of doctors studied the data. The team performed a detailed analysis of the information; which took longer than any thought it should have.

The two of them then returned to the hospital for the assessment of the data, the teams conclusions and diagnosis.

Snow was falling hard that day, the roads were icy the air cold and dense with anticipation. She knew She would need to adapt in some way, She was already preparing Herself for change. She just didn't know how it was going to affect Her yet. Her mother seemed calm as she navigated the streets to the hospital.

She watched from Her car seat, She could easily see Her mother in the rear-view mirror. The eyes moving left to right, as she watched the traffic. The mouth tensing as her mood changed. She made a mental note in Her area of human interest, She knew that one day She would use all of the information that She was collecting. She visualized in Her brain tiny boxes of information, all neatly compartmentalized. Some of the boxes blue, some pink, some appropriately green, some red, orange and purple. All of the 'Big Words' from the games played, all the human reaction to emotional situations, the animated facial expressions, the poker faces, or lack of poker face in some people. The loss of tempers, the smiles, the genuine laughter, love; anger and sadness, frustration, envy, jealousy, She was becoming an expert in placing human reactions into her coloured boxes. She categorized people's emotions so that She could use them as a resource later. By placing them into her coloured boxes She could easily access the information as She needed it, and She would easily know where to find it. For example, the green box would hold any items relating to issues of jealousy or envy; Her own or others. Or genuine growth, green could be a very good box. The red box pertained to anger items. Blue was of course sadness. This box was the largest of the boxes included many smaller boxes of different hues of blue. There was a baby blue box a teal box and a turquoise box. And so on. All of them contained different items filed for different reasons. She put them where She saw fit. Her Brain was a hyper-organized kaleidoscope of colour. And She made it so.

They rode the elevator to the third floor where Her mother spoke to a receptionist and then to a nurse. Then they walked into a room with a large round table and lots of chairs. She sat on Her mother's lap and placed Her head against Her mother's chest. She was most comfortable right there, where She could hear Her mother's heart beat, and feel Her mother's breath. She felt safe, and She felt warm there. She felt protected.

After a few minutes a team of doctors entered the room. All men. They all introduced themselves and then sat in the available chairs. The oldest one spoke first.

"We have spent a great deal of time reviewing the dietary log that you sent to us via your family doctor and we have some questions regarding it before we get started."

Her mother nodded. "Of course, what would you like to

know?"

The grey-haired doctor spoke again. "The log that you sent in was in great detail, containing everything that you had fed your daughter in the thirty-day period? Is that right?"

"That's what I was told to do, yes, that is exactly what I did."

"So for instance, here, this is an example from your diary that you sent in, breakfast; peaches, oatmeal, soymilk, snack; almonds, grapes, water, lunch; brown rice, tofu, snap peas, carrots, sprouts, bok choy, water, dinner; chicken breast, broccoli, sweet potatoes, mushrooms, water, bedtime; soymilk, rice crackers, cheese, avocado,is this accurate, ma'am?"

Her mother looked at the physicians surrounding the table. "If that's what I wrote down for that day, then yes, that is probably accurate, why do you ask?"

"I ask because this is probably the healthiest dietary log that we have ever seen, for anyone, child or adult. She doesn't eat red meat? Drink milk?"

"No, she doesn't like either. She won't touch it. Red meat makes her gag and milk makes her mucosae."

A much younger doctor spoke up. "Ma'am, if I may introduce myself, Hi, I'm Dr. Mike Laroue, I'm a resident here, I'm just new, and I'm honoured to be on this case, so thank you. I have done a lot of reading since we received your daughter's dietary logs, impressive by the way, we see a lot of really bad stuff so I commend you, but any way. Umm, I think your daughter is allergic to wheat. And most likely milk too but seeing as how you don't expose her to that now we are just guessing there."

Her mother shook her head. "I don't understand what you mean, how can someone be allergic to wheat? What does that mean exactly, wheat is in everything, well, no I guess not everything, but She what? She won't be able to eat bread, or cake? Shit!"

"Yes exactly. We don't know that much about it really yet. But what we do know is that Her digestive track is having trouble processing some foods, not all of them however. Natural foods seem to be of no consequence to Her, such as avocados, oranges, bananas, nuts, tomatoes, fish, chicken, etc. You get my point. What happens with wheat is in the actual processing. Gluten is formed which is what holds the bread or the cake together. It's basically like a glue, just imagine that for all intents and purposes today. Your daughter's body doesn't have the enzyme necessary to break the gluten down, so it sits in Her body. Just like plaster of Paris, lining the intestinal track, which then inhibits the absorption of essential nutrients from the good foods that She can eat. We think, I think actually."

Her mother sat and stared at the doctors around the table. She watched her face, She was unsure of what colour this would be filed under, but She knew that before they left this office She would have a clear answer.

Her mother began to speak, not with her angry voice, not with her sad voice, this was her get-to-business voice. "So, let me see if I understand exactly what you are attempting to tell me, for all intents and purposes today. My daughter's body is full of a natural glue that has been building up from gluten, a by-product of wheat. She is not growing at a natural rate because Her body cannot absorb the nutrients essential for growth through the gluten that is lining her intestinal walls. Yes?"

"Yes, exactly what I think. But I could be wrong."

"How many other children have you seen with this?"

Dr. Laroue looked at the other physicians who all looked at the table, the oldest of the doctors spoke again. "None. Your child is the first. We have never encountered this here. But there are documented cases, Dr. Laroue has done a significant amount of research, all of which you are privy to. We are very happy to share our information with you."

Her mother, raised her hand. "That's fine, Doctor, what do we do now, what is the next step, what do I do, for Her?"

"Yes of course, Dr. Laroue, would you like to address those questions?"

"Thank you, yes." Dr. Laroue cleared his throat and continued, "Well, like I said, I commend you, you're already doing an amazing job, we just need to do a little bit of tweaking and I think She should be home free."

"Okay, so what kind of tweaking, and thank you so much for noting that I am doing a great job. Because to be honest, most of the time I feel like it's a losing battle. Trust me. What exactly do you mean by tweaking? Just eliminate wheat products? Breads? No bread, no cake no cookies…?"

He nodded. "Yes exactly, no wheat what so ever in Her diet, no flour products at all, so no flour in gravies, no breads like you said, no pasta, no baked goods, and let's stick with no milk products, no cow's milk I mean. The two items seem to go hand in hand with most of the studies I've seen. I would like to see Her in three months to see how She is doing, check Her weight and Her height of course, and see how She is generally feeling. We are assuming that with the elimination of the gluten, and a few things we will do and talk about later to clean the bowels, She will begin to grow quickly. Once that happens then we will just be monitoring Her progress, and Her diet as time goes on. The older She gets the more She will be able to articulate as well. Which will help us to understand

Her."

Her mother looked at him in disbelief. "What do you mean by that exactly? Understand Her?"

"Well, I just mean that She's not even two years old, by the time She's three she might be able to say a few words. She might be able to speak a little and communicate how She is feeling. Now we are relying on you to tell us. And presumably you, Ma'am, are guessing."

Red Box.

"I think you have failed me, and you have failed Her. In all of your research and studies, and the time that you spent with Her, never once did you attempt to communicate apparently? I am embarrassed for you, all of you, as physicians, as men, and as individuals, representing us as a race. Jesus Christ help us now!"

The doctors all sat mouths agape, looking at Her mother as though she had come undone, when in reality, it had barely begun yet.

"She was completely potty trained, through the night trained by the time She was fourteen months old, gentlemen. Yes, look at me like I am crazy if you must, you're pathetic and rather short-sighted. Fourteen months, never a dirty diaper. She taught Herself to sign before She was a year old. Who does that I ask you? Who? Can't answer me can you? No I didn't think so. She has been speaking in full sentences for months." She looked down at her daughter. "Sweetheart, what is a consequence?"

She took a breath, definitely Red Box. "A consequence is a reaction to an action."

"Can you spell consequence for me please, Honey?"

"Consequence. C.O.N.S.E.Q.U.E.N.C.E. Consequence."

The doctors looked at each other, the grey-haired doctor

asked, "Does anyone sign?"

They all shook their heads no. He spoke again. "Can you spell Pertinent for me."

"Pertinent, of extreme necessity, P.E.R.T.I.N.E.N.T." She looked at her mother for approval, Her mother nodded.

"How about Sabotage?"

"Sabotage, S.A.B.O.T.A.G.E, to deliberately attempt to destroy or harm."

The grey-haired doctor spoke one last time as though there was no one in the room but doctors, ignoring Her presence entirely; "Holy shit. Did anyone even speak to Her at all during all of this testing?"

She spoke to the group of doctors directly herself silently placing the events into her own Blue Box, deeply saddened by their lack of empathy and interest in mankind. "No you did not."

CHAPTER 7

The move was happening, there was no questioning the decision. Her things had been removed, Her toys sold or given away; with only a few favourites packed for the trip.

Her heart was heavy, but She was somewhat excited for the new adventure. She liked the sun and She enjoyed the heat. She was overall, pleased to be going.

Her brother was angry, he had more friends than She did. People that he played with regularly. She had just Her dolls, and Her mother. Her friends were all adults.

She didn't understand children, their lack of decision-making perplexed Her. Crying and temper tantrums were very foreign to Her. To scream and yell in an effort to get your own way seemed to be somewhat counter productive. Rarely did this type of poor behaviour result in the desired outcome. She was one to negotiate, to present Her wishes as eloquently as possible, listening to rational presented to Her from opposition and then bartering until a reasonable transaction could be arranged, where both sides were equally satisfied.

There would be merit in this move, or they just wouldn't be making it. She had to trust in that. She was leaving Her adults that She was comfortable with and would only have Her mother, and Her dad. She was aware that they would meet new people, but they would be foreign. Their language would be different, and their customs rare. She could adapt, She would adhere to the newness, Her mind was fearful but Her heart was curious.

The entire adventure at this point in time was being comfortably placed into a Green Box. Green was a go colour. It was one of growth and adventure, at least in Her world. It signified enlightenment and engagement envy and enrichment. All of these things would potentially occur on the trip, and in reality She had no idea for how long She would be gone.

The plan was not entirely a plan, as it had not been well thought out. It was indeed an idea, one that was more of a whim, and a whim that was being executed. She and Her brother would be caught in the midst, leave their friends, leave their extended family, their home, their toys and the life that they were coming to know.

They would learn a new life, they would meet new friends, they would find a new home, and they would get new toys. They would learn a new language, try new foods, and a new culture.

She would have new doctors and new things to see. She liked the idea, She coloured it green in Her mind, and so the entire situation was placed inside of the Green Box.

Saying good bye would be the most difficult of things for Her. She sat at the top of the stairs with Her magic wand in Her hand, Her breast plate on and Her pixie dust in Her pocket. She felt prepared and yet reluctant to begin Her descent into the depths of the basement.

She was aware that the Woman was there for Her own protection, and although She was not certain from what She was being protected, She was grateful for the presence of Her in the home. There came a comfort in knowing that there was someone prepared to fight the great fight should it happen. Someone willing to take up the sword, ready to die, or rather, equipped for battle on Her behalf. She slept better at night just knowing that the old woman, who still was nameless to Her, was on Her side, for Her and not against Her.

She lifted Her wand and began Her chant, "Um, Strum, Grum, Bore, Bore, Rat, Tat, Tum, Um, Strum, Grum, Peet... Show yourself!"

And it was so.

And the old lady who had once appeared tattered and grey was now just older and pleasant-looking, spoke to Her. "Hello, dear."

"Hello. How are you? I just thought I would come and say good-bye."

"Agh, yer leaving then?" The woman placed her hand on her hip and lit a cigarette.

"Yes, tomorrow I think. Don't have a choice, you know how these things are. I'm just little. I don't make the decisions yet." She pulled at Her socks, bent at the waist, sitting on the bottom stair, looking up at the woman as She inhaled deeply.

"Well, then, that's kind of *unexpected*... I wonder if they know." The woman nodded in an upward motion. "What am I talking about, course they do. So I suppose this will be it for us then, kiddo, I haven't been re-assigned; I don't have any notice to go with you. So you will be on your own now."

She was suddenly frightened of losing the old woman, it hadn't occurred to Her that Her friend was actually going to be left behind in the house. "Can't you come with us? I don't want you to have to stay here all by yourself."

"Aw, that's not how it works, Honey, I won't be here after you go. I'm here for you. Once you're gone there won't be any reason for me to stay. I will just go." The woman lifted her hands and made a hand expression of a puff of air disappearing.

"But where will you go? Will you be okay?" She was overtly empathetic and concerned for others, always.

The woman took another long drag on her cigarette. She was tiny, slim and not very tall. Her hair was neatly done, as if it had been set in curlers and back combed into place. "Oh, Sweetheart, I might just go and make some crab apple jelly somewhere, or maybe I'll sneak away somewhere warm for a while. I've always loved the desert."

"You're joking with me now. I know that. That's fine. I know that I can't hug you. Can you tell me your name, so that I can file you into a box so that someday I will be able to look at your memory at least?"

The woman looked at Her. "Those memory box things you do, that's kind of interesting. Why do you do that anyway?"

"You mean with the colours?"

"Yes, that's what I mean, the colour-coding, why do you do that exactly, I've never seen or heard of anyone doing that before."

She took a deep breath and searched her mind for the words to explain without sounding like a baby. And while wanting to sound grown-up, She also wanted to be brave in sharing her deepest expression of Herself.

"I guess I colour-code and file everything in my mind as a way of immediately dealing with events that could in some way have a profound impact on my life and that I don't feel that I am adequately prepared to deal with. That way I will have them stored away for later. I like to use the colours so that I can find them easy, sort of an easy filing system for me. Orange is my embarrassed colour, red is for things that made me or someone near me angry, green is for growth or envy, things that are great. Pink makes me happy, it's a feel-good colour, every girl likes pink, you get it?"

"Oh yes, I understand, I can see all of the memories there, neatly stored away. Very nice."

"Yeah, it works for me." She was reluctant to say Her good-byes and move back upstairs. She knew that eventually Her time would run out. "You never did tell me what your name is. Or is there a reason why you didn't?"

"I did not. No that's right." The old woman looked away, she placed her hand into the pocket of her cardigan, as though she was looking for something. Feeling for something that wasn't there.

"And so are you going to share with me what your name is? Who you are?"

"I don't think it matters, I was a friend of your great-grandmother's. A very dear friend. That's all. That's all you're getting, now go on, scat, I have things to do here. And Lord knows that there are things for you to get on to doing. Learn your ABCs or your times tables or something. Watch that big purple dinosaur on television. Go now, be a good girl, will you?"

"I will." She stood, as She did, She held out Her hand to the old woman. "I know that we cannot touch, but I want you to know that if we could I would hold your hand."

The woman reached forward, and held her hand close to the little girl's. "And if I was able to, I would protect you forever, *for you will touch many*, but hold few." There were tears streaming down the cheeks of the woman as she spoke, "Pray, love all those who cross your path and seek God in all things. Now go, scat."

With that the woman disappeared, and She gathered her magic wand, her pixie dust, and walked back upstairs to Her family and to Her life where She would continue to file Her memories into coloured boxes, with Her breast plate still on.

CHAPTER 8

They had packed their truck full of the things that they would take and they hit the road. Leaving Canada was not as difficult as one might think. It was winter, snow and ice abounded. The children huddled in the back seat of the pickup truck and covered themselves with blankets. She used the time to catch up on much-needed sleep.

When they had crossed the first border, She woke. There had been discussion with men in uniforms, She could hear the exchange of words in her foggy sleep, Her dad's voice was quite loud.

"Where are you headed today, Sir?" He peeked into the back seat to look at the two children.

'We are driving down to Puerto Vallarta."

The US Border Patrol chuckled. "Is that right? You're driving all the way to Puerto Vallarta? In Mexico? In this truck?" he imagined hearing *"with the two kiddo's in the back? And the pretty little lady there? You nuts man?"* "Have you been there before, sir?"

He was angry, he didn't like any type of confrontation or resistance. "I have been there yes. And yes I am driving there with my wife and two kids, jealous?" He sneered at the officer.

"Sir, why don't you step out of the truck? Turn the vehicle off. Ensure that you have your Passport, Driver's Licence, Vehicle Registration and Valid Insurance please."

"Fuck! What for? What the Fuck, man!" He smashed his

fist into the steering wheel, his face was red, his temples pulsed.

The Border Patrol Officer reached to his belt, his hand on his weapon. "How about we calm down, and step out of the vehicle, sir, now please. Sir, this vehicle is leased, you cannot leave Canada with this vehicle without the proper paperwork for it. Let's quickly and without commotion gather the paperwork, and your documents, and step out of the vehicle, please."

He took a deep breath and look in the rear-view mirror at his son. "I won't be long, buddy, be right back." He grabbed his papers and opened the door to the truck, sliding off of the seat and onto the snow-covered ground. As he walked away the snow crunched and creaked beneath his boots. She liked the sound.

He walked slightly behind the Officer, moving towards the building to the left of the truck. The building wasn't overly large, but was very secure-looking. The roof was flat, the exterior walls were constructed of bricks, light in colour, not the usual deep red that you would expect of bricks. She suspected that the building had been erected in the mid-1970s from the architecture. The style was evident of that period. The building was very linear, simple and clean. A basic sand colour, it looked as though it could use a major renovation.

They entered the door and disappeared. She sat with Her brother and Her mother and She wondered. She wondered why he had been taken inside and She wondered for how long he would be gone.

She prayed. She prayed for lunch, She prayed for a safe trip. She prayed for the woman in the basement who had been left behind. She prayed for Her brother and She prayed for humanity.

She waited patiently.

After a while She fell asleep again.

She woke to the sound of the driver's door opening. She didn't know how long She had been sleeping. She had no idea how long her Dad had been in the building for. She knew that She had to pee, and She knew that Her tummy was growling. And She could use some water.

"Daddy, what happened in there?" She asked.

"Oh, it was nothing, Sweetie, you don't need to worry about it. Let's go now. Who's ready for an adventure?"

Her brother answered quickly. "I'm ready, Dad!" He was always ready for anything that his Dad offered up. Eager to please, and always eager to be included in anything that his Dad was doing.

She looked out the window. She didn't want to be a bother. She didn't want to upset her Dad. But She really needed to say something. "I have to go pee."

In the rear-view mirror her Dad made eye contact. "You'll have to hold it for a while okay? We don't have that far to go to the next town, maybe thirty or forty minutes. Can you do that for Dad? I just really need to get the fuck outta here."

Her mother spoke up. "She can't hold it. I will take Her." She opened the passenger door and removed her daughter from the vehicle. They walked together towards the building in the same way that Her father had done earlier.

"I'm sorry, Mommy." She was crying now. Tears rolling down Her pink cheeks.

"Don't be sorry, Sweet-heart, you can't help it. It's a force of nature. Don't worry about it, okay? Come here, gimme a kiss." She reached down and picked up her tiny little girl and carried her the rest of the way.

Orange Box, her embarrassed and ashamed box. She felt

that She was an inconvenience, that She was making a fuss, and that in some way Her actions were upsetting to Her father. For this She filed everything appropriately in the Orange Box, embarrassed and ashamed that She had had to ask for help.

.

CHAPTER 9

As they approached the building Her need to relieve Her bladder became more and more urgent. Her mother opened the door and they passed into the vestibule, and then they were buzzed through the second set of doors into the main lobby.

The Officer that had been talking to them at their truck was standing behind a counter, doing some paperwork. He looked up at us. His tan uniform was neatly pressed, his tie was held tightly against his chest with a shiny pin. His belt was black, thick and heavy-looking. She could see his gun in the holster on his right hip.

"Ma'am." He nodded at Her mother.

"Could we bother you to use your restroom? My daughter can't hold it, I'm really very sorry."

He moved from behind the counter and came towards where they were standing. "I'll show you where it is. Cute little thing, how old is She?"

"Oh, why thank you, She's two and a half."

"Love the hair, colour is beautiful. She seems small though, for two and half? Tiny I mean."

"She is small, yes." Her mother was not interested in talking much to the officer. She was intent on getting into the restroom.

They entered the restroom and She relieved herself. She made a sour face. Her eyes squinting; her mouth grimacing; her lips pursed in a hard line.

"Why the funny face, Sweetie?"

"It hurts, Mommy."

"It hurts to pee? Oh nuts, we will get you some cranberry juice and some water. How long were you holding it for? Was it a long time?"

She nodded. "I don't remember for how long exactly. Why that officer is so nice to you, but not nice to Dad?"

Her mother smiled at Her. "I don't know the answer to that, my Love, maybe because I didn't give him any reason *not* to be nice to me."

She thought about what Her mother said as they exited the rest room. Essentially She was stressing the golden rule, "do unto others..." She understood clearly what Her mother was suggesting. She questioned, however, why Her Dad did not.

The officer stopped them as they approached the counter on the way out of the building after they had finished in the restroom.

"Ma'am, everything all right?"

"Yes, of course, thank you."

"I mean with your travelling companion, Ma'am, is that your husband?" He nudged his head towards the truck. His uniform was neatly pressed, and had been tailored for him well.

Her mother held Her hand tightly. "Yes that's my husband, why do you ask, is something wrong?"

"Ma'am, how well do you know that man?"

"I'm sorry, why would you ask me that? I'm married to him, so I suppose I know him quite well. Is there something that you think I don't know?"

The officer piled his papers on top of another stack. "You just don't seem like the type to be mixed up with all that garbage I suppose. I can't arrest him today, but I would have liked to. I can tell you that for sure. And since he's going to Mexico again we know he's running. We also know what he's running from. We just can't prove it today. And you seem far too sweet, you seem kind and, well, honestly you're far too pretty to be hanging with the likes of him. Once he's gone we don't care. I hope he never tries to come back to the US or to Canada for that matter. If you need or want to stay, you need only to say something now and I will get your boy from the truck."

Her mother was in shock, she looked at the officer almost dumbfounded, she paused, inhaled deeply before answering, "No, sir, we are fine, thank you for your concern. I'm not sure what you are talking about, but I am sure that you have my husband confused for someone else."

The Officer nodded at her. "Yes, Ma'am, maybe so."

With that we walked out of the building and back to the waiting truck.

She made a mental note, Orange box. Embarrassed… This time though for Her mother.

CHAPTER 10

Juan Maria de Salvatierra was born November 15, 1648 in Milan, Italy, which was part of the great Holy Roman Empire. Of Italian mother and Spanish father,; this Jesuit student of the college of Parma, was fascinated by a book that he was accidentally introduced to, on the 'Indian Missions'. Juan was always easily bored with normal Italian life. He wasn't intrigued by his father's family business, he had no interest in art or wine. His studies at school had been thrilling to him, he had adored the student life and had dreamed of sharing the knowledge he had been lucky enough to absorb.

He had no interest in marrying the young woman that his parents had chosen for him, regardless of how suited she may be, or how grand the dowry she may bring the family. He understood the gravity of the situation for his own family but was rigidly opposed to being strong-armed into an arranged marriage.

The ideology of marriage, so central to their society, and to one's status in that society was cumbersome and somewhat distasteful in Juan's mind. A contractual relationship based on expressed mutual consent, supposedly existing between the husband and wife. Who in most cases had never met or who had met merely for moments. All of it was established on the basis of fortifying the family name. Strengthening blood lines and family affluence. In his eyes it was absurdity.

Juan sought solace within the confines of the Holy Catholic

Church. His hunger to escape the family pressures of marriage were relieved by a deepened connection to the Holy Father. He studied theology day and night and was exalted to professor. Soon he began to teach under graduates, who were as thirsty as he was for the word of God, and for any engagement that was edifying and enriching. His life was fulfilling to him.

In 1670, Pope Clement X succeeded Pope Clement the IX as the 239th Pope in the Vatican, just as Juan was becoming more and more dedicated to God. His own father however, was becoming more desperate with attempts to persuade him again to marry, to settle down and take a bride; to breed children, and be fruitful.

On his own accord Juan entered the Jesuit Order of Priests in Genoa and then in 1675 he sailed for New Spain; which is now known as present-day Mexico. Once in North America Juan became a Professor of Rhetoric at the College of the Holy Spirit, in Puebla, where he settled into a quiet and peaceful life, living on his own; living in holiness, with no wife, living in seclusion from his family, with no dowry, no inheritance, and no intent to advance the family name. He was at Peace.

CHAPTER 11

At night, when the stars were bright in the sky he would see her. Sometimes when the sun had set, and his dinner was done, Juan would wander into the garden behind the church. He would always remove his robes for this. He preferred the comfort of a lighter weight cassock in the evening heat. He enjoyed his time alone, after he had finished Mass, after the teaching was complete for the day and he was finished with Confessions.

He relished in the quiet moments of meditation and prayer, where he and the Lord could interact and reflect. He enjoyed the warm clean air, he enjoyed the Indian people that had fascinated him as a young boy. He believed that his work in Mexico was the Lord's work, that he had been divinely driven to this place.

He shared with the indigenous people the word of God, he evangelized them and encouraged them to share it amongst themselves. His mission was to bring the Holy Catholic Church and its order to this land. God had sent him and he was loyal and he was faithful. He spread the word.

He knew that God was pleased, and as he sat under the stars with a fresh mango and a cup of red wine he began to count the ways. The ways in which he believed he had pleased the Lord, and the ways in which he could please him more.

It wasn't the first time that he had seen her, nor was it the first time that he had heard her voice. She came to him that night with a clear message. Her voice was tender and silky, as it cut through the night air with ease. Like a soft breeze touching his cheek; gently brushing his ear.

Her long dark hair was shiny, and bounced as she walked towards him. Her dress was of the best tailor, crisp, pressed silk. The white garment was bright against the night sky.

He caught her eyes and stood, alarmed by her sudden presence, he wondered if she would stay long. He had seen her a few times over the years, she had come to him but never stayed long. Her beauty was mesmerizing, her skin was like ivory, so smooth-looking that he wanted to reach out and touch it, ever so gently, so as not to disturb her. Her hair flowed like spun silk dancing on her shoulders, her eyes so dark and penetrating. She challenged him; his thoughts were often impure after he would see her.

As she approached his standing figure, he spoke. "I'm Father Juan."

"Yes," she replied, a coy smile came across her lush red lips.

"I was just enjoying the moonlight, I like to count my blessings here with the stars, you see there are so many that I cannot ever run out." He was stammering. His legs felt weak, and his heart was beating faster than normal.

"Yes," she answered.

"Do you count your blessings?" he asked her.

"I do. We all do."

He was perplexed by her answer, for he knew that we didn't all count our blessings. "When you say, we all do, what do you mean exactly? We all do? I would like to think that in a perfect world, which clearly this is not, we would, but regrettably, Miss, I know that not to be the case."

"Faith, Juan, yes it is faith that you must follow, as you have. He is pleased."

Juan cut a piece of his mango and offered it to her, she shook her head, he took a step closer to her and she took a step back.

Juan picked up his cup and gulped his wine. "Who would that be now?"

"Yes. It is exactly whom you believe." She spoke in riddles it seemed.

"Who are you? What is your name? Do you live nearby?" Juan was anxious his heart still beating strong in his chest.

"My name is Miss Mary Mack, and I will be back, you shall share the word, your name will be remembered, from the day that I come back, I will wear black, you shall never lack."

Juan looked into his cup. It was only one third gone. He didn't believe he could possibly be drunk. "I don't understand these things you are rhyming, Miss Mary Mack, I'm frightfully sorry. I'm intrigued but confused."

"Tonight I wear white, my message is light. You walk the path that God paved right. More will come, a girl born to the earth. A message you deliver when the time is near night. Faithful you are, true to your word. Threads were stitched by family hands, to be protected from the moth. By your mother... and her mother, the weaver of your cloth."

She smiled, she turned and she disappeared into the air, like a fog rolling onto the ocean. Juan sat with his cup under the evening stars with his blessings, his sanity and a sense of fear; and he cried. He prayed, and he waited; for clarity, for the child, for the message, and for her to return.

CHAPTER 12

Driving through the Baja Peninsula to La Paz from San Diego is a long drive. It is a drive that should be done at a time of year when weather is not of detriment, when there is ample time for stops and for sleeping. If one decides to make the drive from San Diego, one should most definitely take the time to enjoy the scenery. The Baja Peninsula boasts some of the most spectacular sights in the world. One would be thankful to see boulders by the side of the road the size of great buildings, wild life, greenery, floral and mountain ranges. All of these things should be seen however in the light of day. This trip should not be made in the dark. This is why.

The border crossing at Tijuana, San Ysidro, can take some time; the lines to cross from the United States into Mexico, with a vehicle, can be up to two hours long some times. Walking across the border can be efficient, even liberating for some people, however, when one is moving all of one's things, in a pickup truck, one must wait in the line regardless of how long it might be.

At Tijuana, the Mexican Border Guards, don't care who comes in to Mexico. They may ask to see identification, but for the most part, the majority of individuals entering their country at this point of entry are doing so to escape for a couple of days. The trip is made south of the border to shop for a weekend, and to spend a day exploring. A city in Baja California, which is adjacent to the U.S. border, also called "the corner of Mexico," Tijuana is waiting for travellers to walk through its streets and submerge themselves in its multifaceted and vibrant culture. The eclectic style of the city can hypnotize you with its walls converted into street art expositions, its old marketplaces taken over by independent plastic artists, its historic buildings and its monumental arch, - an architectural icon within its avant-garde style. The history of Tijuana is displayed in the Museo de Historia de Tijuana, located inside the Old Municipal Palace, today called Palacio de Cultura. However, the sights and sounds of the monuments and culture were not to be seen from the line-up at immigration.

After waiting in the truck for nearly two hours, in the hot November sun, it was finally their turn to approach the window. The vehicle crept forward. The children's dad looked at them in the rear-view mirror. He looked frustrated, he was hot and he was agitated. "Nobody say anything, got it." He preferred them to be seen and not heard.

The two kids nodded. What else were they to do? What did he think they were going to say? She wondered if he thought that maybe someone was going to spill the beans and say that he was a shitty dad. That he yelled too much, that he drank too many rums, or that he was mean to their mother. She knew that he didn't treat their mother well. She was sad. She didn't smile much. She was preoccupied and looked tired. Maybe he was worried that She was going to tell that he made Her hold Her pee too often and that She got a bladder infection.

"Buenas Tardes, Señor, a Donde Vas?" She knew that Her dad didn't speak the language of this country. She understood it though, and She knew that Her mother did too. But he had specifically told them to say nothing; so She would remain mute, following his instructions to a tee.

Her father said nothing in response, he looked at the dark-skinned border agent, hoping that he would what? Let it ride this time? Let them through and into his country without an answer? She daydreamed often, She thought of perhaps an old-style Mexican shootout, guns a-blazing, with only one man standing in the end. A white sombrero shining in the sun, as the victor walked off. She didn't think such an endeavour would end well for Her father... "Senor? A donde vas, Senor?" The agent was louder this time, louder and sterner; as though he was demanding an answer. She thought, louder must make it more comprehensible; -in most languages anyway.

"I don't speaka da Mexicano. Do you speaka da English?" Her dad finally responded. He was waving his hands as he was speaking, as if he was trying to sign, or play charades with this poor man. She was immediately embarrassed for him.

The agent looked down at him from the booth window, it was somewhat demeaning to all of them. His tone, the expression on his face and the body language from the window, even a two-year-old could read it loud and clear.

"Yes, sir, I speak English, I also speak French, Italian, and Spanish. In Mexico, sir, you will find many, many people who speak Spanish, but very few Mexicans who speaka da "Mexicano" like you say. Can I see your identification please, sir?"

Her father cleared his throat and then answered, "I thought we could just cross here with no ID."

"Sir, is there a problem? I would like to see your driver's licence please, if I may."

"No, there's no problem it's just that I heard that you guys don't ask for ID here, so I'm just surprised that's all. I wasn't expecting you to ask. I don't think you need to make a federal case out of it. I just don't think you need to see mine when you probably didn't ask for the last guy's, or the guy before that. I mean I make one language fuck up and your gonna fuck me over now? "

"I see," said the Mexican border patrol. "Sir, would you please exit the vehicle, passengers too, I would like to see your identification and I will be conducting a search of the vehicle at this time; you will have the right to return to the vehicle after we have completed our search, and if and before you are taken into custody."

"What the? Are you kidding me?" Her dad was angry. She could see his head turning red, his temples were throbbing, She had seen him get mad like this before, it hadn't turned out well before, and She didn't anticipate that it would end well now.

Mental note to self, Red Box.

"No, sir, I am not joking with you now. Please..." He opened the driver's door with his left hand, he had his right hand on his hip, She guessed that his pistol was holstered there. He held his hand out pointing the way to where they could all wait while the search was being conducted.

Her mother leaned over to her father. "Please tell me that they won't find anything."

"Of course not, what do I look like an idiot?"

She turned away from him. "A little bit yeah, a little bit."

CHAPTER 13

The Sonoran Desert covers over 100,000 square miles, stretching from southern Arizona about 250 miles south of the border into Mexico. Because the Baja California Peninsula was once attached to western Mexico, the Sonoran Desert is found on both sides of the Sea of Cortez and most of Baja California is part of this desert.

The Sonoran Desert in Baja California is divided into four sub-regions, each with its own distinct geography. The San Felipe Desert, in the northeast part of the peninsula, is the driest with an average of five centimetres of rainfall per year. The Gulf Coast Desert is a narrow strip that runs along the Sea of Cortez from Bahia Los Angeles, all the way to the tip of the peninsula. This area receives moisture from tropical storms and nearby mountains which create *"arroyos"* or underground streams.

On the Pacific Side of the Baja, the Vizcaino Desert is the largest sub-region, stretching from El Rosario, 1000 kilometres to the south. Precipitation in this area is low, but vegetation receives moisture from the condensation of heavy coastal fog. South of the Vizcaino is the Magdalena Plains, sometimes the combined area is referred to as the Central Desert. Coastal mangroves, swamps, and large underground aquifers that support agriculture differentiate this region.

Mean annual precipitation on the entire peninsula is 15.3 centimetres, but there are great variances of rainfall throughout the peninsula, and from year to year. There are two main seasons of precipitation in Baja California. Winter storms bring gentle rains from the Pacific, but because of mountain ranges on the peninsula, these storms usually fail to reach the deserts on the Gulf Coast.

The mountains of the peninsula can receive substantial rains and periodically, large amounts of water are washed down the river beds. Even though the arroyos may appear dry most of the year, moisture is retained in the soil and they are lined with shrubs, trees and flowering plants. Because of the twice-yearly rainfall, both winter and summer annuals grow on the peninsula and perennial plants are able to survive as well.

There are more than 110 species of cacti on the peninsula, including the world's largest cactus, the *Cardon.* Cacti have several adaptations to survive the sun and scarce rainfall. Spines on cacti help break up the sun's rays, and thick, waterproof skins prevent water loss. Cacti have extensive root systems that extend horizontally within the top three inches of the soil and are able to capture moisture over a large area.

Many cacti have a barrel shape, which provides a large volume of water storage with a small surface area. Columnar cacti, such as the Cardon and Saguaro, have vertical framework that allows their trunks to expand to store large amounts of water when it is available, then contract when water is scarce.

The Baja California peninsula hosts around 300 species of birds, most of which are coastal or pelagic birds. Many desert birds are carnivores, with a substantial amount of their moisture intake coming from the juices of the animals and insects they feed on.

All of these birds, and plants survive until a drought supersedes. When Wildlife is not sustainable, the food chain becomes smaller. Those at the top of the food chain become ravenous.

The search of the vehicle turned up nothing. No drugs, no concealed weapons. No stolen property. It had all been for nothing, a waste of time, a waste of energy, stolen moments in this life used to prove nothing to no one for nothing to gain nothing and lose nothing but time and dignity.

They were free to go on their way, to enjoy the country. Where Mexicano was the new language. Thinking of it made Her giggle. Mexicano...

She sat in the back of the truck and practised Her songs. She knew many of them. She loved to sing, and to memorize the words. She especially loved Disney movie songs. She could sing for hours, sometimes Her brother would sing along with Her. He liked music too, but wasn't as comfortable as She was with performing. She thrilled at the prospect of entertaining. One day She hoped to sing on a stage, wearing a grand yellow dress like Belle or a flowing blue gown like Cinderella. Bellowing out the tune with everything She had to the beat of 'Colours of the Wind' or 'Beauty and the Beast'.

She slept for what seemed like a long while, and when She woke, it had turned dark. Darkness in the desert was truly as dark as the earth could get. There was no light from anything other than what the stars and the moon were able to provide through the light dusting of cloud. She could see the moon shine through the window, She thought the stars looked closer here than they did at home. She wondered if maybe it was perhaps that they only appeared closer because they were driving closer to the equator.

They were still driving, but She wasn't certain for how long they had been on the highway. Her mouth was sticky inside, and She felt hot. She pushed the blanket off of Herself, and grabbed Her water bottle. Her bladder felt full, with that came a sharp and nagging pain in Her abdomen. She fought the need to say something to Her father. She knew he was opposed to stopping. He relished in the ability to stay ahead of his own schedule, unscheduled stops put a damper on his proficiency of time management. He pleased himself with his own execution of skill.

She could no longer hold it. Her bladder was screaming at Her.

"Dad, I need to go pee. I'm sorry, Dad."

He looked at Her in the rear-view mirror. "There's really no place to stop, can you hold it?" He found these interruptions rather bothersome. The time loss was annoying, and besides he actually didn't see a place to stop. He hadn't seen a gas station or a convenience store for miles.

"I can pull over, but there's no gas station, no toilet, so you will have to go on the side of the road, you okay with that?"

Her mother piped up, "Is that safe out here? In the desert I mean?" She looked at him sideways, she didn't want to alert the children to her unsettled feelings. "I've heard of a few reasons why you might not want to do something like that at night." She thought of the travel books she had picked up from the AMA, the ones that had referenced night creatures like scorpions, coyotes, and snakes. She wondered when the last time was that they had seen a road sign; other than one that identified twists in the roadway.

"Do you know where we are? Do you remember what the last town was?"

He was thinking, she could tell by the way that he held his mouth. His lips were pursed. His eyebrows became furled. "Well, let's talk it out, there was Tijuana, then, Rosarita, Ensenada, Santo Tomas, San Quintin, El Rosario, Chapala,

Punta Prieta, Rosarita again, don't you think they should think about that? Like about calling the towns the same thing? There's two Rosaritas, don't you think it's kind of strange?"

"Just pull over, fuck it! She's gonna explode. She has to pee. Jesus Christ, why can you not just answer the fucking question? Pull over, here, pull over. Pull over, now, PULL OVER!" As the truck swerved quickly to the right and slowed, red dust and sand billowed in a cloud around it.

Her mother opened the passenger door and flipped the seat forward, allowing space for Her to move out. She looked at her brother. "You too?"

"May as well, yeah." Both children moved behind the vehicle and with their mother, out of the dust. The sky was black, like onyx, shiny and still, feathery clouds hung in front of the stars like masks, making it darker than it might have normally been.

They moved quickly, their feet moving steady and sure on the ground. They could hear the truck still softly running, the door ajar, chiming, reminding them that they had left the door open. The sand and pebbles crunched under their shoes, the night air was still warm, but fresh, like a change in season was brewing. It smelled like rain.

Her brother unzipped his shorts and released himself, he made a stream in the sand with his urine, and a silly face as he did it. "Look, Mom, I guess I did have to go after all."

"That's awesome, Honey, I'm glad that you decided to come with us." She could hear the ping, ping, ping of the truck door, she had left it open knowing that it would be a challenge for him to take off and leave them there if the door was ajar. The taillights glowed bright red, in the darkness that surrounded them. She struggled with his lack of empathy towards the children, or maybe it was just lack of interest, she couldn't really figure it out. But she didn't want to risk having him leave them out in the middle of nowhere.

She had to pee as well, so it was good that they had stopped. Her tiny little one had to go badly, She was always so careful about where She would go and how. She was particular about the toilets that She would use, the cleanliness of them. She liked them to be fresh, clean and fragrant, not dirty. She preferred a white toilet to an older coloured toilet like dusty rose or gold. She could use those, but her preference was always white. She didn't like the idea of having to pee into the sand. She really liked a toilet seat. Especially white ones, made from porcelain and She liked silver toilet paper holders. Like at Grandma's house.

Her mother found them a spot, that was out in the open, away from the truck and the road, but nowhere near the cactus, nor the shrubs and bushes. She knew why. Her mother was smart. Her mother knew that near the bushes there could be snakes, and if you were a coyote, and you need a place to hide, it would not be out in the open. You have to hide behind something, like a bush or a shrub. So even though She didn't like the open field She knew that She was safer here.

She turned towards Her brother so that he wouldn't be able to see Her bottom when She peed. She pulled Her shorts down to Her ankles, then Her pink panties, She spread Her feet shoulder width apart; squatted, and holding Her mom's hands relieved Her bladder of what felt like an enormous amount of liquid. It seemed to not ever end, Her bladder continued to empty, a puddle developed quickly in the sand around Her feet.

She looked up and saw Her brother had wandered off a wee bit, he was moving away from where they had set up their desert bathroom, and was straying away from the truck.

Farther into the desert, farther from the highway, farther from where he was supposed to be.

Her bladder was still draining, it was hurting now that it was near empty. Her mom reached into her bag and pulled out a Kleenex for Her to wipe Herself. Her mom always thought of everything, or at least it seemed like it to Her.

She was watching Her brother as he seemed to be toddling off into the darkness. She wondered if there was something drawing him, or was he just meandering? He seemed to be looking for something, his eyes were drawn to the ground, his feet pushing the sand and the dust from side to side as he walked towards a cluster of cactus.

She watched him closely, his red plaid shirt beginning to muddle as the distance grew between them. She finished peeing and wiped herself with the Kleenex that Her mother had provided. She shoved the dirty tissue into Her own pocket, of Her turquoise shorts, as She stood, and looked up to see where Her brother was getting to; She felt responsible for him, despite being the younger of the two of them. Oddly She seemed older in some ways, had always bore a sense of ownership for his safety, and for his well-being.

From behind the knot of shrubs and cactus, She could see two shiny red dots. The dots seemed to be about the size of dimes from where She was standing. She couldn't see if the dots were attached to something or not. It was too dark for Her to see that far into the distance.

"Mommy." Her mother was peeing now, squatting in a similar position to that which She had just been in.

"Yes, Sweetie, Hey, can you see your brother? Geez I look away for two seconds and the boy wanders off."

"Mommy, what's that over there?" She pointed towards the red dots at the cactus bushes. She could still see Her brother's plaid shirt, about 150 feet between where they were standing and the cactus. The red dots were obvious, they were alive and they were glowing. Their presence was discernible, from the distance Her mother could sense the hot predatorial breath, its energy radiating from behind the shrubbery. She knew what it was, and she also knew it wasn't safe to stay where they were.

"Oh, my Jesus Lord. Shit!" Her mother stood and pulled up her pants. She could hear the truck still running, as she took her eyes off her boy for a split second to see if the door was still ajar. She had read about this in the travel books, she hadn't expected it to happen to them however, not when all they had wanted to do was stop to pee. Nothing ever seemed to be easy.

"Sweetie, run to the truck and get in, run as fast as you can, go! Don't look back! Go! Now!"

She did as She was told. She moved like lightning, fast as Her feet would carry Her She ran in the sand. She was crying because She knew that there was something wrong. She knew that what She had seen was evil. She ran, and She ran, and the truck seemed to be so far away from where they had been peeing. She wanted so badly to look back, but She knew that if She did it would slow Her down. So She just ran.

Her mother never had to make a plan, she just instinctively reacted and acted in situations that required her to do so. She pivoted in the sand, and removed her feet from her flip-flops in one swift movement as she burst into a sprint. It appeared to be fifty yards from where she now was to where he was standing. His head was bowed down; he was clearly looking at something in the sand, from the distance it appeared that it must be a flower or something small at the base of the cactus.

Her mother's thighs pumped hard, quads fully engaged, adrenaline pulsing through her veins, sand flying behind her as her feet were smashing into the desert ground. Calves crushing, heart throbbing, fear pulsing through her, seeing her son's predator moving towards her child, stalking him, slowly lurking smelling the air, sniffing the child out, enjoying the musky sweet sweat smell of boy in the air.

Animals of the peninsula display adaptations for the hot, arid conditions of the desert. Most desert creatures are light grey or buff-coloured, an adaptation that provides camouflage and prevents light absorption. Most desert animals adapt to the heat by modifying their behaviour – some limit their activities to cooler hours and locations, while others burrow to avoid the heat of the sun. They become nocturnal, wolf-like, hunters of the night.

The drought in the Sonoran Desert had enriched a hunger in the animal that could be easily satisfied by a human delight. The lack of water had left virtually no plant life for consumption and smaller animals had become scarce.

Members of the dog family and birds use panting as a means of cooling themselves. Some rodents use estivation, a summer or drought version of hibernation, to survive the hottest parts of the year, while others use short periods of dormancy that last only a few hours. Many rodents habituate the desert, like squirrels, gophers, mice, rats and rabbits. They attempt to live amongst each other, relying on their resourcefulness, and adaptability for survival.

The kangaroo rat has morphed its species with special adaptations so it never needs to drink water; obtaining moisture through the seeds it eats, living in burrows with higher humidity, condensing moisture in its nasal passages, and excreting uric acid in a concentrated paste, instead of in liquid form.

Bats are plentiful in the Sonoran Desert and play a very important role as pollinators for flowering cacti and agaves.

Amphibians and reptiles, such as lizards, geckos, and spiny-tailed iguanas, are all common in the desert landscape. These small animals provide excellent nourishment for mammals, which can become opportunistic predators.

Mule deer inhabit Baja California and there is even a rare endemic peninsular variety. Mule deer live in the lower foothills and canyons and have exceptionally large ears, which help to alert them to danger. Adults are prey to mountain lions, while fawns fall prey to coyotes. The Mule Deer were falling victim to the drought, their population adversely affected by the lack of rain and food. The most widespread mammal on the peninsula is the coyote. In many areas, the coyote is the top predator in the food chain. Coyotes are omnivorous, hunting small animals, and eating plant matter such as cactus fruits.

Mountain lions on the peninsula do not live in the desert itself, but in the adjacent mountainous regions. Where mountain lions exist, they become the top predator and play an important role in culling old, weak and sick deer. Mountain lions are mostly nocturnal and capture their prey by ambush, relying on their speed and leaping ability. Here in the desert, the coyote ruled the roost, it may as well have been Wylie himself that was hunting her child, she was determined to save him.

Her pace was electrified, her heart was pounding in her throat, she could see that her child was oblivious to the danger ahead, and the wild dog was relishing in the boy's ignorance of his presence.

Her mother got to the child first, she reached out and placed her two hands around the boy's waist as she lifted his body into the air in one scooping motion. Her body weight shifted as she pivoted in the sand, careful not to turn her back on the ravaged hungry beast. She cautiously changed direction, reversing her steps to where she had just come from.

The coyote is native to North America, it is a smaller animal than its close relative the grey wolf. It is known that ancestors of the coyote have diverged from the grey wolf one to two million years ago. It is believed that there are nineteen subspecies in circulation living in either nuclear families or in loosely knit packs of unrelated individuals.

She had only seen the one wild dog who had emerged from behind the bush. It hadn't occurred to her that the coyote was protecting his den. Time was brewing nicely for a perfectly planned attack by the entire pack.

The six pups that had been crying and had distracted the boy were hidden beneath one of the bushes. The alpha male had observed the young boy wandering towards his own family and had reacted by alerting the others. They were prepared to assault in defence of their own.

Humans are the coyotes only serious enemy. She knew that she had to find within herself an aggression that would be bold enough to overcome the mutt. The dog was growling and snarling, his yellowed fangs exposed, saliva dripping from his jowls, he continued to move towards her. Relentless, he shadowed her movements, with each step she took backwards, he took one towards her.

She continued to back away, moving with extreme caution, sweat beaded on her forehead, and as her breath came faster, it resonated in her ears. All other sounds became out of her reach, the exhaust from the running truck, the ping of the door ajar notification; her son's heartbeat. She heard nothing but her own breath and the voice in her head that instructed her. She bent down and reached with her left hand towards the ground. She grabbed a dead branch from a bush that hadn't survived the dry spell. She threw it in the direction of the coyote, intending to scare him, to grasp and maintain dominance over the animal.

Her elaborate toss of the tree branch did nothing but alert the remaining dogs of the pack to the potential danger of the Alpha male. The remaining Coyotes emerged from behind the cactus clusters quickly and with a thirst to protect the den. The pack thrust forward, barking and growling. The group pushed forward through the sand moonlight now shining off their grey backs.

She continued to back towards the truck, moving more rapidly, fear pulsing through her. The sight of the pack coming at her heightening the alarm, she threw her boy on the ground towards the truck and yelled at him, "RUN!"

CHAPTER 14

Juan Maria de Salvatierra sat behind the church each night with a cup of wine and a heart full of prayer. He waited.

Each night he would repeat what he believed to be exactly what he had done on the night that Mary Mack had last appeared to him.

Each night he retired to his bed, never having seen her again.

Years passed and Juan grew older. Father Juan was committed to his faith and walked the path of the Lord each day. His works were known far and wide, and still he continued to pray and he continued to labour for God.

And each night he would wait for her to return. He would occasionally ask for a special favour in prayer, that he might once again get a glimpse of her, or have just a moment in time to share with her. But alas it seemed that his own prayers were not to be answered.

As he became too old to travel, and he was confined to his quarters in the church, he spent more and more time in prayer. He wrote his papers in the day time, when the light was plentiful, papers that he had been obliged to write for King Phillip V. He was honoured to do so and yet bothered by the task of it.

His beard and his hair grew long as he was no longer able to tend to them. Both of them greyed. He looked like an old man as he lay at night weeping.

"Please, Lord, let her appear that I may understand the message, that I might be clear on what it is that you want of me. Please, Lord, that I might be pleasing to you, and that I may fulfill all that you desired of me."

In his last moments as a man, as a Priest and a member of the cloth, she once again appeared to him. This time she came as a young girl. Her hair was dark, curled in ringlets, which bounced as she moved. Her eyes were piercing dark, her smile bright like the morning sun. Her dress was a beautiful black silk, with buttons all down the back, silver buttons that shone like diamonds.

She smiled at Juan, who had been waiting. "Hello, Mary Mack."

"Hello, Juan, I have come back, I am all dressed in black, with silver buttons, buttons, buttons, all up my back, back, back."

He was so taken with her beauty, he was near speechless. "Yes, Mary, I see."

"It's Mary Mack, I am back, back, back, to take you home, home, home, never again alone, alone, alone."

Juan was ready, he felt that he had served the Lord well, he had done all that he could possibly do as a man, but he wondered in that moment if perhaps he had disappointed his parents. He knew that they had wanted him to marry. They had been depending on it; for the financial survival of the family. He just hadn't been able to sacrifice his own desires for that of his earthly father. He had followed his heart, he had listened to everything that he had been called to do and he had done it well.

He hoped in this moment as he was now about to face his maker that it had not been in vain. That his heart's calling had really been the Lord, that it hadn't been his own desire. He hoped for a greeting of joy and happiness, of great pleasure and pride in what he had achieved.

He looked up at the small girl who was standing before him now, the beautiful young child who had been sent to help him in crossing over. He also wondered if this was his imagination, if perhaps his subconscious mind had created her and was manifesting her in his last moments on earth.

Was she the promise of unrealized desires, his own desires for children that had not become reality due to his choice to follow God? Was she actually a symbol of disappointment? Of heartbreak and broken dreams? A shadow of the children that he didn't have?

Juan cried out, "Lord, am I right with you now?"

He heard nothing. He could still see the girl, he could smell her sweet vanilla scent.

The night air was still; it was humid and heavy. The leaves outside of the window hung restless waiting for a breeze to release them. The heat was all around him, Juan felt trapped, short of breath, the sheets were damp and clung to his body. He closed his eyes as sweat dripped from his limbs and his aching body.

He began to chant. "Hail Mary, full of grace, the Lord is with thee, Blessed art thou amongst women and blessed is the fruit of thy womb Jesus. Holy Mary, Mother of God, Pray for us sinners, now and in the hour of our death, amen." Again and again and again he prayed the rosary, clutching his beads tightly in his hand.

And then it happened for him.

Juan's body became light, he shook it off like he no longer needed it. He could see light everywhere, there was no more darkness. The heaviness of the world escaped him. He reached for Mary's hand, and she took it. With tears streaming down his face, he smiled at her. As they moved on he knew that he no longer needed to answer all of the questions that he had had. He knew that he was right. And he knew that God was not done with him yet.

CHAPTER 15

Her father had gotten out of the truck in a state of panic, he stood behind the tailgate, watching the horror unfold, scared to move, unable to assist his wife from this distance.

In the cab of the truck She sat, She focused on the stars that were shining through the clouds, the ones that She could see. She counted them and as She did, with each one She prayed. The same prayer, over and over, with each new star She saw.

"Dear God, be with us now, save my mother and my brother from the mouths of wolves. Throw a blanket of your love over them as protection and walk with them always, in the caves of darkness and in the absence of light. Be here tonight with abounding strength and triumphant light leading them away from the fight. Amen"

She maintained Her focus, She prayed, and She prayed without ceasing. She held Her tiny hands folded in Her lap, Her lips quivering with fear. She prayed again, and She prayed again.

Until finally a shift occurred; and the clouds parted, exposing additional stars, and the moon shone down brightly, illuminating the dark and desiccated desert. And She knew that She had done well.

CHAPTER 16

As Her mother continued to back away, her young son running away from her towards the truck , his eyes wide with fear; she felt a shift in the energy of the animals. The clouds parted only slightly at first, and then more, until the moon lit the area like a spotlight shining towards a Broadway stage.

The backs of the animals glistened in the moonlight, sparkled like diamonds; their coats normally mangy and ratty were as beautiful as a show dog's shiny cared-for coat. She marvelled at the wonder of it. She stopped moving and held up her hand in dominance. The dogs halted. There was no sound but the muffled rumbling of the running truck and the sound of her own heart beating.

The sand suddenly felt warm under her feet, before she had felt nothing but fear. She continued to hold her hand up to the dogs and the alpha began to back away now. The others followed retreating to back towards the den. She watched them go, and caught her breath. She looked up at the stars, and the night sky, watching the clouds roll over the moon once again.

"Thank you, Jesus." She moved towards where she had come out of her flip-flops and picked them up. She looked at her husband still standing behind the truck, and her son now safely there with him. She knew that her daughter was safely in the cab of the vehicle, and had been for a few minutes. She wondered if he would have intervened had they caught her. Would he have done anything? Would he have attempted to save her or would he have left her to the wolves?

She sat in the front seat of the truck and knew that it was over because it was quiet. There was no longer any barking, no more growling or howling sounds. She could see Her mother moving back towards the vehicle, She could hear Her brother talking to Her father. She thought it appropriate to quickly say thank you. "Thank you, Lord, I know it was You that intervened. I won't forget." And She made a mental note and filed the event into Her Purple Box, for faith events.

CHAPTER 17

The night was beginning to feel long, the road seemed endless with its winding and snaking turns. Occasionally She would gather the courage to look out Her window into the darkness, while they were in the mountain range She was terrified to see nothing below them but the ocean below. She estimated the fall to be near 200 feet to the crest of the water. The truck raced the corners never slowing, never braking. She closed Her eyes and prayed for Her own survival, for that of Her mother and for Her brother. She felt stronger, a strange sensation had come over Her during the coyote incident that She wasn't in complete understanding of. She knew that She was a normal child, with eyes and ears and hands and feet. Her heart pumped blood, and Her lungs functioned as others did. In with the good air, out with the bad, but despite those things, She felt that She was different. She was here for more than just survival, more than just to be. Her life had a purpose, a meaning for existence. She glanced out the window and down again at the ocean below. Crashing onto the cliffs, breaking into great white clouds of mist.

She knew instinctively that Her father would survive anything, She wondered if perhaps he had nine lives like that of a cat. And if that was in fact the case, how many would he have used up already? How many would be left over. She knew that if humans weren't willing to listen to Her thoughts, Jesus would always hear Her. She prayed for Her own soul.

She knew that there was more for Her to do, more to see and that there were things that She was here to learn.

Her father made the decision to drive straight through to La Paz with no stops for sleep. He fancied arriving sooner, rather than later. She didn't understand the concept of rushing to be first and missing the fun along the way. She would rather see the desert in the daylight, perhaps experience the sights, see the cactus and cliffs, the expansive sand dunes and wild life.

They pushed on headed south towards La Paz; with no stops. Her father enjoyed driving through the night because he believed it was to his advantage. Night driving reduced the need to stop for unnecessary pit stops, sight seeing, coyote ambushes or snake fights, there should never be a need to stop period. Without needing to stop for food, there would also be limited access to beverages, which would reduce the need to pee. He anticipated that the children would sleep and he could focus on the road, without needing to listen to Disney Tunes, or the seemingly endless chatter that came from the backseat of the truck.

There would also be no need to stop for food, which would reduce his cost for the trip. Most importantly he wouldn't have to pay for a hotel room which would further increase his savings. With limited access to cash, and no credit cards, he had to think about every penny that they spent. And every penny that was frivolously spent was one penny too much, was one penny that could be spent on something that he wanted, something for himself.

He pushed onward, although even he had to admit the darkness was at time ominous. Blackness from east to west and from the blacktop of the road to as far north as the eye was able to see. An abyss. Clouds obviously covered the stars and the moon, as he wasn't able to make out any of them; their illustrious beauty hidden behind the curtain of the evening sky.

Driving gave him time to think, time to process on his own; he enjoyed the evening air and, he kept the window down to keep himself alert. The highway was unnervingly narrow and in many places barely wide enough for two trucks to safely pass. If they both pulled way over, slowed almost to a halt, and sucked in their side mirrors, they could do it. But it was hard on the nerves, especially if they met on a tight curve, or on one of the cliffs. One wrong move and one of them could end up tumbling off and into the crashing waves below.

Trucks and buses travel the roads day and night, and they are used to it, the drivers are accustomed to the curvy road and its natural hazards. They travel the road hauling provisions to habitations scattered along the roadway on a daily basis. They know each shoulder like they know their own face, like their own hands or the curve of their wife's back. Where there are shoulders, and where the road is lacking shoulders.

The road is frequently littered with hazards, blocked by livestock or pockmarked by treacherous potholes. Often lacking not only shoulders, but guardrails, and bridges, proper striping and road signs. The road is frequently littered with hazards, blocked by livestock or pockmarked by treacherous potholes. The highway can be as dangerous as it is beautiful. In the daytime, you can capture the beauty, at night you are only captive of the dangers.

The Baja's isolation and geology protect ecosystems that harbour hundreds of plant and animal species found nowhere else on Earth. There are more kinds of cactus here than anywhere else in the world, and most of them are found no place else. The beauty of them can be intoxicating, the size of them mesmerizing, even in darkness. Cactus hundreds of years old, soaring to heights that from the truck seemed to be fifty to sixty feet high, with multiple arms.

The challenges presented by the highway's unpredictable asphalt, the surprising communities, the harsh land and hardy inhabitants, spectacular scenery and unique roadside vegetation were making this trip like no other that he had ever driven; he was disappointed that the wife was sleeping through it.

He looked at the turquoise clock on the dash 3:42, she had become kind of lame in his mind. Childbirth had softened her. In the old days she would have been right there beside him, talking, sharing, and laughing. Instead she was sleeping. He took a sip of his cold coffee. Left from earlier in the day. He didn't want to be a hypocrite. Being that he restricted the consumption of fluids for the rest of them. But he really needed the caffeine from the cold coffee to keep himself alert.

He reached over to poke her, just to rustle her enough that she would wake on her own. That way she wouldn't blame him. He was aware of how he needed to manipulate her in order to get what he needed, at least most of the time. She had turned out to be smarter than he had anticipated though.

Just as he poked her, and she started to stir, he saw it in the middle of the road. He slammed on the brakes and his coffee cup flew into the windshield. She woke as her head hit the dash, her dark hair tossing from left to right as her head flopped about the cab. His paper cup ending up in his lap, cold coffee spilling on his shorts. Both children woke up screaming, alarmed at the sudden stop.

He turned around. "You two okay?" Their eyes were wide with shock, but they said nothing.

"What the hell?!" His wife was very awake now.

"Water on the road." He flashed the high beams on so she could see. "Look, we almost hit that at full speed."

He turned around again. "You two clowns okay back there?"

"Yeah, Dad. I'm good," her brother replied. Yawning as he was waking.

The road was completely covered by water. From where they sat it appeared that they had come across a river. A black flowing channel cresting fast in front of them. The highway on which they had driven thus far had essentially disappeared from in front of them. The roadway had been replaced by a rapidly flowing river that crossed the tarmack; as though a bridge had been washed out, or the highway had been built through a gulley that had just recently filled with water. It raged in front of them, and spanned what appeared to be well over two hundred yards from side to side.

"How are we going to get across? It looks as though the road just ends?" Her mother was looking at her husband. "How far across do you think it is?"

He rubbed the back of his head, and then set the coffee cup into the cup holder. "I think it looks like about three football fields, not super far, what do you think we should do?"

She was the rational one of the two of them, level-headed. "Where are we now, how long was I asleep for?"

"I don't know, I have about a third of a tank of gas, so I can't go back, I need to push forward to the next town to fill up, but I don't know how deep it is in the middle there; what if the asphalt has been washed away and the sand beneath has eroded."

"And there is absolutely no way around." She looked behind them into the darkness, and to either side as if looking for a sign, or a signal, to see if there was some way to skirt around the edges of the waterway.

In the backseat the two children were quiet. She had to pee, but didn't dare say a word. She kept Herself still in Her car seat, Her lips pressed tightly together, She rubbed Her head against the back of the seat to comfort Herself.

Her mother looked pretty in the darkness. She seemed alert and provoked. She was problem-solving again. She knew the look that Her mother wore when she leapt into action. She was merely sorry that She saw the look more than She wished or that She needed to.

Her mother looked across at their dad. "Turn on the high beams again." He shook his head, as though he disagreed, but he did it anyway.

Across the water another vehicle responded and turned on their lights. "So there is a car on the other side." He looked at her. "So what."

"So, that means that the water hasn't been here for that long. How long would you wait? It's not as if they would sit there for two or three days. A couple of hours, okay maybe, maybe their vehicle is old, or small. But they aren't going to sit there for days. I can guarantee you that."

"Okay you might have a point, but that still doesn't tell me how deep it is. I can sort of guess better how far it is to the other side though, now that I have a marker on the other side, so that's a bonus."

She was mildly amused. "Yes, true, we can now see into the darkness and have a visual on the other side of the river. Here's what I know from reading those "stupid" books from the AMA. Floodwaters from rapid downpours gush in rivers like this. The ground is too dry for the water to penetrate, and the water just comes too fast. This will probably subside when the sun comes out in the morning. But that would still be three hours from now. So I can pretty much guess that the asphalt would be intact. So it should only be three feet or so deep."

"What if the road isn't flat? What if there is a hill, or a crest in the road?"

She hadn't thought of that. "Good point."

From the backseat, two children under the age of four were listening to the discussion. Both were learning, but both were ever so tired.

"Where is the air intake on this vehicle?"

He looked at her sideways, "Air intake is on the top front of the grill, with the lift from the tires we probably have forty-two maybe forty-five inches of clearance." The 1994 Chevy Pickup was a Z-71 model, with the four by four package, with air intake placement on the top front of the grill. "I see what you are thinking; we drive head on into it. Go right through it and hope for the best. The water won't penetrate the air system of the truck because the intake should be higher than the water will likely reach, and the rest will dry. The only unknown will of course be a sudden drop in the road."

Her mother looked behind them and noticed that they were no longer alone on the road, there were other cars and trucks stopped behind them. There were people getting out of their vehicles, lighting cigarettes and walking towards the water's edge.

"So here's what I'm thinking, I will drive, I take the wheel. You get out and walk in front of the truck, I will follow you into the water, you will be able to tell if the road is going to drop or if it is suddenly going to start to slope. You can signal me and I can reverse. If we get water into the air system the truck is tits. So we can try but if it gets too deep then we have to back it up."

He looked at her uncertain, he didn't want to get into the water. It was flowing fast, and he was pretty sure it would be cold. He thought of suggesting that she walk it, but then he realized that she was only five foot five, he was six feet tall. He was the obvious choice. And of course there was the fact that he was a man; he hated that, he hated that he had to do the shit jobs all the time.

"Fine." He looked back at the two in the back seat, he held his hand out to his son. "Buddy, if I don't see you again, take care." He smiled and shook his little hand. He pulled his sunglasses from the collar of his t-shirt and placed them on the seat of the truck and took the change out of the pockets of his shorts. He pulled his flip-flops off and opened the driver's door of the truck.

Her brother radiated at the acknowledgement, at the grand gesture in perhaps his father's final moments. He had noticed him, and not Her.

CHAPTER 18

She watched from the back seat as Her dad began to walk into the water in front of the truck. She wondered how deep the water would get? What if he disappeared completely? She rubbed Her head into Her car seat hard. She found it comforting to rub Her hair against something that was firm. Sometimes She would rub it until a nest formed on the back of Her head. A ball of hair knotted into a lump that Her mother would have to cut out with scissors.

She thought of his bare feet on the asphalt; the tiny rocks and grit that would be beneath his heels, under his toes, and rubbing on his arches. She pulled Her own feet up into Her seat, and now sat cross-legged. She felt cold.

"Mommy, I feel cold, and I have to go pee." She lifted Her hand up to Her mouth and thought about placing Her fingers inside Her lips and onto Her tongue. Self-gratification from sucking.

Her mother was very slowly inching the truck into the water behind their dad. "Sweet-heart, can you hold it just for a few minutes? We won't be long and then when we cross this water, you can go."

Her mother's tone was gentle, and genuine. She believed her. She nodded and looked out the window. A small crowd was forming around them. She saw many faces, all of them had darker skin than She had Herself. She liked the way they looked. They wore clothes that were kind of old-looking and their hair was shiny, black almost. Even in the dark She could see that. They seemed to have nice smiles. And they laughed. They smoked cigarettes and they laughed.

She turned her head and looked back, there were a lot of cars and trucks parked on the road behind them, She assumed that's where they had all come from. Her family was the source of entertainment. Interesting. Amusing and entertaining, yes She had to agree.

"Mommy, how deep is that water?"

"We don't know for sure, that's why your dad is walking in first."

Her brother spoke. "So what if he disappears into the water? Do we go forward? Or do we go back? Who will save him?"

Her mother looked at them both in the rear-view mirror. "Funny question, but very relevant, and so I would be obliged to answer in the most honest manner possible. I would like to suggest that he is in fact going to make it past half way, at which time he will probably either jump onto the hood of the truck or just keep walking. I do not believe, that he will need saving; I don't think that this water is more than thirty-six inches deep. Which would only come up to your dad's hip more or less. So just about enough to rinse out that coffee that he spilled."

She looked at Her mother and smiled, She thought about him slipping and falling under the water, She envisioned him thrashing about, his arms splashing and throwing water around, his feet coming out from under him and thrusting him towards the surface, his head bobbing in and out of the river, his mouth taking in water, him trying to scream in vain as the under current pulled him away from the truck, away from the crowd away from help, and into the coyote-infested desert.

She rubbed Her head into the car seat again. She hated that he made Her angry, She hated that he made Her feel hate. She wanted to love him, and yet he made it so difficult. The circle had to stop, She had to stop the perpetual motion of anger and resentment and hatred. She knew that it was up to Her to change this cycle of energy. She had been told, and She had accepted, and yet it was so hard. She closed her eyes. If only for a moment to compose herself. To catch herself from the negativity. To capture a positive moment in time where she could relish in the sound of tranquil constructive energy.

Her brother continued to watch. She peeked out one eye, She could see him leaning forward, eagerly watching their dad as he waded into the water. He was smiling at the crowd of onlookers, waving through the now open window, secretly pretending in his mind that the vehicle was a Royal one, and that he was the Prince, being driven across the river by his servants, perhaps as though the Prince of Egypt would have been crossing the Red Sea. She chuckled silently to herself; such an imbecile. It was almost as though She could actually read his mind.

Their mother continued to push forward with the truck, the water still rushing beneath them, and now coming up the sides of the bright electric-blue vehicle. She could hear the sound of the water as it rose up the passenger door near where She was seated. A crowd of local people were cheering and clapping; their dad was in the water nearly up to his waist and not yet at the halfway mark of the river. He was picking up speed, moving faster, no longer wading but now water jogging, nearly running.

Their mother was accelerating as she followed him deeper and deeper into the river. The truck ploughed through the water, splitting the river in two, the water cresting and falling off to the side, not hitting the top of the grill, avoiding the air intake by design.

The shouting and cheering became louder as they got closer to the middle of the river bed. "Malditos Gringos Locos, *Crazy fucking White guys.*" There was a lot of laughing and cajoling. She enjoyed this very much.

Her dad slapped the hood of the truck and shouted at their mother, "Pin it, don't stop until we reach the next town, I'll jump in the back, see you on the other side."

Her mother did just as he had said, and they made it across the water. The mexicans on that side of the water were just as excited, they hooted and hollered, just as loud and clapped and honked their horns. However, none of them retreated to their cars and attempted to cross the river. They stayed planted right where they were, waiting for the sun to come, waiting for mother nature to take care of business, waiting for their God to dry the river.

She saw in that evening she had trusted the same God as these local people, however, Hers had taken them safely across the river by faith, instead of asking Her to wait for something to change.

CHAPTER 19

Her mother was very sad one day, not long after their arrival in Puerto Vallarta. She sat alone, on the beach watching the waves as they crashed against the shore. She wanted to go to her, to comfort her and offer a hug or hold her hand. But She left her to grieve on her own.

There had been a telephone call, from Canada. Her mother had spoken and then had cried. She knew that someone close to Her mother had probably died. She also knew that death was actually a blessing, and that sadness overwhelms the living, but that the one who passes is reborn. It is a joyous time in heaven. She had read about it in the New Testament that She had, and She and the old woman who had lived in the basement, had talked about it once.

A few days later there was another phone call for Her mother, and then some banking things were done. Then things started to change for them, and then Her mother became Madam.

CHAPTER 20

Adjustment to life in Mexico had been more of a challenge than She had anticipated. Upon arriving in the country, they had set up a nice house with plenty of rooms and a pool for swimming, a beautiful garden and servants' quarters. She and Her brother had gotten settled into a private school which She actually liked very much at the onset. They wore cute uniforms and studied in Spanish, English and French.

Her greatest challenge seemed to be the language barrier on all fronts. The teachers didn't understand Her. Which was something that She had not yet encountered, a communication barrier. The new Nanny didn't understand Her, the children at school didn't understand Her. She was a lonely white girl with red hair who spent Her lunch hours and recess alone, and She never got what She wanted to eat because when She asked for ham they thought She said chicken. She was becoming frustrated and disheartened with the situation.

Although the local children were learning English, they weren't doing it quickly; they all spoke with thick accents, and had a difficult time with certain consonants. Y's sounded like J's so yes sounded like jes.

She was having just as much difficulty with Spanish. She had been completely immersed. If She wanted a glass of juice from the Nanny She had to ask for it in Spanish. The Nanny was not about to learn English, and had no understanding what so ever of the English language. It was becoming exhausting.

She did the only thing that She knew worked well for Her, and that was to pray about it. She asked God for help.

At the new school after a few weeks, She sat alone one day during the lunch break eating Her quesadillas and noticed that across the playground, was another little girl playing hopscotch all alone. The School included preschool grades all the way through to grade nine, She was of course just in pre-kinder, which was normally for four-year-olds. She was only three, however, She was smarter than most, of course; except for the language challenge.

The little girl who was playing hopscotch looked Her way and waved. Excitement raced through Her. Purple Box! She would remember this! She had believed She was going to be making a friend today. She had prayed for it. She would be able to go home and tell Her mother.

She picked up Her things and placed them back into Her lunch box, closed it, and walked towards the little girl on the other side of the playground. The lines for the hopscotch court were painted on the pavement in bright yellow. Home base at the top of the court was a traditional semicircle. Mary Mack stood in the semicircle waiting for Her to approach.

"Hi, do you speak English?" She pushed Her hair behind her ear.

"Hello, I'm Mary Mack." The little girl smiled up at Her as she reached down to grab her stone from the hopscotch board.

"Hi, it's nice to meet you, can I play too?" She was excited, but noticed that the young girl wasn't wearing a uniform as She was. "Hey how come you don't have a uniform like me?"

"I only wear black, with silver buttons, all down my back."

She looked at the dress, it was very chic, she was drawn to it, or to the girl, to an energy that she possessed. "Cool, can we play together?"

Mary Mack nodded. "Yes, and if you like, I will come back."

"Fun! I love to play! I'm not very good though, can you teach me?"

Mary Mack was quick to respond. "But of course, my Dear, but you must first understand the basics of the game. Hopscotch was first played by Roman children, but the first English-speaking children began to play, during the seventeenth century. The rock we use to mark our spot is actually called a stone. Now I will go first, so that I can show you." Mary moved behind the first square of the court. "I am going to put my stone on the first square." She placed her stone carefully onto the first stone. "Then I am going to hop over the first stone, like that see." Skipping on one foot, Mary Mack breezed through the court hopping on single squares on one foot and on the side-by-side squares straddled. Once in home base she turned around and came back towards Her, picked up her stone and smiled at Her. "Do you see how easy it is?"

"Yes, I can do that! Can I try now, Mary Mack?"

"Of course! It's your turn now! Do it just like I did." And so She did.

She enjoyed Her time with Mary Mack, and felt a sense of trust with Her new friend. She opened up to her. "Mary, can I tell you something? "

"Well, yes, I have the knack, knack, knack, to lend an ear, ear, ear, or just be near, near, near."

And so She shared Her fears of the Spanish language, Her difficulties with adjusting and Mary Mack listened. And then Mary promised to help Her. The girls played until the lunch bell rang, She hadn't eaten much of Her lunch, but she didn't care. She had enjoyed having some company. "Okay, Mary, I have to go to my class now, who is your teacher?"

Mary began to move away, "Thanks for speaking with me, I love the sound of your accent, you're really getting the language now. I have enjoyed our time together, and I loved speaking with you. I hope that we can spend more time together talking. I came to play today, I can come another day if you like, so I'll be back." She winked at Her as she moved away.

"Great! Bye, Mary!"

"It's Mary Mack!" Mary waved at Her as She ran off towards Her classroom with Her lunch box and a smile on Her face.

She entered the classroom and took Her seat as she was expected to do.

Miss Alicia, Her teacher approached. "Hi, Sweetie, I noticed you were playing hopscotch out there."

She bent over and pushed Her lunch kit under Her desk, she answered her teacher in the language of the classroom, which had been proving to be difficult for Her until today. "Claro que si, Senorita Alicia, lo estaba disfrutando tanto! Me diverti realmente." *"Oh yes, Miss Alicia, I was, I was enjoying it so much. I really had fun."*

Miss Alicia cocked her head to one side, the teacher listened to the child; the same child who had been struggling with the language, and the transition into the new school, and was now clearly in full command of the language. "And now you speak Spanish? Without any accent at all? How did this happen?"

She stopped and looked ahead at the chalkboard and realized that not only was She understanding, but that She was also able to speak. "Yes, Miss Alicia, I suppose I do. Is that all right? I assume that it will be better for everyone. Much easier I mean if I speak Spanish. That way you don't have to teach me. I could help you also to teach the children English if you like."

The teacher stood looking over Her, not sure what to say, or what to do next. "I see, I would like to see you after school please."

She was not certain why it was suddenly a problem that She understood the language. She enjoyed it immensely. Math was easier. Art class was more fun that afternoon, when She was able to actually interact and share Her beliefs and opinions. Finger painting had never been so much fun.

The final bell rang and She began to gather Her things. She took Her Beauty and the Beast back pack from Her hook and placed Her lunch box and Her sweater inside. She was hoping that Miss Alicia was going to forget about the meeting she had requested. Slowly She placed the rest of Her things inside of the bag and turned around.

She was surprised to see Miss Alicia standing with the Head Lady of the School; Lady Gonzalez, and Her mother. That meant that Miss Alicia had called Her mother at work. That meant that She was going to be in some kind of trouble. Orange Box; which was really too bad because today had been a Purple Box day.

Her mother spoke first. "Hi, Sweet-heart, how was your day?"

Her mother hugged Her. Her mother always smelled lovely, like flowers, She heard people tell her that she smelled beautiful. It was comforting to Her.

"It was really good, Mommy, I made a new friend."

Her mother's voice escalated one octave. "Oh that's great, Honey! I'm so glad! Miss Alicia just wants us to talk for a few minutes and then you and I can go home okay?"

"Where's my brother?"

"Oh your brother is going to take the school bus home, just like usual, he doesn't even know that I am here. Okay? Shall we sit down?"

Lady Gonzalez spoke in English. "Yes please let's all sit." Everyone took a seat around a large round crafting table. The table was low to the ground, suited for children, not for adults, with smaller chairs as well.

Miss Alicia spoke next, directing the question to Her. "Can you explain to me please what happened today?"

She looked at Her mother for support. Her mother held Her tiny hand and nodded, not having any idea of what had transpired. "I played hopscotch at lunch time."

Miss Alicia smiled. "Jes, but I mean with the language, before lunch you don't speak Spanish and then after lunch, you speak Spanish perfectly."

She looked down at Her shoes and then at Lady Gonzalez. She was not able to lie. She was incapable of creating a story to which would please and appease the situation. She told them the truth as She knew it.

"I was having my lunch, and then the girl that was playing hopscotch, she waved at me, I didn't want to be alone any more. So I went and I played hopscotch with her, and then when I came back after the bell I could speak Spanish but I don't know how it happened, I swear."

Miss Alicia furrowed her brow, she had been watching Her playing hopscotch alone, through the lunch hour. "Which girl were you playing with?"

"Mary Mack." Her mother squeezed Her hand.

Lady Gonzalez cleared her throat. "I don't believe that we have a student, named Mary Mack at the school."

She smiled, pleased with herself. "Oh no you don't, she wasn't wearing a uniform, so I asked her about that, and she said she wasn't from around here. But she said she would come back."

Miss Alicia nodded. "Okay, well, I think that more importantly we need to address the fact that you have learned a language over the lunch hour." She clicked her nails on the table top.

Lady Gonzalez nodded in agreement. "Yes, ladies, this is of concern to us. Impossible, it's simply impossible. I cannot agree with Miss Alicia more. I am going to want to have some testing done, in order to assess the depth of understanding of the language. Is that all right with you, Madam?"

Her mother was surprised on many fronts, her child had apparently learned a language today, to her this seemed like an accomplishment rather than an issue, however she could see how they could be alarmed by Her intelligence. She was also playing with someone on the playground that was not a student of the school. This was a problem. Security was supposed to be one of the school's highest priorities, she wondered how this could ever happen. Lady Gonzalez was concerned with testing, but her mother didn't see the need for more testing. Further analysis of her child, that was not actually necessary for her child, and for what? So that they could write an article or a paper on the school and their achievements? Perhaps not.

"I'm sorry, Lady Gonzalez, what was your question again?" She pulled her small child into her lap.

"Testing, Madam, are you all right with testing? I think it is of utmost importance that we get to the bottom of this. I can arrange to have the testing done here at the school, and it won't take up more than a couple of days of class time. There will be no cost to you personally."

Her mother laughed. "Oh, well that's a relief! Just what exactly are you going to be testing for, Lady Gonzalez? Are you looking for accent? Are you testing for comprehension? Pronunciation? No, no thank you, I honestly don't see the need for any sort of testing. I think that my daughter is just fine."

Miss Alicia spoke out." We just want to understand Her better, that's all."

Red Box.

Her mother took a breath. "You want to understand Her? Now you do? Now because She has done something that you don't understand? Why not yesterday or last week? When She was struggling to understand. Why not this morning, ladies, when She was eating alone? I gave you my answer and my answer is no, no testing. Let Her be."

"Well, Madam, I am disappointed with your decision, we could learn so much."

"Lady Gonzalez, please, you can learn so much just from being around Her. You don't need to subject Her to tests. Let's move on please. Are we done, ladies?" Her mother had reached the end of her game.

"Thank you for coming in. We will take this under advisement." Lady Gonzalez shook Her mother's hand as they moved towards the classroom doorway.

She and Her mother walked down the hallway towards the exit.

"Are you mad with me, Mommy?"

Her mother squeezed Her hand with tears in her eyes. "Never, Baby, never."

CHAPTER 21

Juan had done well adjusting to his new orders. He enjoyed the defined instruction and specific rules that applied to the work he was to do.

He robed himself and prepared for today's assignment. He headed to his debriefing and then put on his sandals. The hood of his robe was to be left hanging down tonight, exposing his long grey hair and beard.

He walked down Ignacio de Vallarta with passion, his mission was clear and concise. He had become somewhat of an expert at these expeditions, and spent as little time as necessary in the field.

He saw his destination and crossed the roadway without looking. He had not become accustomed to the traffic and types of vehicles that people now moved themselves in from place to place. He much preferred a good old-fashioned horse. A horse was reliable and didn't make as much noise or cause as much damage to the eco system as these things did. Cars they called them; some of them were actually quite large. Made of metal and tin. He found the entire thing quite perplexing.

A few of the vehicles honked at him, which was a relief, meaning that they could in fact see him.

At the front of her place of business, he peered through the glass. It was full of people. Most of them were eating. All of them seemed to be enjoying themselves, smiling, drinking wine, laughing.

He pulled the stainless steel handle on the glass door. It moved towards him and he stepped through. There was music playing inside, he quite liked the choice of sounds she had made there. He found music soothing to his soul.

He looked from left to right. Scanning the room for her.

His large physical presence made him impossible to not notice. Diners began to set down their forks. The head waiter approached.

"Hola, Amigo, can I help you?"

Juan looked around again, he must find her. He shook his head no.

He saw many people eating and enjoying wine, tables full of smiling faces. There was a bar to the side, and a cashier. He saw a set of double doors at the back of the room that he assumed led to the kitchen area and there was a narrow hallway on the left that must have been the restrooms.

"Okay, restrooms are for customers only, Buddy, so you're going to have to move it along okay?"

Juan stood his ground, he straightened up and placed his walking stick firmly on the floor. The bartender snickered, *'careful, everybody, Jesus is in the house.'*

Laughter began to break in the restaurant, nervous laughter, because Juan did in fact resemble nineteenth-century depictions of Jesus Christ. And then she emerged from the kitchen, through the double doors at the back of the room, he saw her before she saw him.

She came through the kitchen doors with a tray full of plates, her green silk dress protected by a clean white apron, her long dark hair neatly tied up in a bun. Her skin glowing from the sun, her smile bright, intoxicating.

The two of them made eye contact. Juan smiled at her. She

delivered the plates to the table that was waiting for their dinner and then moved towards Juan.

"Hello." She reached out her hand to take Juan's.

He was pleased. "Hello." He received her hand and kissed it.

"How can I help you?" She was gentle, kind, accepting and generous. Just as he was told to expect.

"A piece of bread, Madam, and a little water… if you can spare it?"

She quickly scanned the room. There was a table at the side of the restaurant that was available, waiting to be set. "Please, be my guest." She led him to the table and pulled out the chair for him. He sat. She placed her hand on his walking stick and asked, "May I set this aside for you?"

Juan shook his head. "I mustn't let that out of my sight… you understand."

"Of course, here is fine then?" She leaned his stick against the side of the table next to him.

He nodded.

She motioned to her staff to set the table and to bring water and bread.

"What can we get you to eat? Would you like to see a menu?"

Juan was again pleased. "This is plenty, thank you. The Lord is with thee."

"A man cannot survive on bread alone, I will have them prepare a feast for you. Would you like wine with your meal?"

"I have no money to pay you tonight."

Madam smiled at Juan. "I was not expecting you to."

"Will you be so kind as to join me." Juan hadn't anticipated her to be so amicable, but was pleased with her reception of him.

She agreed.

The food came and to his delight was rich with Spanish flavours. A Creole that tasted like his mother's with prawns, over a bed of Spanish rice. His taste buds were in heaven. She had opened for them a bottle of wine that soothed his soul. He ate in silence. She sat sipping her wine and patiently waiting for him to finish his meal.

He looked at her when he was done, wiped his chin and said, "Delightful, Madam, I thank you kindly."

She had a warm glow that he liked. She was good.

"You are very welcome. How long have you been travelling?"

He chuckled. "Oh a very, very long time, yes indeed."

She held her wine glass. "And what brings you here?"

Juan looked up at her over his own glass of wine. "You."

She was startled, he could tell, he had expected her to be slightly frightened, and so she should be. "Me? Good heavens what do you mean?"

He had accumulated a few breadcrumbs in his beard which he noticed and brushed away. He was certain now that she had no idea who he was or why he was here, which made his reception all that much sweeter. "You, have brought me here, I have travelled here tonight from afar for you, Madam."

She sat staring at him, one of the wait staff approached the table. "Can I bring you some dessert, Sir? Or coffee maybe? A Cappuccino?"

"No thank you. No sweets for me. My sufficiency is suffonsified. Thank you for being so incredibly generous."

Madam snickered, "My grandmother says that; 'my sufficiency is suffonsified' funny… Anything else then?"

"No thank you Madam."

Madam looked up at the waiter and politely asked him to

excuse himself. He scurried off to do something else. Backing away from the table, as if afraid to turn his back on the visitor.

Juan continued. "You are no longer on the right path. You will be corrected. I cannot tell you when, I cannot tell you how. But I can tell you that you made a choice somewhere that was not approved." Juan pointed in an upward direction. "You will be redirected therefore."

She twisted her fingers around the wine glass. "Who are you?"

"You know *of* who I am, that is all that matters. You have a great kindness in you, He is pleased. I must go, thank you for a lovely meal. May I clean the floors or do some dishes? Something to repay you?"

Madam shook her head no. "No please, it was my pleasure."

Juan stood and took his walking stick, he moved towards the door and looked back at her. She was unaware of her beauty. He liked the sense of humility that she possessed. He nodded his head in thanks and moved through the doorway and into the street. Juan disappeared into the crowd leaving behind a restaurant full of patrons with questions as to his identity. And Her mother with questions as to the meaning of his message.

CHAPTER 22

Weeks passed and Her schooling situation hadn't changed. She continued to eat alone at lunch time under the Banyan tree. Her lunch box was always filled with exciting treats, She would read Her books and once in a while She would watch the other girls skipping or playing games with the boys. Sadly She was never included. She was frightfully alone, forlorn and lonely.

Finally Mary Mack returned. When She saw Mary Mack from across the playground She was ecstatic. She wanted to yell out to her, but feared looking like an idiot to the other kids so She kept quiet. She didn't need to be putting anything into an Orange Box today.

She picked up Her lunch items, threw them into Her lunch box, and ran over to the other side of the school yard. "Hey, Hi, Mary Mack, where have you been? You said you would come back!"

"Hi there! I did, I did come back." Mary Mack swung her black silk dress from left to right. "See the silver buttons all down my back? If you would like you could play with my elephant, we could jump over the fence and never come back."

She looked at Mary Mack inquisitively. Although she spoke in riddles and rhymes, it made some sense to Her. The idea of running away today was of some intrigue to Her, of disappearing and chasing big dreams. In Her own mind, that was what Mary Mack was eluding to. Of course there was the incredible idea that perhaps she was in fact suggesting that she actually had an elephant somewhere under her dress but it was highly doubtful.

"I would love to play with you today, Mary Mack. Can we whisk ourselves away to someplace I've never been? To a land of macaroons and fancy shoes? Of glass tables and Stirling Silver Roses. Have you ever seen a Stirling Rose, Mary?"

Mary Mack nodded in agreement with Her, She continued, "Oh I just love them, Mary Mack, they are the most beautiful of all the roses, and there are the Angel Face which are a very close second. Both are lavender roses, which of course signify enchantment and love at first sight, both are considered quite rare. The colour is distinctly silver and lavender with a traditional rose smell."

Mary Mack was impressed with Her knowledge and questioned Her further. "And so tell me, do you know more about the origin of these two flowers? And if not, could you please find out, for our next meeting. It is of great importance for a woman to know of the things in which she speaks. If you choose to speak of something to which you are interested, you must always be completely abreast of the facts, and of as many opinions as possible, about the subject that you are presenting. No one appreciates a woman with nothing between her ears. Of a pretty face they bore, of a rich mind will entertain and entice for centuries."

She smiled at Mary Mack and agreed that indeed She would investigate the roses further. "Can we play, Mary?"

"We are playing now, listen, did you hear? I think it's nearly time for you to go back, don't be scared, don't be afraid, your mother will have your back, the tide will turn, your path may change, but you will not lack, listen to your heart, and pray for all, for your own desires will fall, far you will go, countries you will see, when you get lost, look for me." A wind blew into Her face, dust and leaves hit Her on the cheek and She closed Her eyes. And Mary Mack was gone again.

CHAPTER 23

Lady Gonzalez phoned the residence, looking for Her mother late in the afternoon on a Thursday. It would have seemed to everyone that She was the perfect student. She did not interrupt in class, Her homework was always done, She was never late nor absent.

She was a straight-A student, and Her teachers had been instructed to mark Her hard. They diligently applied a more structured and difficult curve to Her assignments and tests than to any other student.

She only worked harder because of it. She studied more, learned more, and became more and more enlightened and enriched from Her hunger for knowledge.

The phone rang. "Bueno, Hello."

"Hello, this is Lady Gonzalez from the American School calling, may I speak with Madam please."

"Jes, one moment, Lady Gonzalez."

"Hello, Lady Gonzalez, this is Madam, how can I help you?"

"Madam, if I could have a moment of your time, I think we should have a discussion about Her and Her studies."

Madam set down her coffee, and switched ears with the telephone receiver, "Is there a problem, Lady Gonzalez? I was of the impression that She was doing remarkably well at the school."

"Yes, well, I suppose from an academic stand point one

could assume that. All things considered one would get that impression from Her marks. She does seem to study incredibly diligently and we could anticipate that She would continue to advance at the expected rate, however, the board has met and discussed Her overall progress and we just don't believe that the American School is the ideal fit for Her. She does not seem to have adjusted socially, and quite frankly, Madam, social interaction is a grand part of the educational experience. We believe, the board, the teaching staff and myself of course, feel that Her needs would be better met elsewhere, perhaps home schooled? Or the British School? The programs there are more adaptable, they utilize the Montessori system, which for Her might just be an excellent fit. She is just too different from the other children here at the American school. I'm sure that you understand."

Madam was offended, tears filled her eyes and anger filled her heart. She wasn't certain what exactly she should be saying. She had two children. And if one was not welcome in the school then neither one of them would be attending.

"Actually I don't understand, I have always encouraged both of my children to be different, rather than the same as everyone. I pity the children in your school, Lady, who all fit into your mould. That they should all only be as good as you allow them to be and never anything more. That they should only strive to be just good enough to fit in and not bold enough to stand out. I am happy to pull both of the children from the school and we will move to an alternate. Thank you for your time, I trust that you will have a cheque ready for me tomorrow for the endowment?"

"It will take us a few weeks, Madam, to prepare a cheque for you, I hope you understand the position we are in, we cannot prepare that kind of cash in less than twenty-four hours."

Madam took a breath. "And yet Lady Gonzalez, at the time of enrolment, you insisted on having it in less than twenty-four hours, regardless of my situation, so pardon me for not understanding nor caring for your position at this time, but I will be there tomorrow by three in the afternoon and I will expect a cheque for the entire amount of the endowment that I provided. It was my understanding after-all that all of that money was to be secure in trust."

"You really do not need to take such an aggressive stance, Madam! It is very difficult for us, a small establishment to secure those types of funds in a short amount of time, all I am asking for is a few weeks for our accounting team to facilitate the process." Lady Gonzalez was breathing erratically.

Madam was beginning to feel more and more annoyed, she pulled at the telephone cord, which was coiled and twisted into a knot, "If you didn't have an accounting "team" then perhaps you wouldn't have issues with facilitating my request, which frankly is a simple one. If you need assistance, my attorney would be more than happy to step in, of that I'm quite certain."

"That won't be necessary, I will see what we can do, honestly you are a very difficult woman to deal with, I can see why they say you have a heart of stone. Please do not send the children to school tomorrow. I will arrange to have their things ready to be picked up by end of day. Good bye, Madam!"

Madam replaced the receiver in its cradle and moved down the hallway towards the children's bedrooms. She paused in the hallway to fully digest the bitterness of Lady Gonzalez's comments. She found it hard to believe that people actually spoke about her that way. Did they really think she had a heart of stone? Could it be possible that she was perceived as such a horrible woman?

She wondered how exactly she would explain the situation and decided that the truth was always the easiest and most palatable meal.

She knocked first on her daughter's door. "Sweet-heart, can I come in?"

"Yes, of course, Mommy." Madam entered the pretty room. She had decorated it in shades of blue, like the ocean, cool and calm with silk and gauze fabrics draping over the bed, to create a mosquito netting to protect Her while She slept at night.

Madam sat on the chair in the corner, watching Her play with Her dolls. She seemed to be interacting with them, talking to them, She was role playing. "Sweet-heart, have you been having trouble at school? Anything odd happen that you would like to talk to me about?"

She looked up at Her mother, and with sincerity, smiled and shook Her head. "No, Mommy, I try really hard. I do everything they ask. I do my best just like I promised I would."

Madam felt weeping brewing in her own throat, tears cresting in her own eyes; she desperately didn't want to have to tell Her and yet she didn't have an option. "Honey, I think we are going to look for another school."

She stopped playing with Her dolls and looked at Her mother. "What do you mean, Mommy? Did I do something wrong?" She started to cry then, Her words were difficult for Her to annunciate, She had a terrible time finishing Her thought. "I really have been doing my very best. And I tried not to make any of the teachers mad with me. I didn't play with any of the children because they don't like me and I eat alone every day except for when Mary Mack comes to see me."

"I know you do your best every day, and I am very proud of you. I will find a wonderful school for you, Honey, don't worry. I don't want you to feel like you have done anything wrong, this is not about you. This is about a school that is not certain how to educate a youngster that doesn't quite fit into their cookie-cutter mould. You just happen to be a little different than most of the kids that they normally see." Madam reached out and touched her daughter's nose. "Which is exactly why I love you as much as I do. Because you are different. You are special, you are important, and God has huge plans for you. That I know for sure."

"What if they don't like me at the new school that you find for me?"

Madam hugged her little girl, looked out the window at the ocean, felt the cool breeze from the water on her golden skin and said, "This was meant to be, sometimes God has to shove us to where He needs us; this will be good, trust me, they will love you there. Where ever that may be, I can feel it in my bones."

CHAPTER 24

The sun beat down on Her, Her bare shoulders were hot. She wore a hat that protected Her auburn hair from the sun, and covered most of Her face.

She pushed Her foot around in the sand, watching the other children play. Their sand castles were only mediocre and She wondered why they got so excited about such simple pleasures. Simpletons.

She looked out to the horizon and counted the sail boats, one, two, tois, cuatro, cinco, six, sept, huit, nine, ten, once, a speed boat and three jet skis. In her mind She began to calculate the ratios of the water vessels. Eleven to one, eleven sailboats to one speed boat and three jet skis, she could factor the the likelihood that they might crash into one another. The speed boat was of course travelling at a rate in extreme excess to the sailboats, and the jet skis used no particular pattern of movement. It was possible, but not probable that one of the captains would err and there could in fact be a terrible crash.

She watched the waves rolling on the beach, the sound of each crash brought Her a profound amount of joy. The power and vastness of the water was intense and mystical. It sang to Her.

Her brother was playing catch with another little boy, about his age, and the Nanny who was supposed to be watching them was talking to a man. She had become quite involved in the conversation and seemed to have almost forgotten about her precious cargo.

The Nanny's name was Luz, which meant "light". It was an interesting choice of name for a woman, although She didn't seem to believe that it was quite suited to her. Luz did not shine like some of the people, she didn't glow nor did she radiate any type of positive energy. She was just one-dimensional, flat and rather a bore.

The water crested and crashed over and over again, white foam never ceasing to roll onto the beach. When She enjoyed something, She would do her best to find out all that she could about it. She would ask others, She would read what She could, and She would research whatever might be available on this new thing called the internet.

Ocean foam, the type of foam created by the agitation of the ocean water particularly when it contains higher concentrations of dissolved organic matter like proteins, is derived from sources such as the offshore breakdown of algal blooms. These compounds can act as surfactants or foaming agents. As the ocean water is churned by breaking waves in the surf zone adjacent to the shore, the presence of these surfactants under these turbulent conditions traps air, forming persistent bubbles that stick to each other through surface tension, and that is how the ocean makes the foam.

She loved to watch it roll into the shore, and pull out leaving only traces of its existence. She got up from where she was sitting and moved towards the water's edge. She thought She might just like to put Her toes into the foam, just to feel it cool and fresh on Her hot feet.

She looked left to right, checking the whereabouts of Her brother and the Nanny, both were still occupied so She decided to move ahead on her own.

Sand stuck to the back of Her tiny thighs, while Her bikini

bottom was wet from sitting. She stood with Her feet in the cool water, feeling instant relief from the scorching sun. Reaching down with Her hands She splashed them and rinsed in the pulling ocean. She sat again on Her bum in the wet sand, feeling the water lapping back and forth.

The waves mesmerized Her, the energy that they created, the pure strength and momentum, ebbing and flowing over the water as if held captive by the wind. She found the power was intoxicating. She could smell the salt in the air, She could feel it on Her skin, the breeze soothingly cooling Her, as it created more and more energy in the water. The rolling waves becoming stronger and more deliberate; more intense.

With an increase in the wind, came larger waves. They seemed to Her to increase in size, rolling and crashing louder and more often. The height of the water was rising around Her, where She was just a moment ago sitting with only her bottom in the water, now it was cresting around her chest. She liked the feel of it. It came in cool and then left Her quickly to the sun's beating rays, toasting Her skin.

She tipped Her head back, allowing the sun to strike Her delicate face. Her blue sun hat fell from Her head and into the water, exposing Her luscious auburn hair. With the retracting wave, the hat was pulled away from where She sat and off into the ocean. In a split second it was gone, Her hair now cascading down onto Her shoulders, gleaming in the heat of the sun.

She could still see it, swirly and tossing in the water. She jumped to Her feet and attempted to grab it. She chased the hat and jumped in the water, splashing and giggling as She shoved Her hands towards the floating head cover. She knew that if She lost this hat She would be in trouble, She would disappoint Her mother. She didn't like the feeling of disappointment, or how it looked on others. It made Her feel small and defeated, and not loved. Her tiny feet moved quickly, Her hands and arms grabbing and pulling towards the cherished hat. The water was becoming deeper. She feared losing anything, but She dreaded losing something that Her mother had given Her.

She looked to where She had come from at the shore, to where She had been sitting before the hat had fallen in the water. From where She was now standing, it seemed to be farther than She was allowed to go out into the sea. She knew that Her mother would not be pleased that She had decided to go on Her own, nor that She had gone so far.

She weighed the consequences of losing the hat and Her mother finding out that She had gone into the water unsupervised. She decided that She must retrieve the hat. Without question, that was the greater and less ominous of the two choices.

She could hear the laughter of Her brother and his friends as they played catch, throwing the ball back and forth, running and jumping. She could hear the voice of Luz the Nanny as she chatted with the strange man.

She forged on, determined to save the hat from peril.

She stepped forward, and just as She reached out to grab Her hat, her foot landed on the jagged edge of a living coral, sharp and cutting. She immediately lost Her footing and slipped into the water.

The power of the ocean grabbed the small child, and tossed Her to the left and to the right. She circled around and around and tumbled with each rolling wave. Her small body bounced and jack knifed into the ocean floor, crashing Her hard limbs against its sandy covered concrete bottom.

Her arms flapping wildly under the water, She lost all sense of direction. By instinct Her mouth opened for air, but all She took in was salt water, acidic on Her tongue, burning her throat. She continued to roll with the waves, not seeing Her hat, no longer seeing the shore. She could no longer feel the sun on Her warm body, the freshness of the salt water was now bitter. Like battery acid in Her lungs and vinegar in Her belly the water had lost its sweet lure.

The world to Her became very dark in an instant. All light and beauty escaped as She fell once more to the rocky sand base of the ocean floor. Her body lost the will to fight the waves; Her mind became robust with memories and visions.

CHAPTER 25

She saw the handsome shiny man, from Her birthday party. His face was clear to Her as She sank towards the bottom of the ocean.

She could see that he was attempting to communicate, to speak outright to Her. The water morphed the sound of his voice and She had to struggle to understand what he was saying to Her.

"Not now, Her, hold on, I have them coming for you now."

She smiled up at him, from where She was She could see only his face and darkness all around Her. An abyss. She knew that She must know him, She knew that She had seen him at Her party and it did occur to Her that he should not be under the water. She was under the water and this caused sufficient enough concern. One person drowning was probably enough for one day. Her thoughts raced and Her mind drifted.

"You have been chosen, Her, now isn't your time. I am protecting you now, you mustn't give up, they are coming for you."

She suddenly felt completely at peace. She was void of fear, and above the need to fight. She effortlessly floated in the water next to him. Wanting to touch him but not able to reach him.

He appeared to be near and yet was outside of the limits of Her grasp. Her fingers extended towards where She believed he was standing. But nothing prevailed. No contact, no realization of the physical man.

She looked over Her shoulder and She could see a small figure on the bottom of the ocean, lying lifeless; a solid form, with auburn hair cascading over the ocean floor.

"Not now, Her." His voice boomed now, it was louder, it was clear and it resonated with Her. "It's not time for you, you have much work to do, there is a plan for your life, you must go back. I have them coming for you now."

She looked back again at the figure on the ocean floor and understood that it must be Herself. She heard his message but longed to go with him. She didn't know why but She felt a stronger pull towards him than She did to the body lying on the bottom of the ocean.

She wanted to speak to him, She wanted to ask who he was, how She knew him, how he knew Her, what his name was, where he had come from, why he was there with Her under the water. She wanted to go with him to where he was going. She wanted to move on to a different place, to see different things, and *feel* differently. She tried to follow but he was moving too fast, moving away from Her now, deeper and deeper into the water.

She saw algae around Herself and the most brightly coloured fish. Swimming close to Her now. Her hand tried to grasp a bright yellow long-nosed butterfly fish. She knew of this fish because She had read about it, in a journal that She had seen at the doctor's office.

The lifeless figure on the ocean floor was now in the midst of a flurry of activity. There was a swimmer, it looked like a man, or a large boy was near Her. He had grabbed Her, he picked Her up and was swimming towards the surface of the water.

It was the man that Luz had been talking to. The man that

had been with Her nanny, a stranger had Her in his arms. She raced back towards where the two of them were. The water felt warm again, it was no longer cold and icy. She could hear him now, his heart was beating strong, and his blood was rushing through his veins. She could feel the warmth of his skin on Her own as they crested the surface of the water.

He lay Her body on the sand, She could hear the cries of Her brother and Luz the Nanny. The lazy mexican Nanny was sobbing but doing nothing to assist in this moment of grave need.

Her brother cried, while the stranger turned Her on Her side, then rolled her onto Her back again. He began mouth-to-mouth, attempting to breathe life into Her limp body. He used his hands to perform CPR, pumping Her chest between breaths into Her tiny mouth.

Her hair lay soaking and matted with sand and algae on the beach. Her skin was pale, almost blue. Her lips were void of any pinkness what so ever. She looked dead. The stranger cried out, "Ahora chicita, aliento! Por Favor! Breath! Breath for the love of Jesus, Breath!"

In that moment She snapped. Time stopped for a moment and She snapped back into consciousness, back to where She could do what She came to do.

"Not now, Her, this is not your time." She comforted in the idea that there were those who were here to watch over Her. She was here with a purpose, a plan, She had a mission to fulfill. She took a breath, and choked on salt water as She vomited on the sand. She was surrounded by crowds of people, who watched Her gagging and struggling for air. Her head was pounding. She looked up to the blue sky, quietly said Her thanks, "Thank you Jesus" and then She looked through Her boxes for a special one, a Pink Box.

CHAPTER 26

Abraham was an acquaintance of the family through the Church. He was a gentle, caring man, and he was handsome. He was tall, perhaps six feet or slightly more, and slender but strong, with a full head of thick dark hair. He sang in the church choir on Wednesdays and on Sunday mornings and on Tuesdays he led a Bible study at the Barbershop on Calle Juarez.

His clothes were not plentiful, but he was always neat and pressed. His shoes were polished, his tie straight. His Bible was always with him.

He had moved to town from Guadalajara, apparently because his wife had found a job here. And then she had become very ill and then she had died very suddenly. Then he was alone, with just the Church and his Bible. He was very kind, and he was always very thoughtful. He prayed a lot. He seemed gentle.

Her Mother hired him one day when he came by the house to see if she might have any odd jobs or extra work. He claimed that he could and would do anything, and that he would never let her down. There was already a Nanny, and a maid, and there wasn't much need for anything else, but Her mother always wanted to help people, and she said that if you helped people by giving them work they were helping themselves, and so Abraham started to work for the family as the Butler.

A Butler normally is responsible for a vast number of jobs

within a household. The word "butler" comes from the Anglo-Norman buteler, a variant form of the Old Norman butelier, or as they say in France, the Old French botellier, who is an officer in charge of the king's wine bottles.

The role of the butler, for centuries, has been that of the chief steward of a household, an attendant entrusted with the care and serving of wine and other bottled beverages, which in ancient times might have represented a considerable portion of the household's assets. Which is really all very complicated but actually means that he was in charge of the bottles within the household.

In Britain, the butler was originally a middle-ranking member of the staff of a grand household. In the seventeenth and eighteenth centuries, the butler gradually became the senior, most usually male, member of a household's staff in the very grandest of households. Butlers in the past would be attired in a special uniform, distinct from the livery of junior servants, but today a butler is more likely to wear a business suit or business casual clothing and appear in uniform only on special occasions.

Butlers were head of a strict service hierarchy and therein held a position of power and respect within the household. They held a more managerial role than "hands on"—more so than serving, they officiated in service for the family. For example, although the butler was at the door to greet and announce the arrival of a formal guest, the door was actually *opened* by a footman, who would receive the guest's hat and coat. Even though the butler helped his employer into his coat, the coat had been handed to the butler by a footman.

Even the highest-ranking butler would "pitch in" when necessary, such as during a staff shortage, to ensure that the household ran smoothly, although some evidence suggests this was so even during normal times.

Beginning around the early 1920s, following World War I, employment in domestic service occupations began a sharp overall decline in Western European countries, and even more markedly in the United States. Even so, there were still around 30,000 butlers employed in Britain by World War II. As few as one hundred were estimated to remain by the mid-1980s, however, their value in Mexico was becoming more and more interesting due to a surge in young wealthy entrepreneurs in the 1990s with thanks to the Free Trade Agreement between neighboring partners the United States and Canada.

A modern Mexican Butler may be called upon to do whatever household and personal duty their employers deemed fitting, in the goal of freeing their employers to carry out their own personal and professional affairs. The image of tray-wielding butlers, who specialise in serving tables and decanting wine, is now anachronistic. Employers are far more interested in a butler who is capable of managing a full array of household affairs—from providing the traditional dinner service, to acting as valet, to managing high-tech electronic systems and multiple homes with complex staff.

While in truly grand houses the modern butler may still function exclusively as a top-ranked household affairs manager; in lesser homes, such as those of dual-income middle-class professionals, they perform a full array of household and personal assistant duties, including mundane housekeeping like laundry and ironing, grocery shopping, and chauffeuring children. Butlers today may also be situated within their employer's corporate settings, seeing to jets and yachts and managing the family fleet of cars.

Along with these changes of scope and context of work, a butler's attire has changed. Whereas butlers have traditionally worn a special uniform that separated them from junior servants, and although this is still often the case; butlers today may wear more casual clothing geared for climate, while exchanging it for formal business attire only upon special service occasions. There are cultural distinctions, as well. In the United States, butlers may frequently don a polo shirt and slacks, in Mexico where heat is a factor, Bermuda shorts are often considered acceptable in place of slacks or pants.

A butler's duties would differ from the nanny greatly and also from the housemaids. The nanny is responsible for the children, and for their primary needs. Which seems relatively simple. The nanny however will at times rely on the butler for assistance when she becomes overtaxed by her employer on occasion. For example, if the nanny is required to be in two places at one time, she may request assistance from the butler, but never from a housemaid.

Once a nanny has utilized the service of a butler and he has not failed her, she will begin to depend on him as a support system. He can press school uniforms, pack lunches, ensure that homework is complete, drive to and from events, wash clothing if needed, and appear at extracurricular sport practices, all while gaining the admiration and trust of the youngsters, and without the employer ever being aware of him having any involvement whatsoever with her children. A good butler can make a mediocre nanny appear to be Mary Poppins to a proprietor.

Thus it was with Abraham. He began to assist the nanny with the pressing of the uniforms, and the packing of the lunches. It was nothing at first.

Nanny would ask him to help with soccer practice, "could he just this once take Master to practice as little Miss had a play date after school." And so Abraham obliged.

Weeks rolled into months and Abraham continued with his Butler duties, he managed the cars, and maintained the exterior of the property, he performed the shopping after the housemaid had provided him a detailed list. He enjoyed ironing and so he did that every day. He especially liked ironing his employer's dresses. He took extra care with the beautiful silks, ensuring that they hung just right. She always looked so lovely in them. Madam reminded him of his late wife. It was important to Abraham that this new family, *his* new family presented well.

When he was needed he would perform any type of maintenance around the house, and light housekeeping as it was needed, although he was rarely called upon to clean anything. It was more likely that the nanny would call him to request small favours with regards to the children. Driving, homework-related, pressing clothing and preparing their lunches, he didn't mind, he enjoyed the children immensely.

Abraham missed his wife, there was barely a moment that he didn't think of her. He went to church, he prayed, he continued his Bible studies, and he drowned himself in his work. He assumed that one day the pain would subside and he would be able to move on.

One Friday in May Nanny called before dawn. "Abraham, Bueno, Hello, Abraham."

He answered the phone reluctantly this time, without knowing why. He had always jumped at every opportunity to be of service, but for some reason today, he was slow to motivate. "Yes, hello, Nanny, what is it?"

"Abraham, listen, I need you to help out today, the Madam is off to Guadalajara late in the afternoon, and the children have soccer and ballet, both at the same time after school, I can't do both. So, I also have to get my hair done."

He groaned. "What time?"

"Which?" She snapped at him.

"The children, what time do you need me? Madam left me a list of things to do for her today as well so I am quite obligated already. I'm not sure if you realize or not that I too have a job, and it is not yours. Yours is to care for the children."

Nanny was quite taken aback by Abraham's lack of enthusiasm, and was offended by his potential lack of interest in her needs, "Fine, look if you cannot help me then I will just do my very best on my own and I guess that I will just have to tell Madam that you were not willing to help out. Don't worry I was perfectly able to do this job before you came along and I am perfectly capable of doing it now."

Abraham laughed at her. "Oh is that right, Nanny? You're perfectly capable are you? Well, let's just see about that shall we? Madam doesn't know that I cover half of your duties does she? I wonder how she will feel about that? Was it your hair you were planning to get done today? Or your nails? I wonder how Madam would feel about that? Isn't today payday? Perhaps I shall ask for half of your pay for half of your work that I have been doing."

Nanny was furious. "You listen to me, you stupid bible-thumping, Jesus-loving queer, do not cross me, do you hear me? You will regret it! I was here first and I will be here last. Do not threaten me. Do you hear me? Who do you think you are? You are just the butler, and she only gave you the job because she felt sorry for you, because your sad, sad wife died. Fucking pathetic."

Abraham's blood was boiling, her language was appalling, her tone and the context of her message were very intimidating. His anger burst. "Oh is that right, Nanny? You will make me regret it? You Bitch!" He wanted to reach through the phone and squeeze her neck until no air would reach her lungs. Until her eyes would pop from her head and her body would rattle and shake in spasms.

"You should have just helped me today, you stupid mother fucker." And with that Nanny hung up the phone.

CHAPTER 27

Miss Mary Mack was a tiny-framed young girl whose dark curly hair bounced as she skipped. Her skin was as soft as ivory cashmere, clean and void of any marks or freckles. From her smile shone the sun, bright and becoming. She skipped and she sang in riddles, passing messages to those in need.

I'm Miss Mary Mack, Mack, Mack
All dressed in black, black, black
With silver buttons, buttons, buttons
All down my back, back, back.
Go ask your mother, mother, mother
for fifty cents, cents, cents
To see the elephants, elephants, elephants
Jump the fence, fence, fence.
They jump so high, high, high
they reach the sky, sky, sky
And don't come back, back, back
I wonder why, why why
Why won't talk, talk, talk
Why can't walk, walk, walk
Why can't eat, eat, eat
But proves your defeat feat feat
Go ask your mother, mother, mother
For five cents more, more, more
To see the elephants, elephants, elephants
Jump out the door, door, door.

They stooped so low, low, low
They stubbed their ego, toe, toe
And that was the end, end, end,
Of the elephant show, show, show!

Mary Mack never knew when or where she would be sent. Mary Mack was on stand by and always ready to report for duty. She was captivating, she was smart and eloquent, she almost always spoke in riddles, at least at first. Her message was often delivered in the form of a rhyme, which would ensure that the receiver would be required to listen in order to decode the message. It wasn't always easy for them, and it wasn't always completed with success.

There had been times when her messages had been unheard. She had spoken them just fine, but the context of the message had fallen on deaf ears. That saddened her, and in a way hardened her heart a little bit, if that was still possible.

She loved each and every mission that she went on, and never enjoyed seeing one of her people fall. If they fell from grace it was because they chose something that wasn't becoming of God. It was simple really. Each plan was to be executed. If the individual was off-track by a simple choice, there would be an intervention; a correction of sorts. He did give each and every individual free will, which opened the floodgates of opportunity and chance. In reality, however, there were certain people that had distinctive plans, and those plans needed to be executed regardless of their own choices. Hence the interventions, we introduce to you "Miss Mary Mack…" She loved the dramatic effect of it all. She revelled in the concept and was thrilled to have been a part of it for so long. She did good work, she met important people, and made a difference. She had to believe that. She hung on to it. It was all she had.

CHAPTER 28

Abraham was very near full panic. He knew one thing for sure, Nanny was going to make certain that he paid for losing his temper this morning. He didn't know a lot about women, he hadn't had a lot of experience or an abundance of success with the likes of them in the dating department. But one thing that he had been able to comprehend in his thirty-two years was that women were not always rational, and rarely could one negotiate with an angry woman. Nanny was livid.

He paced his tiny apartment; the television repeated the same news over and over. His shoes squeaked on the terra cotta tiles, as he walked the same seven-foot path repeatedly. He feared wearing a tread into the tiles. He needed a plan. He needed to keep this job. He would have to kill Nanny. There was no other way to salvage this situation.

He would kill Nanny and he would dispose of the body. The timing was near perfect. Madam was going to Guadalajara for a few days on her business trip, and the children could be cared for by one of the house maids. No one would even notice that Nanny was missing for days. He could continue his work as though nothing was array.

How should he do it though? Choking? Poison? He could stab her but that could hypothetically increase his odds of capture. He pictured the blood, the mess and the need for cleaning. The chaos involved would be problematic. He wondered if there would be some way in which he could kill her with a delayed response. In some way knock her off, where she would die on her own three hours after leaving work, or after seeing herself out of the house at least.

He knew a lot of doctors through the church and thought of inquiring with one of them. Just for the sake of asking and nothing more. He called Dr. Pena on the phone.

"Bueno, Dr. Pena, Hello, Abraham here, how are you today, sir?" He waited for the appropriate response before engaging in his leading yet necessary questions.

Dr. Pena had been a doctor of Internal Medicine and then a professor of the general surgery, at the University of Guadalajara. In his later years he had opted for a secondary degree in medicine focusing on naturopathic studies, specifically the origins of the iris.

Abraham respected the good doctor's opinion and was certain that regardless of whether or not the doc approved of his decision to kill the Nanny, he would most likely help him to plot against her. At the very least once he had shared with him his desire to kill her, the doctor would become an accessory. So he wouldn't be in this alone.

"Good, Abraham, Gracias, nice to hear from you, how have you been?"

"Fine, thank you." Abraham was slightly frustrated with the small talk. He desperately wanted to just jump into the junk of it. He wanted to tell someone how awful Nanny had been to him. How she had been abusing him at work, how she took advantage and then when he finally stood up to her and said no she went psycho on him. "Actually, Dr. Pena, do you have time to talk? Could I come to see you today? Maybe even this morning?"

"Abraham, are you ill? Should you see the hospital?" Dr. Pena responded.

"No, no, nothing like that, I, it's just that, I need to talk to someone that is able to listen to me, and that is mature enough not to judge me poorly, Sir. You understand."

Dr. Pena assumed that it was an affair of the heart, perhaps that this had something to do with a woman, conceivably a one-night stand or a mistress had been taken. Or worse perhaps Abraham had become involved with a married woman.

"I see, well, I can check the book, give me a second." The doctor set the phone down quietly.

He returned to the phone quickly. "Yes, Abraham, I have openings from eleven until one-thirty, I suppose that someone was anticipating that I would take a lunch break, perhaps head home to Adele for a snack and a siesta. Why don't you come by for eleven, we can walk in the park and then we can stop for a bowl of soup at Don Pedro's. It should give us plenty of time to talk and I might even have time to fit in a short nap before my two o'clock appointments show up."

Abraham was pleased with this, this to him was something that he could quite easily live with, it would benefit him greatly to meet with Dr. Pena. He would be fed and he could see the doctor, poke and prod him for information and be at the school to pick up the children as scheduled for three o'clock.

"Yes, that works very well thank you. I will be at your office for eleven this morning, thank you, Sir."

"Very well, Abraham, see you then." Dr. Pena replaced the receiver in its cradle, pondered this conversation and the potential discussion later that morning. He then picked up the phone again and called his wife Adele to let her know that he would not be home for lunch.

CHAPTER 29

Abraham arrived at the school promptly at three, just as he had done for months before. He had had plenty of time after meeting with Dr. Pena to have the suburban cleaned and polished, and he had stopped to pick up a few groceries that the house maids had called him for.

He still had heard nothing from Nanny, but he had taken the advice of the Doctor and had decided that the best thing to do was pray for her. So he would do nothing. He was ill at ease, but intended to do nothing but his job and focus on moving forward.

He saw Her run from the school with Her lunch box and backpack in hand, waving at him frantically. "Abraham, Abraham." She smiled as She neared the vehicle.

He stood next to the rear passenger door, where She would always enter the vehicle. He knew his job, and She knew his place. They were comfortable with each other, but there was an unspoken respect and a kindness between them.

"Hiya!"

He reached his hand toward Hers and She grabbed on, She pulled him down towards Her and hugged him. "Hello, Misses, how was your day?"

"Fine, Abraham, thank you." He relieved her of Her bags and opened the door for Her. She climbed into the back seat of the Suburban and he turned to see Her brother coming towards them.

She questioned him, "Abraham, why do I need to learn French?" She was inquisitive and normally eager to learn as much as She could, Abraham found Her question intriguing and somewhat alarming. He wondered what happened to Her at school that day that had upset Her to the point that She would not be interested in learning.

"Hello, Master, how are we today?" He took the bags from her brother and continued holding the door. "I'm sorry, Misses, but I can't answer that for you, that is a question for your mother."

Her brother laughed. "Hey, Abraham, elle pense que le francais est trop dur." He swung himself into the backseat of the truck next to his sister. There was a fondness between them, a closeness. She cared for him, nurtured and protected him from things that they could not see, he aspired to protect Her from the things that they could see.

"I do not! I just don't see why we need to speak so many languages! I'm only five!"

Her brother piped up, "I'm doing Mandarin next, I think, what do you think, Abraham? I was reading the other day that the Chinese population is expected to grow exponentially over the next fifteen years and that in fact they could be controlling the world's markets by 2020. What do you think about that? Hey? Sounds kind of far out right? I mean no way, but what ever, I'm only six right? Stupid. That's what Dad said when I told him. He said it was dumb, that it would never happen. But it makes sense, because they have this plan, Abraham, like I was reading that they have this whole family control thing, so they get paid if they have a boy, and they don't if they have a girl, and if they get more than one child in a family then they have to pay additional tax. It's the government's way of controlling the growth of the population. And Hong Kong which has been under British rule since 1842 is being returned to Chinese Sovereignty with a promise of continued democracy. I just don't see how that's possible though because China is communist. And there's lots of other cool stuff too that I read about that I tell you. Stuff that they are inventing in China and Korea. Mostly electronic stuff, but lots of cutting edge things. Just let me know if you would like to hear about it."

Abraham was busy thinking about his own things and really had no interest what so ever in listening to the child. "Yes of course I would love to hear about it, but just not right now because I have a really bad headache and as you can see the traffic today is horrible. Can you please sit down and do up your seat belt, Master? Thank you kindly."

Abraham was nervous about seeing Nanny, he thought about Dr. Pena's reaction to his request for advice. And now that he was thinking about it, he realized that perhaps it sounded a bit offside. He didn't believe that he would have actually killed Nanny, but in his mind it had been a soothing matter.

The children had begun to banter about something that had happened during the lunch break at school. He turned up the volume of the radio so that he wouldn't have to listen to them. The endless chatter on some days was more than he could bear. His thoughts returned to Nanny and what he might say to her when he saw her, and worse, what she might say to him.

He knew that she was not going to be any sort of sensible or kind. He predicted anger and vile language, more profanities. His thoughts raced through different scenarios. None of which ended well for him. He thought about his discussion with Dr. Pena and understood the doctor's rationale, but was still seriously thinking about killing the bitch.

The mind is an awful thing at times, a steel trap in which one can find yourself locked up and lost. Listening to the voices of loved ones gone, lovers who have left, friends who you no longer call amigos. The voices of your negative emotions, the parts of your psyche that the heart doesn't want to deal with but that your brain isn't quite done with yet. Your memories just keep vomiting them up, hurling the voices up and into your frontal lobe where you can hear them. Where they can shout at you. Where they are able to make sense. Where they are able to rationalize, negotiate and barter on your behalf.

CHAPTER 30

As they approached the house he could see her waiting out front of the gates. Arms crossed in front of her chest, her white sweater and skirt neatly pressed as always. The drive down to the house was arched with beautiful big Cecropia trees. At this time of year they were very lush, and a dark green, full of leaves and vibrant in colour. The Madam had had bougainvilleas planted in rich reds and pinks along the driveway, which drooped and hung over deeply nestled blue agave making the long entrance festive and appealing to visitors during all seasons.

Abraham normally adored driving up towards the family home. He took pride in working for this family, for the woman that had hired him when he had so desperately needed a job. He appreciated the things that this family had provided, and the incredible opportunities that they had given him while under their employ. The children and Madam had become his whole life. His world revolved around serving them. He couldn't allow a self-serving manipulative nanny to take that away. He wouldn't. There was just no way.

He could see the scowl on her face as he approached. He was doing his very best to maintain an air of casual imperviousness for the children's sake.

"Oh look! There's Nanny!" Both children adored their nanny, and couldn't wait to see her every day after school. It was of utmost importance to Abraham that the children were kept out of their affairs and protected of any of the ugliness that may or may not occur. "Indeed, there she is, waiting for you as she does every day! She must be so excited to see you."

The Misses was the first to speak. "Why would she be excited, Abraham? Today is just a normal day, nothing to be excited about." She was frightfully abrupt at times and painfully direct.

Abraham answered Her as directly as he could without hurting Her feelings. "Misses, I just mean that Nanny must be glad that you are here."

She thought it was an odd thing to say, even if She was only five, She looked at Abraham. He was not himself today. Of that She was certain. He was tense, She had been able to see it in his neck while he was driving, and his temples had been pulsing. She had noticed it while She and Her brother were talking. Abraham had turned up the music, thinking that they wouldn't notice his distance from them today while they were chattering.

Normally, Abraham was very engaged in their conversation, he seemed to even enjoy participating with them and never told them that he was too busy or not interested. She found it very rare that he had not become engrossed in Her brother's titbits about China. He was upset about something, or something was bothering him, She would make certain to find out what it was.

CHAPTER 31

Nanny was prepared, and was ready for Abraham when he arrived with the children. She knew that he would be the gentleman and would follow through with his responsibilities and pick them up as he was employed to do. She could always count on him to be predictable if nothing else.

Nanny waited for Abraham to open the door to the Suburban for the children, she made eye contact with both children, and then took their bags from Abraham. She reached up and took the hand of the little Misses and helped Her out of the truck, and then the Master. She hugged both children and kissed them on the cheek. "Hola mis hijitos, how was your day, did you learn anything of great value today at school?"

She of course answered Nanny first, "Yes, Nanny, many things, but I'm afraid that I don't understand why I must be subjected to the French language. It is pompous and frankly I find it a bit of a bore. I would much rather learn Italian or perhaps even as brother suggested, Mandarin, it would be more useful you see, Nanny."

"Oh yes, Misses, well, that's very interesting, for sure, but your mother she decides these things. So we just have to make sure that you do them. And you are just so very beautiful today, look at how shiny your hair is today. Did you brush it yourself this morning? It looks so red today, doesn't it, Abraham? It's such a lovely colour, misses, and now you must get ready for ballet class, let's go and find your things for that and get your hair into a proper bun for class, so Abraham is going to drive you there today. Isn't that right, Abraham?" Nanny looked at Abraham sideways, daring him to cross her.

Abraham looked at the Misses, Her hair was indeed beautiful, it was a colour that was not normally seen in these parts of the country. Auburn… he had heard someone refer to it as auburn. It was a shade of reddish brown that was mostly only seen in movies. And it glistened, in the sunlight as though a million diamonds were hiding in her scalp. It was rare for sure, his mind drifted back to his conversation with Dr. Pena and his steadfast position on not killing the nanny.

"Of course, Nanny, yes I will take the Misses anywhere She needs to go. Providing of course that you have all of Her things ready and if She is willing to come with me."

She looked at Abraham and smiled. "Of course I will come with you, silly. I will go and get ready now. How long until we leave?"

Abraham looked at his watch. He looked at Her brother and at Nanny, he put his hand into his pocket and silently thanked his God for the perfect plan of revenge. Nanny would never recover from this. He felt giddy inside, he was so happy with himself. He refrained from smiling, controlled his voice and cleared his throat.

"Well, Miss, I think if we leave in thirty minutes we should be in top shape. Is your brother going to join us today? I think that's a grand idea, why don't you come, Master? You and I can go for an ice cream while the Misses is at ballet… sound like fun to you?"

"Oh yeah! I love ice cream!"

"And I know that you do, Master! This will be so good! And Nanny can have a wonderful afternoon doing whatever it is that Nanny likes to do when she doesn't have children to care for. Hurry, hurry, let's get ourselves ready and we shall be off."

The children ran off to their bedrooms to change their clothes, Nanny scowled at him, " How dare you, you watch yourself, Abraham."

"Oh, silly me, did I offend you, Nanny? I must have temporarily lost my senses. I trust that you will be all right while we are gone? Hmm? You should know where to find us? Yes? And where would we find you, Nanny? If we should need to find you that is? Where would we look for you, Nanny?"

"Fuck off, you crazy bastard. If I need you, I will call. You just worry about what you are doing, you hear me? You are on a need-to-know basis from now on. Make sure they get something to eat later. And not just ice cream, you know how Madam feels about that. Make sure She gets to the ballet studio on time for class and don't piss me off again, Abraham, or you will be fucking sorry that you did. I can promise you that."

Abraham's blood was boiling on the inside, but he refused to allow Nanny to see just how fuming he was. He balled his hat tightly into his palms, wringing it out as though it was wet. His plan was falling into place magically, Nanny was like putty in his hands, and his plan hadn't really had any thought put into it.

"I will do everything in my power, Nanny, to see that I get the job done today. I won't ask again where you are, but you can ask as many times as you like where I am, and I am very certain that you will. Now if you will excuse me I will ready myself for our excursion."

Nanny shook her head. "This is what I'm talking about, you are a nut job, Abraham, you don't make any sense, ever! Just go, get going or you're going to be late, and then there will be that to deal with." Nanny smoothed her skirt as she watched Abraham walk away from her. She was smiling, she had won, he had caved like a deck of cards in a sea breeze. Her mother had told her that she would have a way with men, that she would be able to control them, to get her way with ease. Her mother though, had thought that she would have to use her body, using sex to manipulate men, she had just used her brain. Her mother was old and stupid and uneducated. Nanny suddenly thought that she might only stay at this job for a short while longer. Maybe it was coming time for a change, perhaps she was meant for bigger things, maybe big business or maybe even politics.

CHAPTER 32

With both children back in the Suburban, and Her ready for ballet, Abraham started towards el Centro. When he reached the Malecon he scoped out a decent parking spot and pulled in on an angle.

"Okay, everybody grab their things please." He turned the vehicle off and opened the driver's door.

Her brother spoke first. "Why are you parking here? It's so far to the Ballet Studio?"

"We are going to have to walk for a bit today, is that okay, Master?"

"Well, I just don't understand why, there's a whole parking lot at the studio, and when Mom drives we park right there. If we park here we have to walk like all the way across the downtown. And it's really hot, and She is going to be late for class."

She said nothing. She was mute.

Abraham placed the keys to the vehicle on the seat and closed the door. He opened the rear passenger door so that the children could get out and picked up Misses' bag. He peeked inside to see if there was anything that they might be able to use, and then threw it into the back of the truck.

"Okay let's get a move on, come on, let's get going, so that we aren't late."

The children did as they were told and started walking with Abraham away from the Suburban and onto the cobblestone-paved streets. The sun was hot, beating down on them. Neither one of the children wore hats, both were very fair-skinned and were never out in the hot sun unprotected. The late afternoon sun was very unforgiving for gringos. Her skin was very fair, her brother could see that She was very quickly becoming heat stroked.

"Abraham, She is too hot! She needs a hat, or else you need to get Her inside. She isn't supposed to be outside at this time of day. The sun is too bright for Her."

Abraham had never had children of his own, and he had never had to deal with a gringo child with odd-coloured hair and white skin. He was quick on his toes though; he was quick to think, and very quick to respond in crisis situations. "No problem, Master, let's just cross over the street there," he pointed across to the other side of the road, " and then down a block there is an ice cream shop, we will go in there for a break. It is a little hot even for me today."

Her brother questioned the decision. "And what about Her ballet class?" He was becoming uncomfortable with the decision-making process already.

"Today I think we might just have to miss ballet class, but it's only just one class, no big deal, instead we will have lots of fun. We can stop for that ice cream and then we can go go-carting if you like, and we can go to the piñata factory, to see them make the piñatas. Maybe even we can have them make a special one for you!"

She was not pleased. She loved Her ballet class, it was Her favourite thing to do. Missing ballet was not an option for Her. Most certainly not something that She would do by choice. And She would not under any circumstances chose piñatas over ballet, ever. This had somehow gone terribly wrong and She was extremely displeased.

Her brother spoke. "So go-carting hey? But isn't the track all the way out by the marina? That's such a long way! And you left the truck way back by McDonald's! I like that idea though, I guess we could grab a taxi, did you bring some money, Abraham?"

"Yes of course I have some money! Lots and lots of money! Now let's just pop in here and have some ice cream and we can discuss the rest of our afternoon plans. Yes?" He held the door open for them.

"What's your flavour, Master? What kind would you like?"

"Well, I like chocolate, like Mom, but She can't have any."

Abraham looked aghast. "What do you mean She can't have any? Why not?"

She finally spoke. "I'm lactose intolerant. Ice cream makes me vomit and gives me the shits."

Abraham's mouth opened in surprise, he was at a loss for words. He had never heard such language from a five-year-old.

"Also gluten intolerant, and I am a vegetarian, I don't eat anything that ever used any type of respiratory system for survival. It's just wrong in my opinion. Cannibalism of sorts; in my mind anyway. You can do whatever you want. I choose not to. I am not pleased with the choices that you have made today, your choices have negatively affected my program, and you did so without asking me. This was ill-advised. The consequences of these actions will not be pleasant for you."

Abraham was taken aback by the diction of this tiny five-year-old girl standing in front of him. He had never heard someone so small use such big words, and to be honest most adults didn't speak so directly, and most of the people he dealt with struggled with articulation of the English language, at least in this country.

"Well, I am sorry that you are lactose intolerant, but I don't know what that is, to be truthful, and I don't know what gluten is either. I do eat meat, and lots of it. I don't understand vegetarians, and don't care much for them. Plants also breathe. Read up on it. You are fucking five years old. Suck on that. I am the adult and I am going to make the decisions today. We are going go-carting because I like it, I don't like ballet, I think it's a bore. And then we will do more stuff that I like. And maybe we will even stop for some tacos, tacos de cabeza, do you know what those are?"

She was disgusted. "Do I look like I don't understand basic language to you? Yes I know what they are. And no I will not eat head tacos. You may eat as many as you like. But there is no part of the head of any cow, not the eyes, nor the brain, the lips or tongue that is going to be ingested by my body. So suck on that, Abraham." She looked around for familiar faces, She saw none. "I want to go home, or I want to call my mother."

Abraham was now ordering the ice creams for himself and Her brother. "No."

She started to move towards the door to exit the ice cream shop, Abraham grabbed hold of Her bun on the top of Her head with his free hand, and pulled Her back towards him. "You are not going anywhere, why don't you sit down and behave yourself? Be nice... just this once? Yes?"

She sat down at the table with Abraham and Her brother, not because She chose to be nice, as he suggested but because She didn't see any other option. She didn't view voiding one's opinions and desires as being nice. It was more like being manipulated or moulded. At five years old She had very strong feelings on the subject already. She crossed Her arms in front of Her chest and sat with Her back to Abraham.

She listened to the two of them while they rattled on about

go-carting, and car racing. The Indianapolis 500, the Grand Prix, the Can Am, Her brother loved cars and was in love with the idea of racing. She became more and more frustrated and angry with the amount of time that they were wasting; however She was determined to get moving. She looked at Abraham with Her sweetest face. "Can we go now?"

Abraham was pleased that She looked less hostile. "Yes of course, let's get moving."

They left the ice cream shop and hailed a taxi, which took them to the go- cart track north of the city centre, near the marina. There they spent a few hours speeding around the track. She let her hair down and gave it a go. She actually enjoyed herself, tried driving, and had a good time. It may not have been the ballet, but racing was more fun than She had anticipated it would be. In that afternoon She found a reckless abandonment that She didn't know She could possess. One that if contained could provide Her with pleasure, but if let loose could lead Her to destruction. She was very aware of the powers that were given. Aware and very afraid at the same time.

Her brother was over-the-moon happy. He found a jumping-for-joy kind of happy at the track. A profound pleasure that ran deep into his boots, a love for driving, for shifting, and steering, for manoeuvring around the obstacles and pile-ons. He knew this was for him.

CHAPTER 33

Senora Gomez was concerned. Never once had She missed a ballet class. She was a young student, only five, but showed such promise. She decided that it was imperative that she contact Madam, something had to be wrong. In her stomach she had a feeling that the child was in danger. She pulled the child's file from the filing cabinet and retrieved the cell phone number for the parent. She dialled.

Ring, Ring. "Bueno, Hello..."

"Hello, Madam, Senora Gomez calling, from the Shanti Ballet studio."

"Yes, Senora, hello, is there a problem?"

"Well, actually, Madam, yes there is. I'm very sorry to bother you, Madam, but She wasn't in class today. And as you are aware, She has never ever missed a class. I am concerned."

Her mother was immediately alarmed. "Senora, I am in Guadalajara today on business, but as you know Nanny ensures that She never misses any of her ballet classes. I will call Nanny to see what happened, can I call you back?"

"Yes of course, Madam, I'm very sorry to have inconvenienced you, I was just very concerned for Her. She has never missed a class you know. I appreciate the call back if you have a moment. Thank you so much, gracias."

"Of course, Senora. I'll call you back as soon as I know something." With that both women hung up.

Her mother dialled the number for Nanny.

Ring ring, ring ring, ring ring. "*Hola, you have reached Nanny, I am so sorry that I can't take your call, but if you leave a message after the beep I will call you back as soon as I have a free moment. Gracias!*"

She hung up and dialled her husband's number, it was busy.

She hung up and dialled Abraham's number.

Ring ring, ring ring, ring ring. "*Hello, this is Abraham, sorry that I have missed you. Please leave your name and number and I will get back to you.*"

Fuck.

She held the receiver in her hand. Instinct told her to move quickly. She called the airline and booked a flight for within the hour, she then called her assistant and filled him in quickly, he would cancel her appointments and arranged for a driver to pick her up in Guadalajara and whisk her to the airport, and another driver to pick her up at the airport in Puerto Vallarta to take her to the residence. She would continue to attempt phone contact with Nanny, her husband and Abraham.

CHAPTER 34

Abraham could feel his phone vibrating in his pocket, he quickly pulled it out and flipped the front up to see who was calling.

Madam.

He knew that she would catch up to him, he knew that his time would be limited and so now he knew that he must make his next move. The taxi trundled on through the streets of downtown Puerto Vallarta, easing its way towards the bridge that would carry them into old town. He now felt anxious and ill at ease. It was dark now. The sun had gone down, so at least he didn't need to worry about having Her out in the heat.

"Listen, man can you move this taxi a little faster for me please, I need to get there today, you know what I'm saying?"

The driver looked at Abraham in the rear-view mirror, he quietly wondered what this guy was doing with two gringo children who were clearly of a very different class of people. He thought about calling his boss but he didn't know how he would do that without alerting the guy in the back seat. He was driving slow because he didn't really want to drop them off. He had kids of his own. He knew the little girl's face was disturbed. She looked tired and hungry. He would pull over as soon as opportunity presented itself, with the intention of calling dispatch for help.

"Listen, cabrone, I can only go as fast as the traffic is moving, there's so many people today, cruise ships in town today; and you know what, I gotta make a quick stop here to go pee. I'm only gonna be just a second." The taxi driver pulled his cab over to the left side of the road and stopped by the curb. He opened the driver's door and stepped out. Looking back at Abraham only briefly.

Abraham was upset. He wanted badly to get to the other side of town. The children were hungry, he knew that. He didn't want anyone to be angry with him, and he had to make a delivery, and he needed to get to the bus. Ridiculous, who stops to go pee? Instinct told him to move.

He grabbed the hands of both children and exited the vehicle quickly. They headed down the street on foot, and disappeared into a crowd of tourists walking from the malecon.

CHAPTER 35

Madam's plane landed in Puerto Vallarta and her driver was waiting for her. The entire process had taken her less than two hours. She had still been unable to reach either Nanny or Abraham, but her husband was en route and would meet her at their residence.

She arrived at the residence to find Nanny lounging at the kitchen table enjoying coffee with the housemaid. Nanny jumped to her feet as Madam entered the room, as did the maid.

"Madam, we weren't expecting you until tomorrow morning. Welcome back."

Madam was livid. "Nanny, where are my children?"

"Well, Madam, they are at ballet class of course." Nanny looked confused.

"Nanny, Ballet class runs from four in the afternoon until five thirty. It is now nearly seven thirty. Both children are to be in your care at all times. I will ask you again, and I would caution you to think before you speak. Where are my children?"

"Madam, it was Abraham, he insisted on taking them today, he said that he didn't mind, and that you had asked him to help out more, he said he would be helping me by helping you, so I agreed to allow him to take the children to ballet. I have been here waiting for them to return."

"And when I called? You didn't answer, why? Your phone

that I pay for goes to voicemail, why is that, Nanny? Why have you not been answering my calls for the past two hours?"

'Oh, Madam, I'm terribly sorry, I must have had the ringer turned off. My mistake, madam. I'm so very sorry."

"Well, Nanny, Abraham did not take the children to Her ballet class. Senora Gomez called me to let me know that She was a no-show for class today, which was alarming to her as She has never missed a class ever."

"What! He didn't take Her? Where did they go? Where are they now?"

"Well, that I don't know, Nanny. But I do know that you were not doing what you were supposed to be doing today. You are paid to care for my children and to ensure their safety at all times. Clearly today you were not doing that."

"I am very sorry, Madam."

"I am going to call the police. I have been trying to reach Abraham for two hours and he also is not answering. I am not finished with you yet, Nanny. But you are excused for now."

"Thank you, madam." Nanny excused herself and retreated to her quarters. She felt like throwing up.

Madam picked up the telephone receiver and dialled the number for the police head quarters just as her husband came through the door. She nodded at him as he placed his briefcase on the dining room table.

"Bueno, Police Headquarters, how may I direct your call?"

"Chief Alvarez please. This is an emergency."

"One Moment while I transfer you directly." The line clicked three times, and then rang again.

"Alvarez."

Chief Alvarez was the youngest police chief that Puerto Vallarta had ever seen. He was appointed at the age of thirty-nine, and within just six months of active duty as Chief had cleaned up the streets and had made a serious dent in crime. He had worked hard as a young lieutenant in the Army and then had become a very decorated Police Officer. He had never been married, but fancied the ladies. Especially the pretty ones, and recently he had taken a liking to foreign ladies. One in particular.

"Jorge? Bueno, hello, it's me."

"Hello, how are you? I'm surprised to hear from you."

"Yes, Jorge, it's my children. I don't know where they are."

Chief Alvarez could sense the panic in her voice. "How long?"

"A few hours."

"Who was the last to see them?"

"Nanny I guess, they were with Abraham, our butler. He was supposed to drive them to Her ballet class, but they never arrived. I was in Guadalajara, Senora Gomez called me from the ballet school to let me know that She hadn't shown for Her training class today. I came back as soon as I could get a flight."

"Are you at your residence?"

"Yes."

Alvarez looked at his watch. "I will be there in ten minutes, I am going to dispatch a city wide search for the children right now. What is the proper spelling of their names? With that I can get their photos from the Canadian Consular, and I can have that information to all of my on-duty officers within twenty minutes. Don't worry. I will find them."

Madam spelled the children's names and turned to her husband. She had filled him in on the phone earlier, with the information that she had at that time. Now she knew that they had been missing since four in the afternoon. It was now almost eight.

She then quickly relayed her recent discussion with Nanny to her husband, he couldn't help but question nanny's involvement.

"It just doesn't make sense to me. Abraham has been a great employee. Something had to have happened. Why would he just take the children?"

Madam answered him. "I agree with you. It doesn't make any sense at all. But I think that the best thing we can do is let one of Jorge's men talk to Nanny. She will buckle like a house of cards in a light breeze. Or better yet, let's put Jorge in with her."

"Good, I like it. Do it. If he doesn't get our kids back, though, I'm going to kill her. Because she has done something, I know it in my gut, so she's as good as dead. Just so you know." He threw his glass against the wall and stormed out of the room.

CHAPTER 36

Abraham knew that they must be moving to their next destination swiftly. He was beginning to feel a bit of pressure and excitement all the same. He was beginning to have anxiety about using his cell phone. He wondered if they were even on to him yet. He looked at the time. It was just after eight.

He opened the flip cover and dialled. He listened to a pre-recorded message for the travel times which wasn't ideal, but all of his questions were answered.

The children were very quiet, he was aware that they must be hungry. But he was reluctant to enter a restaurant to feed them. He thought about perhaps getting food from a food truck, maybe tacos or quesadillas. It was going to be a long trip tonight and the idea of doing it on an empty stomach was less than appealing.

They moved onto a side street that he knew had good food. He wasn't certain about the whole vegetarian thing, but if She were hungry enough She would eat. That he was certain of, his mother had taught him that. His own mother had withheld food at times. Poor behaviour had resulted in withholding love, withholding food and lashings. He was not a fan of any of them, but he had learned from the experience that if one were hungry, one would eat.

CHAPTER 37

Chief Alvarez arrived at the residence followed by three marked police vehicles. One car and two pick up trucks, loaded with uniformed officers. As he had promised, he had contacted the Canadian Consular and had informed her of the missing children. She had consequently contacted the Canadian Embassy in Guadalajara, and Toronto. She then contacted the immigration office in Puerto Vallarta and revoked the children's visas, and placed travel restrictions on their Canadian Passports, without which they would not be able to cross any border out of Mexico. Her biggest concern was not in them leaving the country however; it was what could happen to them within the borders of Mexico. Alvarez agreed to keep her abreast of the investigation.

Madam was waiting at the front door. "Jorge, thank you for coming."

"Of course." He hugged her and inhaled deeply as he did so. He found her fragrance highly satisfying. "Has anything developed since we spoke?"

"Nothing, no. Except that they were here after school, their backpacks are here and their lunch boxes. So they came home and then left again."

"Okay, I need to speak first to Nanny, where is she? And I am going to have each one of my officers speak to the other staff members, friends and I will need a list of anyone that may have had contact with the children, yourselves and your staff in the past twenty-four hours. These people may have clues for us. This is very time sensitive so I need everyone to co-operate. I also need the cell phone numbers for Nanny and for Abraham; we are going to do a twenty-four-hour recall on both numbers. And also someone is going to have to speak to your husband as well. Is he here?"

"Yes of course. Everyone is here. Please bring them in. Anything you need, Jorge."

Alvarez pulled his radio from his hip, he spoke into it and seconds later his men climbed the front steps and entered through the front door. Their uniforms were brilliant white, they removed their navy baseball hats, which bore gold crests as they crossed the threshold, all of them were wearing bulletproof vests, and heavy combat boots.

Alvarez directed all of them with specific instructions and then walked the hallway towards Nanny's quarters. He knocked once and then opened the door. Nanny's room was small but very beautifully decorated, not plain but very designer. Jorge thought it interesting that Madam elevated experiences even for the hired help.

Nanny was frantically packing her suitcase when he entered. "Hello, I am Chief Alvarez, are you going somewhere, Nanny?"

She was crying, sobbing almost uncontrollably. "I am getting fired, this is just in preparation."

"Do you know why I am here, Miss?"

Nanny wiped her nose on her sleeve, her mascara was running, her eyes now red, and beginning to swell. "Of course, the children are missing, Madam thinks that monster Abraham, he's the butler, she thinks that he has done something terrible to them."

"Why do you think you are getting fired, Nanny? Did you

do something wrong?" Alvarez always found theatrical women entertaining, some men would become angered by the drama, and he was immensely amused.

"She said that it was my responsibility to care for them, and so now; they are missing so I guess I am getting fired. I'm not stupid you know. I'm very smart."

"Of course you're very smart, Nanny, no one thinks otherwise. Madam thinks you're very smart or she wouldn't have you caring for her children. Do you not believe that it is your responsibility to care for them?"

"Yes, but, well, really it's her responsibility, she is their mother, not me. I am just working here you know. I do my best and all, but really I just work here. It's her job to care for them; she can't blame me for this. She is always working, Chief Alvarez, I do my best, and I work really hard."

"I see. That's too bad. That she's always working I mean. Can you tell me about your day today? Walk me through it step by step please."

"Yes, of course, well, Madam was in Guadalajara, you know sometimes she travels, so the children had to go to school, I made the lunches and got them ready and on the bus at six-forty-five."

Jorge interrupted. "I see, so the school bus picks them up then? Where does that happen?"

"Yes, the bus gets them right out front, brings them back too if we need it. At the bottom of the driveway."

"Okay, so tell me, the children get onto the bus in the morning at six forty-five approximately, then they are off to school, and then what does your day look like, Nanny? So you are free from just before seven in the morning until when?"

"Well, no, no I'm not free, I have other responsibilities. I have the children's laundry to do. And I have to ensure that all of their scheduling is done. And of course I have to see to Her dietary needs. Special shopping and things, that's all part of my job too, and Madam expects me to take them to all of their extracurricular activities, and play dates."

Nanny was making excuses and justifying her time. Alvarez probed deeper. "I see, Nanny, how has it been for you having Abraham as the butler here? Have you become friends?"

"Well, you know, I don't think anybody really can be friends with Abraham. He just keeps to himself really. He's very private. You know his wife died, and since then, Chief Alvarez, he really is just a shell of a man. I don't think he has relations with women, you know what I mean. The Madam, she only gave him the job because she felt sorry for him, you know, poor Abraham and everything. So here he is and he is kind of a dead weight for the rest of us. I mean he helps and stuff, but really we have to cover for him."

"Really? That's interesting, how so?" Alvarez texted his lieutenant who was at the church interviewing the pastor; he wanted to know everything he could about Abraham and his personal life.

"Well, there's sometimes you know that he just doesn't pull his weight, like, I probably shouldn't tell you this, but you know with what's happened to the kids and everything and I just feel awful." Alvarez nodded.

"Yes, yes, Nanny, you must tell me, it is imperative, please."

"Well, just yesterday you know I asked him to just do this one little thing and he lost his temper. And he said he was going to make me pay for it. Now I wonder if this is his way of getting back at me. I feel so awful, and I wonder if all of this time that he has been working here, if he was unstable.

You know, sick in the head. Nobody could blame the poor man, after everything that happened with his wife. But the children…" Nanny began to sob again. "Do you think Madam is going to fire me?"

"I'm sorry I can't answer that, so yesterday, he said he was going to make you pay for it? When you say that he lost his temper, how exactly did that happen, Nanny? What did he do exactly that made it clear to you that he had lost his temper?"

"Well, he was yelling at me, and he threatened me."

"He was yelling at you? And how did he threaten you, Nanny? Can you be specific please? I will need the details."

"Well, he said he was going to make me pay for it." She twisted her hair in her left hand.

"Sorry I need to interrupt you there. What was it that he was going to make you pay for? I think I missed that part." Alvarez leaned on the window sill, reading a text message from one of his officers.

"Oh of course, yes, well, I had asked him to pick up the children from school. And then he said that Madam had left him quite a list of things to do, and that he couldn't do it; and so I said to him that She had ballet class and that if She came on the bus She would be late. And that I really needed him to help me out, just this once. And he said he just couldn't and that he had some personal things to take care of, so I said, that if he wasn't able to pick the children up that I would be obliged to tell Madam, and he said he would make me pay for it."

"See, Nanny, that just doesn't make sense to me. Would you like me to tell you why?"

Nanny was still crying. Alvarez hated teary women. He liked his women strong, determined, intelligent and articulate. There was no hiding the fact the he had a soft spot for hair and long legs, but without the rest of the package looks were just a fading mirage. One day he hoped, one day.

This crying broad was too much for him though, drama he enjoyed, but the crying was too much; he needed air. The amusing theatrics were beginning to grow tiresome. He had moved close to the window, and wanted to open it but didn't want to seem rude to her. He needed her to cave, he just hoped that he could make her crumble quickly so that he could get on with this and find these poor kids.

"Do you mind if I open this window? Gracias, I'm going to tell you why I think this story is bullshit, Nanny. But first I am going to tell you that I have officers speaking to every person that knows this family, that knows the children, Abraham, and you. Anyone that may have had contact with you, or Abraham, in the past week. There are people that have come forward voluntarily, to offer information already. It is my job, Nanny, to find these children. It is in everyone's best interest to find them alive. Do you understand what I am saying to you, Nanny? If that crazy bastard kills them, Nanny, the blood will be on all of our hands."

Nanny's sobs were racking her body uncontrollably. "Listen to me, woman. Get control of yourself, Nanny, Nanny. Stop crying. Listen to me. If you cannot help me then I will put you in prison, Nanny. If we do not find those children we will have an international incident on our hands. The Canadians will come down on me, Nanny, they will crush me hard, they will stomp on me until I cannot get any air; I cannot have that. Not on my watch, and not because you wanted to get your fucking hair done on Madam's dime. Oh yes I know all about it already, you lying bitch."

Nanny wiped her nose on her sweater sleeve. "But I don't know where he would have taken them."

"I need you to tell me the truth, tell me the truth about what happened so that I can find them. Do you understand me, do you? Because if you do not, we can just go now, Nanny, I have a nice place for you, in a nice underground cell, in the rainy season, nanny, it fills up with water. So your skin will rot, and all of that hair will fall out of your head. There's no place to get dry, no place to hide from the water, no place to lie down or take a shit. When you take a shit, nanny, it floats around and then you live in it. It's on you like moisturizer. How does that sound to you? Hey? Makes this place look like a fucking palace with Madam hey? Makes the children seem like a dream job, tell me the truth so I don't have to take you there, and my guards, they are going to like you a lot... ya I think so maybe... chica."

And so Nanny unravelled the truth, the housemaid, the taxi driver, the clerk at the go-cart track, and Dr. Pena all came forward and shared what they knew, the Suburban was found parked close to the Malecon, and the Chief began to quickly put all of the pieces together in an attempt to find them.

CHAPTER 38

Abraham knew that they were looking for him now. He had seen his photo on the television while they were eating their dinner. He wasn't certain how Madam managed to get shit done so fast in this town, when local, national people couldn't get anything accomplished, but he kind of respected her for it.

So now they were hiding. He had purchased tickets for the bus to Guadalajara at ten-thirty. So they had just another hour to kill. Or rather to hide. Once they arrived in Guadalajara they would purchase tickets to Mexico City and then once they were there he would have new passports made. He could take them south to Brazil where his first thought was to sell them.

He knew that the girl with the pretty hair would fetch a decent price. But the boy maybe even more. Blonde hair, blue eyes, three languages, and he was smart. Who knows, how much he could get for the two of them; but for certain Abraham was not returning to Puerto Vallarta. His day had not turned out the way that he had planned it. That was for sure.

When he had gotten up in the morning his plan was to kill the Nanny. To potentially torture and then murder the one that was so dreadfully threatening to him. That might have been easier, in the end. He pulled his hat down over his face as far as he could and attempted to watch the television as the children ate their tacos. There was a city wide man hunt for him. Abraham couldn't help but smile. Never in his life would he have thought that a simpleton such as himself would have experienced such fame.

The girl had been quiet for quite some time. Mute, and had barely eaten a thing. He supposed that maybe She really was a vegetarian. He watched Her out of the corner of his eye. She was struggling to chew. She picked at the tortilla, and ate the onion, cilantro and cabbage, for sure a fucking vegetarian. Holy Mother of God. Who would have thought? A five-year-old with a sincere belief system. Was She stubborn or was She honestly as unwaveringly genuine as She openly appears?

He listened to the report on the television about how the children's passports had been restricted.

'Like he cared', he didn't have their passports anyway, and he was planning on getting new ones for them as soon as they arrived in Mexico City. Abraham was disappointed that there was no direct bus to the big city. The trip to Mexico City through Guadalajara created a slight delay for him, and a source of frustration more than anything. He was also certain that for every time that he had to make a change or stop he risked getting caught. For him that was not an option.

He rushed the children to finish their food so that they could walk over to the bus station. He would pick up the ticket that he had reserved on the phone and then they would load and be on their way. He was confident that they were home free.

A walking street vendor was selling cotton candy in colours of pink and blue. His white pants were dirty, and rolled up on the bottom exposing his sandalled feet. His T-shirt bore the logo Vive Mexico and was threadbare but was worn with pride. His grin pulled his lips from ear to ear, exposing yellowed teeth.

"Algodon de Azucar," he shouted, '*Cotton Candy*'.

Her brother was intrigued and since he had such a sweet tooth was quite interested in perhaps a blue bag of the sweet and tasty treat.

"Abraham, can we have some cotton candy?"

"No, not right now, we need to get to the bus station. Here we go, let's cross here."

Abraham pointed them to where he wanted to cross. She saw a restaurant that She was familiar with. She pulled from Her memories trying to remember why She knew the sign out front. El Escondite, She was certain that she had heard the name before.

"But I want Cotton Candy, I want a blue bag. I'm tired. And why are we going to the bus station anyway?" Her brother was tired and cranky, he was dragging his feet as they moved on the cobble stones. She was becoming frustrated with the situation. Her head was aching. A throbbing between Her eyes. She had experienced this pain before but it had gone away quickly. It seemed to intensify as they moved further and further from the residence. She longed for Her mother.

As they stepped up onto the curb on the opposite side of the street, She looked up at the sign of the restaurant again and remembered where She knew it from. She looked back towards the taco stand that they had just eaten at; and to the Cotton Candy vendor as he wandered down the street away from them. The sky was dark, She wasn't certain of the time, but She knew from the way that She felt that it had to be long past Her bedtime.

"Abraham, I have to use the toilet." She pulled at the back of his shirt as he attempted to steer them down the street and towards the bus station.

"Sorry, doll face, you will just have to hold that pee until we get onto the bus, then you can go. There will be a bathroom on there."

"Nope, this isn't pee, oh no, Abraham!" She raised Her

voice so that people inside of the open-windowed restaurant would be able to hear Her. "I'm gonna poop my pants."

Abraham was shamed by Her outburst. He had never had children and would never have imagined that one would be so outwardly upfront about private things.

"Well, fine, let's see if we can slip into this restaurant and use their bathroom quickly. Okay? Just do what ever you need to do to not do that business in your pants, I can't have that."

"Ooohhh, okaaaayy, Abraham, I'm trying to hold it."

As they moved through the doorway and into the restaurant She winked at Her brother, ever so discreetly so that Abraham wouldn't notice. She knew, that Her brother had clued in that She was up to something, She had never pooped Her pants. She was potty-trained when She was fourteen months old.

As soon as they were through the doorway She saw what She was hoping for. The owner of the establishment, who was an acquaintance of their parents. She remembered their parents speaking with him after a church event one Sunday morning. She knew his name, She only hoped that he would remember their faces without Her having to say anything to him.

Abraham approached him and asked nicely if She could use the bathroom.

Senor Sebastian Chavez smiled at Abraham without looking up and said, "I'm terribly sorry, but we reserve the right to limit the usage of our facilities to restaurant patrons only."

Abraham nodded in acknowledgment. "Yes, normally I would understand, but it seems we have a bit of an emergency with my girl here. Could She just for a quick moment slip into the ladies' room. I promise She won't leave a mess and She won't be but a minute."

Senor Chavez looked over at the girl and immediately was

in awe of the colour of Her hair. He also was in awe that this man was in Her accompaniment. He recognized the children, he knew that this man was not one of their parents. "Of course, fine, but please tell Her to be quick. If you will excuse me for a moment, I have a table that is in need of attendance."

Abraham removed his hat and thanked the restaurant owner. "Of course, thank you, Senor." He nudged Her towards the bathroom. "Go ahead, be quick."

She took a deep breath, for courage, and in front of the restaurant full of people she raised her voice, "Thank you so much, Abraham, for letting me go Poop, I don't think I could have held it any longer, especially not on the bus."

Abraham grabbed Her by the hair and pulled Her towards the bathroom door. "What do you think you are doing? Get in there and do your business and hurry up. Do you think I'm stupid or something?"

She looked at him sideways as She moved into the bathroom and closed the door. "Maybe something, yes." Now She was alone, and Her brother was on the other side of the door. She felt terrible that She had created a wall between them and wondered what Abraham was going to do. She sat on the toilet and began to pray. She placed Her head into Her tiny hands, and closed Her eyes.

"Jesus, I know that you are with me now. I know that you walk beside me, and when I am not able to, you carry me. I thank you for your faithfulness during my continued wavering and doubting of You and your grace and presence, Lord. I need you now, Jesus. It has not been my way to ask for things for myself, but tonight, Lord, I am scared. I need my Mommy, I don't know what he is doing with us or why and I don't understand what is going on. I pray that for the Cotton Candy Vendor that he had a good day today and that he is able to abundantly feed his family. For Nanny I pray for a new sense of self, that she be able to see herself for all of the great things that you have given to her and all of the wonderful gifts that she has. I ask for my brother, courage if this journey must continue on, Lord. For Abraham I ask forgiveness, compassion, empathy and understanding of those who will persecute him, Lord. Forgive him, Lord, he knows not what he does... For my mother and father if this ends badly I ask that you help them to heal, and fill their hearts with love. And for me, maybe some decent food, I cannot eat the stuff he gave me, seriously bad, Lord, for this and all of your heavenly gifts, I ask of thee in Jesus name I pray. Amen."

She decided that She may as well pee while She was in the bathroom, so She set on to do that. Quietly She began to hum the beginning bars to Amazing Grace. Involuntarily She began to sing, softly first, and then louder, as though the song came from not inside of Her, but as though it channelled through Her, from another place. Her voice was clear, each note enunciated and pitched to near magical perfection.

The hymn as it flowed from Her tiny frame filled the patron-occupied restaurant. The heavenly song was heard by all of the diners with such clarity that not an eye was dry. The room was rejoicing in the sound of the Lord as it penetrated the hearts of everyone present.

CHAPTER 39

Señor Sebastian Chavez knew the faces of these children, he was certain of that. He moved toward a table at the rear of the restaurant that he knew would be near to completing their entrees and asked quickly if he could remove a plate. Once he had the plate in hand he retreated to the kitchen, threw the plate onto the stainless steel counter top and pulled his cell phone out of his pocket.

As quickly as he was able he dialled information and asked for the number to the private residence of Madam, he waited while the call was connected.

CHAPTER 40

Chief Alvarez and his officers were busy questioning nearly everyone in town that knew the family, or the children in some capacity. Alvarez was determined that he would find them. And that he would find them before he would be obligated to call in the Federales. Once the Canadian Government requested Federal intervention, he would lose jurisdiction and he would most definitely lose face. He figured he might have until midnight, which gave him just over an hour maybe an hour and a half to find two kids in a town of seven hundred and fifty thousand locals and tourists. Like two needles in a haystack, for him there should be nothing to it. He chuckled to himself quietly, if he didn't find the children his career would be over, at thirty-nine he would be lining up for work at the chicken ranch. Plucking feathers and gathering eggs would be the highlight of his days.

The questioning was going well but was producing little in the way of leads. He had all officers on duty and any available off-duty officers now walking the streets, going door to door. Perhaps in eyes of some this was overkill. Would he do the same if the children were Mexican? Most likely not, for two reasons, first he believed that if the children were native, they never would have been taken in the first place, and second he wouldn't haved needed to involve Canadian Government.

Instinctively he had made the decision to make the call to the Canadians to make it easier for Madam, his insatiable desire for her had impelled him to involve her Government at the onset. Had he been stronger, more confident, perhaps he would have more time now. If he had been more of a man and less of a pussy-hungry little boy he might have taken control of the situation from the get-go. Instead he let his animal instincts take over and do his thinking for him. Now he would be paying the consequence. He hated himself for wanting her so badly.

Alvarez had been told that he had just thirty minutes to find the children. Los Federales would be calling in the Marshalls, and bringing in choppers. Once that happened there was no hope for a happy ending for anyone, especially Abraham.

The residence phone began to ring. Madam glanced at him for approval. He nodded for her to answer.

"Bueno, Hello."

"Madam, Hello, Sebastian Chavez, here, disturbing news, your two children are in my restaurant, Madam, your daughter, She needed to use the restroom. And so they are here, but I for the life of me do not understand why they would be on this side of town."

"What? Sebastian! How did they get there?" Alvarez grabbed the phone from her.

"Chief Alvarez, here, where are you exactly?"

"Hello, yes, Sebastian Chavez, Restaurant El Escondita.

Alvarez was thrilled. "Stall them if you can, Señor, keep them there, officers are on the way, we are less than two minutes out. Are the children alone, sir?"

"Of course, I will do my best, but no they are not alone. They are with a mexican gentleman, early thirties."

Alvarez signalled to his commanding officer. "Thank you for notifying us, Señor, we appreciate the call." Sebastian closed the front of his flip phone. He wondered what was going on exactly that the Police Chief himself was with the Madam at her residence. He found that particularly odd.

He knew that he had done the right thing in following his instincts. These children were in some kind of trouble.

CHAPTER 41

Juan Maria de Salvatierra dressed himself in his walking robes. White in colour, hooded like those of the Franciscan Monks. Around his waist he tied a simple rope and knotted it in a basic fisherman's knot. He slipped his feet into basic sandals, good for walking, of which he would be doing much on this journey.

His hair and beard he quickly combed, which had both now turned from light brown to grey to almost white. There were strands of grey and bits of coarse wiry dark hairs still to be found in the long beard, but he liked that it trailed long past the middle of his chest.

He grabbed his walking stick and a piece of bread and felt that he was fully prepared for today's journey. He was pleased that he was being sent for this assignment. He had over the years been on many, but this one came to him with special purpose. A much higher intent than normal and with the potential for significant impact. He felt that he was well prepared and worthy of the cause. He set out with the intention of making an impact.

CHAPTER 42

Alvarez dispatched his officers to the restaurant and told Madam that he would be back with the children. Of course he really had no idea of what the outcome of this would be, but he did know that he would be doing nothing but his very best to ensure the safety of those children.

He got into his own vehicle and placed his red rotating beacon light on the roof of his vehicle. He accelerated down the hill with sirens blaring and lights flashing. He fancied himself a true officer in charge. He glanced at his watch, he was three minutes from the restaurant if he kept up this speed, and if there wasn't a parade crossing the bridge to Old Town.

He could hear the soft sound of sirens from all sides. He used his radio to call the station and inform all of them to approach in silence. He thought the element of surprise was perhaps his last upper hand in this situation. The bus station was located just down the street from the restaurant where the children had been located, he could assume that the plan had been to take them outside of the city limits by Greyhound, with the hope of being undetected of course.

Jorge's mind wandered to Madam, he had never wanted a woman so much as her. He could only fathom that the boundary between them ignited his desire. He had shown her of his affection and had been very diplomatically with big words and a ton of empathy, shot down. When he lay in bed at night he imagined what her skin would feel like, and how her hair would feel in his hands. Her aroma was intoxicating; he couldn't resist the urge to inhale deeply whenever he encountered her. Her perfume, would linger in his mind for days after; somewhat satisfying a carnal need that was his most protected secret.

Her decision to say no to his advancements had only made him want her more. The forbidden fruit was much sweeter than what was available at the public market. His instinct told him that if he found these children and returned them to her safely, he might have a chance with her. He didn't hope for marriage, he knew she was committed to her husband, but if he could have just one night with her he might stand a chance at being the other man. He could live with that.

He approached the bridge to Old Town and slowed his vehicle. The crowd of pedestrians walking on the roadway began to part and he was able to move forward. He honked and used his loudspeaker to get the traffic moving. "POLICIA, POLICIA, adelante, move to the left por favor!" Taxis with their Latin music resonating out the windows, and the high-pitched squeal of Selena occupied the night air.

CHAPTER 43

Abraham felt an urgency to move on. He pulled the boy close to him, and waited outside of the restroom for the little girl. The walls were painted a soft orange, a buttery salmon that made the hallway seem warmer than it was, and made Abraham feel anxious.

He knocked on the door. "Hey, hurry up in there, what are you doing?"

She sat patiently on the toilet, finished Her prayer and nodded. "Just a minute, I'm almost done." She got up, wiped Herself, pulled up Her shorts and washed Her hands. She could barely reach the soap and so had to hoist Herself up and lean in on Her abdomen. Her feet were dangling six inches from the floor when Abraham pushed the door open.

"Come on, time to go."

She thought him rude, presumptuous and overbearing. "I don't like you much any more. You are not being very nice today. I'm not sure what you think you are up to, but I can tell you that it doesn't end well. I was just washing my hands. The germ cycle and all you know, it ends with me."

Abraham was enraged with the situation and extremely frustrated with her forwardness. "What ever happened to children who speak when spoken to?"

"You did speak to me, you asked me what was taking so long. I was washing my hands."

He grabbed Her and the boy and moved toward the end of

the hallway. If they moved to the left they would enter back into the main court of the restaurant. If they moved right they could exit through the kitchen and out the back. Abraham chose right.

He had the hand of one child in each of his own. He moved quickly past the stainless steel serving station, the cooktops and refrigerators. Sweat was running down the centre of his back, and pooling at the nape of his spine. His pants were soaked around the waistline. His face drenched with sweat, he saw the doorway to the lane.

Without saying a word to anyone, the three of them slipped through the doorway and into the crowded streets once more. They were now back on track, Abraham was pleased that they would be moving swiftly now. Towards the bus station and towards his freedom; he felt elated, excited with the prospect of a new adventure, a new civilization to explore. This bus would take him one step closer to where he wanted to be.

CHAPTER 44

Juan walked down the street towards the bus station gathering attention despite his desire to remain discreet. He looked down at his own sandals and determined that perhaps a flip-flop would have been more unidentifiable than the strappy leather Roman footwear that he had chosen. Of course his robes were always an issue as well, he just hadn't been able to bring himself to dress like this generation of individuals. He found their clothing to be appalling.

He pulled his hood up over his head, hiding his hair, but enhancing the appearance of his considerable physical size. He crossed the street without stopping to look for cars. A Taxi driver honked at him and when met with his gaze the driver sank deep into his seat. Juan's eyes were dark and penetrating, his beard was long, his lips always pressed in a strong and determined expression, never smiling.

He placed his hand on the hood of the taxi and stopped. He looked into the eyes of the driver, and without saying anything sent a clear and effective message of passage. God Speed, walk carefully.

He could see the children, with Abraham moving through the crowd, now very close to the bus station. He quickened his pace so as to reach them before they reached the front entrance, which would be littered with people.

He saw colours of orange and turquoise, pinks and yellows, he was aghast at the choices made for a basic human necessity.

A simple robe was now embellished with studs and glitter; and were nearly always in bright colours. Long gone were the colours of the cloth as he had known them, basic white and brown, blacks and grey. Simplicity it seemed to him left this world long ago. Having been replaced by false prophets of material items, humans filled their lives with things, things which promised happiness, clothing that could make them appear to be something other than that which they were, stuff that could fill a void once filled by God, once filled by loved ones. He was saddened for the race, saddened for the earth and hopeful for a change.

He was close to them now, within arm's reach of Abraham. He planned to subtly take care of his business here when the sound of a siren alerted Abraham and his head turned to the left. The two men's eyes met.

Juan reached forward despite the alteration to the plan and placed his hand on Abraham's head, holding him just long enough for a slight compression of time, delaying his movements just long enough for his touch to have an affect. Just as his palm made contact with the top of the head, Juan looked to the heavens and shouted out, "Lord, have mercy, for he knows not what he has done." He released and moved into the crowd with nothing more than a quick glance back to assess the effect his touch had had on the once spiritually driven man who loved the Lord, loved working for Madam, loved these children and hungered for the love of his long-lost wife.

CHAPTER 45

Alvarez approached the bus station after turning off of Ignacio de Vallarta, he arrived at El Escondita, the restaurant where Sebastian Chavez had allowed Abraham and the children to use the restroom facilities. His cruiser lurched to a stop.

He saw Sebastian as soon as he had entered the front door, and nodded at him. Sebastian pointed to the hallway that led to the restrooms, looking rather ashen himself. The main dining room of the restaurant was only one third full, and at this time of night diners were mostly locals. Jorge was pleased to see this. Less tourists meant less explanations in the morning papers.

Alvarez cautiously approached the hallway, noting that his men were now arriving as well. The doors to both the men's and the ladies' restrooms were closed. He moved to the ladies first. With his right hand he cautiously pushed the door open, revealing an empty space. He stepped back and opened the men's doorway, again, there was nothing. He saw another corner at the other end of the hallway. He moved forward, disappointed to find that one end took restaurant patrons back to the dining room, the other direction was an entrance to the kitchen.

Jorge took a deep breath. He could hear his men moving through the building behind him. He hoped that he would turn this corner and find the three hiding in the bodega. He was disappointed and furious to find not only that they were not there, but that the emergency exit to the lane way was ajar. He picked up a bag that was presumably trash from the ground and placed it carefully into the trash can, turned around and re-entered the restaurant.

He approached Sebastian Chavez with his hands in the air. He sometimes had a hard time dealing with people, especially when they didn't execute a plan as it had been placed. "What happened here, Señor, the man and the children are gone from your establishment?"

Sebastian looked shocked. "No, no they are still in the restroom."

Jorge headed out the front door, and shouted over his shoulder. "No, Señor, they are not. We will be back, don't go home tonight, Sir."

He looked left and right, quickly assessing the area, bus station. Now it made sense to him. He took off on foot, his men all moved into their marked vehicles and approached the station in silence. He had been adamant about not drawing excessive attention from the crowds, or scaring the children.

He could see them ahead, waiting in line to board. He sprinted. When he was within thirty metres, he called out, "Abraham, Abraham."

CHAPTER 46

Abraham turned his face in the direction of the person calling him. He was dressed in plain clothes and without his glasses and from this distance it was foggy, but he was certain that it was the chief of police; Jorge Alvarez. Wonderboy. He thought it amazing that the man didn't have a cape and crest, and perhaps a new name ending in 'man'. He would fit right in with all of the rest of the superheroes, Batman, Superman, Spiderman… all doing their part for society.

He knew that he had reached the end of the road. He respected the abilities of Madam, his grudge had never been with her after all, and his intention had never been to hurt the children. In fact that morning when he woke, he had intended to kill Nanny. Things had definitely taken a turn for the worse. He chuckled to himself as he watched the Police Chief run towards them.

The children were holding hands, comforting each other in silence while they waited to be saved from their captor.

Alvarez's men surrounded the building leaving no opportunity for escape. Abraham lifted his hands to the air knowing that he would never again see the light of day.

The Police Chief read him his rights and clearly stated the charge, handcuffed him and placed him in the back of one of the pick up trucks. Abraham would be escorted through the streets, in a display of triumph for the police department, from the station to the courthouse, where he would spend the night in a very dark cell. In the morning he would be transported to the jail where he would spend a very long time in solitude.

Jorge was pleased with his achievements, although he quietly reflected that he did owe a grateful handshake to the restaurant owner. Had Sebastian Chavez not called, he might not have found these children tonight. He made a mental note to send the man a bottle of whisky expressing his gratitude.

Abraham was spent, exhaustion over came him as they placed him into the back of the pick up truck. He looked at the faces of the children and wept. His carefully laid out plan had never been to involve them. In the end he had lost the battle to the nanny. He felt ashamed that he had engaged her, that he had taken her bait and that he had let the entire charade continue for as long as it had. He was about to spend a good part of the rest of his life behind bars because his own ego had not allowed him to walk away from a woman that meant nothing to him. He thought of his wife, and of ending his own life. In his own anger earlier in the day the thought hadn't occurred to him. Now that he was facing a potential eternity in prison, he relished in the idea of spending moments with her, self sacrifice now seemed a better option. Holding her and looking into her eyes, hearing the sound of her laughter; it would have been a more desirable ending for himself.

As the truck began to pull away from the bus station he made eye contact with Her. From where he now sat She looked so tiny, so petite, but Her eyes were so dark and penetrating She appeared not old, but wise. She raised Her tiny hand and waved to him. "Bye-bye, Abraham, thank you for the go-carts." He could see that tears were rolling down Her cheeks, in almost the same pattern as his own. With a head full of questions and a heart full of regret, Abraham disappeared into the night, in the back of a police pick up truck through the busy streets of Puerto Vallarta.

CHAPTER 47

Finding Nanny's replacement was quite an endeavour. Extra caution was being taken considering the circumstances that just had passed. Her mother was happy to take time from work, and ensure that the process was completed in a manner that was effective and efficient. But most importantly it was imperative that the right woman be placed in the care of her children. Madam decided to involve the children in the selection process which took some time. In the end, a very cherished employee from Madam's business was offered the job, which included the new nanny and her husband moving onto the property to live.

Guadalupe-"Lupita" Reyes was a rotund woman, who regretfully had not been fortunate enough to have children of her own. She was quite pleased to have a new experience on her horizon and one where she would be involved with children twenty-four hours a day seven days a week.

Lupita had met her husband at the tender age of fifteen, they had fallen madly in love and had married before she celebrated her sixteenth birthday. The two of them were a match made in heaven, enjoying the same activities, the same foods, and a romance worthy of a motion picture. Their only disappointment in their lives together had been their inability to conceive and sustain a pregnancy.

After a few months of working with the children, a routine was found; everyone began to relax, and Lupita started to love both of the Madam's children like they were her own.

She entered the room one day. "Lupita! Can we go to the beach?"

Lupita was touched, this tiny little child spoke Spanish better than she did herself, and without any accent at all. "No, Mija, not today, today we have so many chores to complete, but perhaps tomorrow hey? What do you think?"

"I think that we have too many chores and not enough time for the things that we like to do. That is what I think."

The new nanny chuckled. "Yes, well, I can understand why you would feel that way but sometimes in life we have to do our work first, and then we get to play."

She was certain that by the time She was done here She would be able to convince Lupita to go to the beach, at least for a couple of hours. "Listen for today, why don't we go, and then do the chores when we get back?"

Nanny thought about it for a split second and then discarded the thought. "No, no, look I have to work. And then we can play. You can help me if you like, because we might get to the beach faster if we share the chores, what do you think of that hmm?"

She looked at Lupita out of the corner of Her eye and laughed. "I think you are trying to get me to do your work for you, that's what I think!"

"No, Chiquita, hee, hee, never, all right let's go, vaminose. To the beach."

And so they went, and the relationship was so, it grew and it was good, and She was safe from harm.

As they walked together to the beach, She could hear voices all around Her. She wanted to ask Lupita about it without sounding silly. "Lupita, can you hear the cars on the main road over there?"

"Jes, my love, I can hear da cars, is this a new game we are playing?"

She thought then about how She should answer that question. "Sort of yes, do you hear what I hear is what we are going to call it."

"Okay then, I'm ready to go."

"Do you hear, the sound of the airplane way off in the distance?"

"No. I'm too old for dat."

"Okay, do you hear the sound of your own heartbeat?"

Lupita stopped walking, and placed her hand on her chest. "I can feel it, mammy, does that count?"

She smiled at Her Nanny. "No, can you hear me breathing?"

"Jes, I can hear dat just fine." Lupita was enjoying the game very much.

"Can you hear the sound of the man speaking about his daughter?"

"No, Mammy, I don't hear any man talking."

The sun was warm on them as they continued to walk towards the beach, She continued to probe. "Do you hear the sound of a little girl talking?"

"Just you, mammy." Lupita laughed out loud and grabbed Her hand. She held Her tight, never wanting to lose Her. "I do love you so, precioso baby."

Now that She knew that Lupita couldn't hear them She wondered why She was hearing them. She thought She might discuss the matter with Her mother later. For today however they would enjoy the sun and the sand and a lovely day just the two of them.

Lupita wanted to play the game more, and asked why they weren't playing.

"We aren't playing because you can't hear anything, Lupita! I'm the only one that can hear anything!"

Lupita laughed out loud and suggested that they build a sand castle. The sun was hot on their skin. Toasting them lightly as they played on the beach, just the two of them. The sand was perfect that day for building. The sand stayed together in a ball when it was rolled around in their hands. Just wet enough to pack densely without crumbling. Lupita had brought some of her favourite sand tools from home, a small shovel, a scoop and metal bucket, she never used plastic tools, plastics just didn't do the trick in a professional manner. They dug a water hole, a well, not a moat, this would serve as their water supply for the construction of the castle. It would replenish itself through out the day, rules of the tide. The sand that had been excavated for the water hole was piled into a one-foot high, three-foot round mound that would be levelled and then serve as the base of the castle. Their foundation, the added height would provide them some drainage for all the water they would use during construction; the two of them had become self-proclaimed experts, in castle management. Each time they chose to build, the structure was larger and stronger than the one before. Like their friendship the key was in a strong foundation. Each of them had been hurt in the past and both She and Lupita were guarded in their relationship, but had begun to trust one another.

"Lupita, if you can't hear the voices that I hear, then what is it exactly that I am hearing? Do you think that maybe I am crazy?"

Lupita placed a small bucket of sand on top of the castle to begin the formation of a tower. "Do I think you are crazy, well, that question is one that I have never before been asked when one is expecting a serious answer. I know that you are not joking with me now. So I am going to have to think about how I should choose my words okay?"

She played with a handful of sand and looked off towards the horizon. Waves crested and fell, repeating a similar but different pattern each time. The path of the ocean was never quite exactly as it was ever before but it was always moving in a pattern that to the naked eye looked familiar. She thought about how each and every person's life was very much like that. Moving about, in waves and crests, heaving and falling, repeating similar movements without great passion. Without great pleasure or gratification. As if completing a dance that was known but not enjoyed, like a language that was spoken but not understood. She sat still and watched the water as She waited for Her nanny to find the words that she needed and She hoped to never just heave and fall, She wanted to not just roll through this life breathing and waving through each and every day waiting for the next one to start so that she could hope for the end. She wanted more. She wanted expression and gratefulness, and a full bounty. She wanted passion and rich taste buds. Electrifying experiences and the tango. She wanted to surf on the waves as they crested and to embrace the wind with such vigour that it would run from Her in trepidation. She wanted to take the world by the balls and scream "*I am here now, I am doing this now, I was sent to show you how.*"

Lupita spoke, "No, no I don't think you are crazy. But I don't understand it. I would like to, but I don't. Maybe you can explain it to me. If you would like to share it with me, I mean."

"Well, sometimes I just hear voices, sometimes they are clear, like I can hear them as clear as I can hear you now. And then other times they are mumbled. Like foggy, or as if they are stuck in a fog." She continued to play with the sand between Her feet. Rolling and pulling it with Her tiny hands.

Lupita nodded. "So are they always the same voices, or are they different?"

"Different, rarely ever the same."

"And what types of things do you hear? Do they talk about the weather? Or do they ask for fashion advice? Do they need directions? What kind of stuff do they need, mammy?" Lupita's interest was genuine. She loved the child and was curious.

"Well, it depends. Some of them just want to know where they are. Some of them want me to help them find their families or maybe they need me to get a message to a family member. You know what I mean?"

"No, I don't get it."

"Well, like the people that I hear, I don't think they, you know," she nodded her head from side to side, "I don't think they are still living."

Lupita dropped the scoop that she had been playing with. "You mean, you think you are hearing dead people?"

"I dunno, maybe."

Lupita was now the one staring out at the ocean. The deep sapphire water was alluring, drawing to her. She had always loved the beach, the sand, the cool breeze the coconuts and the surf. "You're not crazy. I know that for sure. I don't know anything about communicating with spirits, or the afterlife, but I can tell you this, I know that something happens to all of the energy that we have in our bodies after we die. Something has to happen to it. It just doesn't make sense that our body dies and so does life for the soul and the spirit. So I believe that there is a possibility that something is communicating with you. But I don't have any understanding greater than that. Maybe you can help me to learn. Okay? How does that sound? Have you talked to your mother about this?"

She pushed her hair back from Her face, exposing Her freckled forehead. "No, she has had so much going on, and with all of that stuff that happened with Abraham I just didn't want to bother her."

"When did it start? The voices I mean? When did you hear them the first time?"

"The first time I remember I was when I was just little, we had an old woman who lived in the basement. She was there to protect me she said. But when we moved here I had to leave her behind. I think though that the voices got louder after the thing with Abraham. Or maybe before, I dunno. It's hard to remember really."

Lupita made a mental note to talk to Madam later that day, after She was settled for the evening and had gone to bed. This was pretty important. Important enough that it might even warrant a trip to see Madam at her place of business.

CHAPTER 48

Mary Mack watched Her sleeping from the window sill. The drapes fluttered and billowed as the night draft gently filled the room. Her black silk dress was crisply pressed, silver buttons fell down her back in a neat row, one on top of the other. She enjoyed sitting on the ledge of the window but wished that it was easier to access. It was always a bit of a chore to open the window when it was so tightly closed. For her to facilitate the opening of the window without waking the child was a challenge and was physically demanding as well. She wished that someone would think to just leave the windows open.

She pushed her dark ringlets behind her ear, listening for instructions, listening for direction. She watched Her sleeping, Her breathing light, Her chest rising and falling, Her auburn hair slightly damp from the heat and humidity. The night was filled with activity. The shadows rumbled and roared, footsteps hurried and scurried in the darkness where the naked eye saw obscured shapes and heard awkward sounds.

Mary Mack was dutifully Her servant, sent to protect Her, when She said Her prayers, She was unaware that they were already answered.

"Now I lay me down to sleep, I pray the Lord my Soul to keep, and Angels watch me through the night, until I wake in the morning light… Amen."

Mary Mack sat on the window sill, watching for predators, and waited.

CHAPTER 49

Lupita walked to Madam's restaurant. The evening was humid, the air was hot and heavy. She began to sweat as she walked, her feet felt hot and swollen in her shoes, she wished she had taken the bus now. There were crowds of people all over the downtown core. The Malecon was covered with tourists in brightly coloured tunics and tank tops. She watched them as she walked and wondered how it had become that it was appropriate to behave in such a manner. People had lost self-respect. There was no matter of dignity in the world any more. She wondered where it had gone, and when. When had ladies lost their desire to act as women? When had it become the norm to dress like strippers and act like prostitutes? And they wondered why men no longer respected them. They wondered why men didn't call them in the morning? Why was that even a question? Why should that even be a matter for consideration? Why were young ladies placing themselves in situations where they were under valued?

She walked on, her feet still sweating, her heart pulsing from the pace of her gait. She was relieved to see the building just a few blocks off in the distance. She silently prayed that the air conditioning would be blowing at full capacity.

She entered and asked to speak to Madam after greeting the staff, all of whom she knew well. The room was gloriously decorated and was full of people enjoying a late dinner.

Madam came out from the back office and greeted her. "Hello, Lupita, how are you? So wonderful to see you, what brings you here tonight?"

"I was hoping to speak with you, Madam. I know that you must be worried about the children, but I can assure you that both of them are sleeping, and I made certain that they were both showered and that their homework was complete before I left."

"Of course. So Maria is there at the residence with them then?"

"Yes, and Justo, he is there I didn't think you would mind considering the circumstances."

Madam took a sip of water. "Of course I don't mind if your husband is there, Lupita. How is Justo? I haven't seen him for quite some time?"

"He's just fine, Ma'am. He loves his work and his health is good, so there is nothing for him to complain about. The Good Lord wouldn't like that anyway, so best he doesn't do that." Lupita took the glass that had been offered and held it in her hand but didn't drink from it.

"Lupita, what did you want to talk to me about? You seem a little bit agitated, or upset. Is it something that one of the children has done? Or one of the other staff?"

"Oh heavens, no, Ma'am, I love my job, and I just thank you, every day for having me work for you. I mean, I loved working for you before, but now with the children it's just so much more, and I think that She is really starting to trust me, and She is starting to open up to me now."

Madam took another sip of water. "She seems to be relaxing a bit, I noticed that She is sleeping better, She is having less nightmares. Which is very positive. I am grateful for that. How is her brother doing? Do you think he is adjusting as well?"

Lupita smiled. "You know, Madam, he is just a beautiful

little boy. He never seems to be upset about anything. He's always happy. And he is very protective of Her. He cares for Her very much. He is good. Right now we don't need to worry about him."

"And so, Lupita, do you think we need to worry about Her?"

Lupita chose her words carefully. She knew that on her walk here she had been attempting to distract herself. Send her mind to places other than thinking of Her and Her spirits. Now however she must address them head on.

"Madam, I don't think we need to worry about Her exactly, but I do think we need to talk about Her. There are things about Her that are different from other children, Ma'am. I think you know that. I also think that is why you have chosen me for the job. I appreciate this and I am taking this very seriously. I know that you have had many people tell you that She is different, and some of them have suggested that different is not a good thing. That in Her case, it is a bad thing. I just don't believe that. Madam, I'm not entirely certain how to tell you this, but She believes that She hears the voices of spirits, and I kind of think She might. I know that if it's not true then that makes me crazy, but I just believe Her. She doesn't have any reason to lie to me, and honestly I don't have any reason to lie to you. There is no benefit to making up a story that makes me look like a crazy woman. So I am here with you now, a woman, a nanny, a caregiver of your child, telling you that your baby, your little girl who is only five years old? Is She five? Yes? Okay, five years old is hearing the voices of dead people."

"Yes She is just five years old. And, well, Lupita, that is a lot to take in. I have to be honest, I am not entirely certain what I believe any more. But I can't deny that She exhibits certain character traits, abilities and gifts if you will that I can't explain. And believe me I have tried. I lay in bed many nights asking the good Lord why my child, why Her? And you know I have never gotten an answer. So am I surprised that you think She hears the voices of dead people, or spirits? No, Lupita, no I am not surprised. I am not surprised at anything that She can do. Nor will I be surprised at anything that She accomplishes. I know one thing to be true, this child was placed here for something. Something big, we have no idea what that might be, and we certainly have no idea what our role in that might be. But She is here for something, Lupita. And I know that it is our duty to serve and protect Her. It is an honour. That is what we are here for. Don't forget that."

Lupita drank her entire glass of water in one gulp. She wiped her brow with the palm of her hand. "Yes, Madam."

"If you want out, Lupita, just say so now, I will understand. But if you are in, then you're in, She loves you. Don't hurt Her."

"No, Madam, I won't I love Her too. Like my own, no disrespect."

"Of course not. I love Her more than you can possibly imagine, which is why I am trusting you with Her." Madam stood from her chair. She straightened her skirt and gently touched her hair.

Lupita thought her to be the picture of simple elegance. It seemed to be so uncomplicated for Madam. She wore very little make-up, from what she could tell, not more than lipstick and mascara, her hair was long and never out of place, it was dark like melted chocolate, and hung in loose curls. She was a natural beauty; effortless, timeless, flawless. Lupita realized that she was a bit envious. Not jealous, but she envied the raw beauty of her boss. She had a glow that radiated when she dealt with individuals, one that put them at ease. Her gestures exuded strength but invited people to know her, made them feel as though they were part of her world. When in reality they were nowhere even near her own orbit. She kept everyone at arm's length. At a safe and comfortable distance to where she could observe and control every situation. She was powerful, Lupita watched her as she stood, as she straightened her skirt, she was confident and assured. She never questioned her own decisions, she wasn't afraid to ask for forgiveness when she made a mistake, but was humble enough to know that when she did err the honourable thing to do was acknowledge it.

Lupita stood as well, she picked up her handbag and set down the glass which was now empty. She smiled at Madam. "Thank you for seeing me, I know that you are busy."

"I'm never too busy for you, please remember that, the children are the most important and cherished people in my life. Anything that they need, or you need, Lupita, please make sure that you let me know. No matter what it is."

"Yes, Ma'am, I will. And what will you have me do about Her voices? I don't hear them, I can't pretend to, and I won't lie to Her. I'm not certain how I should handle the situation."

"Just be Her friend, that's all She wants, Lupita, She knows that you can't hear them, She just needs to know that you aren't judging Her for hearing them. That would break Her heart. I fear that She might be more fragile than we know."

Lupita nodded. "I will do everything in my power to ensure that She is well, Madam."

"Thank You, Lupita, I appreciate that my children are finally with someone who is genuinely caring for them."

Lupita left and took a taxi back which Madam had provided funds for. She was grateful, and very relieved to not have to walk back the two and a half miles to the residence as it was mostly an uphill climb.

She kissed her husband who was sitting in the living room watching the television and then looked in on both children who were sleeping soundly, she closed the window in Her bedroom and shook her head as she did so. She hadn't left it open. She made a mental note to ask Justo and Maria if either of them had opened it. She knew that Madam didn't like the mosquitos anywhere near Her, and so she was always careful to ensure that it was securely closed.

Lupita moved next to the bed and straightened the netting above it. Tying it closed at the end safeguarding this precious child from the dangers of malaria and dengue fever. Dengue fever is a painful, debilitating mosquito-borne disease caused by any one of four closely related dengue viruses. The virus is related to the viruses that cause West Nile infection and yellow fever. Lupita knew that Madam had been infected as a teen, and so she was overly protective of the children.

Most cases of Dengue occur in tropical areas of the world. It is transmitted by the bite of an Aedes mosquito infected with a dengue virus. The mosquito becomes infected when it bites a person with dengue virus in their blood. It can only be spread by the bite of a mosquito and can't be spread directly from one person to another person. Infection can incubate for up to six days and result in mild flu-like symptoms such as headache, nausea, severe joint and muscle pain, vomiting, fatigue and bleeding of the gums. In cases where an individual's immune system has been compromised in some way; say perhaps by stress on the gastrointestinal system from dietary restrictions, symptoms can be much worse. Damage to the lymph and blood vessels, enlargement of the liver, failure of the circulatory system, shock and death.

Lupita made certain that the mosquito netting was fixed firmly around the child and then she moved into the room of the boy and did the same. She would exercise the utmost caution in every way possible to ensure the safety of these children while they were under her watch.

CHAPTER 50

Juan Maria de Salvatierra was again preparing for a return to duty. It had been requested by higher powers, that he return to execute functions of his role, that were significant and vital to the overall success of the mission. He prepared himself, as he knew that he should, in his robes and sandals. He knelt, and he prayed, as he always did; for humanity, for Mother Earth and all of her creatures, large and small, for the seasons and the wind that changes them. He prayed for the lives that had come and gone, and those that were coming. Those that had served the Lord, and those that would. In his thoughts he held tight to his belief in the Trinity, in all that is good and right, and he trusted in what the plan was for the future. He believed in his faith journey as he always had. He continued on and relied on the Lord for his needs. He wanted for nothing.

In his time as a man he had done good work, of that he was certain. When he had landed at Bahia Concepcion, on the Baja Peninsula, he had wanted nothing but to evangelize. To share the word of the Lord with people, that had not yet had the chance to hear it. He had, had to learn their language in order to spread the gospel. And so by faith, he had learned indigenous tongues.

And by mastering their languages, he was able to explore and establish missions throughout the Baja California. He became known as the Apostle of California, before he died in 1717; while writing the history of California for King Phillip V.

He read the scroll of instructions which he held in his hand; in its entirety. It was descriptive and detailed. He was clear on his assignment and was adequately prepared. He took his walking stick, and his cross, pulled his large hood over his head, and he set out on this leg of his journey.

This part of his work was the most difficult for him, he found it a challenge to engage in any type of battle; having given his entire living life to prayer, peace and to building the church of God. He was grateful that it was not required of him often, and that he had the power of the Lord on his side. He held his sword with faith, and courage; he was steadfast with the knowledge that he was walking within God's grace.

He appreciated that he had been assigned to protect Her, that in his own journey, he would be included in all and everything good and plentiful that She would do for Mother Earth. He had been chosen because of his own good works, to serve Her.

The black Angel approached Juan, his mouth twisted in a wretched sneer, eyes dark and withdrawn. He had fallen so long ago, that he had lost hope of ever returning to the light; his sights solely on destruction and the capture of those who lost hope in the promise of everlasting life. Those who therefore filled their days with the pangs of hate. The Black Angel's sole purpose was to destroy Her, his intent today to take out the great Juan, easing a direct path to Her.

The two met face to face. Juan held up his sword. His white robes blowing in the wind, his hair free; he felt strong. The Black Angel's wings were extended making him appear grander, larger than life. They exchanged words.

"You could just let me have Her." His breath was as wretched as his skin, appalling, dirty and diseased.

"Never."

"I could reward you. You could have all of your heart's desires Juan. I'm not as bad as I look." He had a knack for promising more than he could deliver.

"Never." Juan shook his head.

"You could have your own children, I can give you everything you have ever wanted, Juan."

"Never."

"I will never let Her live, you know that. I will destroy Her, and you will watch me do it. It will pain you greatly. Like a silver bullet through your heart, Juan."

"I will never let Her out of my sight. We will protect Her both day and night. You will never beat us in battle. We are trained warriors. We will win this fight."

"As you wish, then a battle it shall be. I will defeat you. Remember you were human... once. You cannot win, Juan. You must know this. This war will rage until the end of Her days... Or mine..." He laughed. "Which ever comes first."

Juan raised his sword again, prepared to engage in battle. "I came ready for you today, and I will be prepared for you tomorrow. I was a simple man of the cloth once, but I am a warrior of the Lord, and a servant of Her today and forever more. Raise your sword!"

"Nah, I think I would rather try to outsmart you. Let's try something different shall we, Juan. Swords are just getting so, blah, these days. It's rather old. It's the 1990s after all, let's try a battle using our wits shall we? I bet you don't even know what I am capable of entirely. You've seen me do many things, but I'm still learning. So now you are going to have to learn some of my new tricks." He was laughing again, a deep-throated kind of laugh that sounded like he had liquid caught in his voice box. "I can only imagine how this one is going to unfold. Here's what we are going to do, Juanito. I am going to create a sort of smoke screen, Juan, steal some stuff, by using the something called the internet. I won't tell you what or how, but it will be your job to figure out what I've been up to, and then you will have to react. She will be involved somehow… or She will be in harm's way… I really can't say. I remember that time when I sent the Black Plague; that was before you; really lovely outcome though. The First World War, and of course the Second, awful that was. And there was AIDS, and Black Monday in '87, that one was Fun! The financial crash oh how it tumbled and toiled and the people, Juan, they went crazy… you weren't part of that either were you, Juan? No different team… Well, let's see how this one unravels, it might be similar, or it might not… How does that sound… ready set GO!"

Juan had no idea what he was talking about, he took a step back, set down his sword and placed his hand on his hip. "What exactly is the internet?"

The black angel, smiled coyly at him. "Oh Dear, Dear, Juan, if I were to tell you it would spoil all of my fun now wouldn't it? And besides, it's up to you to fix what ever problems that I can cause for Her, you know that; so Giddy up! There's work to be done!"

"You will never win! I can guarantee you that! We will not surrender Her. He is willing to sacrifice as many as are necessary to ensure that She reaches maturity and is able to fulfil Her plan. She will prevail. He will concur you. Mother Earth will survive."

"Tsk, tsk, Juan, you really under estimate me still… we shall see, run along then, trouble awaits you. I shall see you in the shadows. And tell Mary Mack to stop with those silly rhyming things she does… it gets on my nerves. Takes too much time to figure out what the hell she is trying to say half the time."

Juan backed out of the room feeling like he had been sandbagged. He hadn't expected to be completely shot in the dark. He had anticipated an old-fashioned battle today. He was comfortable with things that he knew. This was not something that he really felt he had time for. But She was worth it. He would make time, he would figure out what the internet was. He would figure out how one would possibly plan and execute destruction on it and how it could possibly affect Her. And then of course what he could do to keep Her safe and on Her objective.

He would not however tell Mary Mack to stop rhyming.

CHAPTER 51

Chief Alvarez made a point of not contacting Madam for months after the kidnapping incident had been put to rest. After the trial had been completed, and the sentencing of Abraham had been done, he chose to allow the dust to settle. He honestly found it far too difficult to be in the same room as the woman.

He missed seeing the children however, he found both of them quite engaging. He never thought he would even consider the idea of liking an individual who hadn't reached adulthood, let alone enjoy them, but these two were different. They were smart, they were both witty, and wildly entertaining.

He had taken pleasure in watching them both during the trial, as twisted and sick as that made him sound as a man. Both of the children were articulate, when they testified and yet neither one of them said anything negative about Abraham. Both shared very positive stories, that he had fed them, that he had taken them to the go-cart track, which had been very pleasing. He had taken them for ice cream, of course She hadn't eaten any, he had gotten water and candy for them when they asked for it.

Alvarez believed it was for this reason that the Judge was lenient in his sentencing. He couldn't help but wonder what type of parent, allows their child who had been kidnapped to testify on behalf of the kidnapper? He wondered what went on in her head and since he couldn't figure it out, he had to stay away from her.

She was more than he was prepared to involve himself with, and he certainly couldn't trust himself with her, or to be around her. The smell of her was intoxicating to him, her hair, her skin, the sound of her voice even. He had a hard time even focusing on his work if she managed to drifted into his thoughts. He would never understand her alignment with her husband. To him, that was one of life's greatest mysteries. There didn't seem to be a passion, or boundless love, it seemed to be more of an arrangement, or business deal. The concept of which made him scratch his head in wonder. His own idea of a great marriage would be full of desire, and love, a shared passion for life. He couldn't fathom a bland and tasteless sharing of daily routines with no hope for excitement or celebration. He would rather, just continue to live his life alone, a silly and very dedicated police chief.

He leaned back in his chair and closed his eyes. Madam's face continued to haunt him. He picked up his cell phone and flipped through the contact list until he came to her number. With his thumb hovering over the number he sat for a few moments, pondering the decision of whether to call or not to call. His brain told him no, and yet his heart kept telling him yes, call, yes call.

His thumb pushed on the number, within seconds it was ringing.

"Hello, Jorge, is that you?"

"Yes, how are you?"

"I'm fine thank you, I'm surprised to hear from you, it's been a while." Madam looked out the window of her office into the street. The afternoon heat radiated from the cobble stone sidewalk, tourists chattered as they walked past, bright coloured shopping bags filling their hands.

Jorge responded, his mind filled with thoughts that he wished he could wash away, "I know, I'm sorry, I've been busy with work, how have you been?"

"I have been well, now that the trial is over, things have gotten back to normal and the children are settled. We had visitors from Canada, my brother and some friends, it's been a little bit hectic, but things are good."

"It's nice to hear your voice, Madam."

"You too, Jorge."

"Have dinner with me? Tomorrow?" Jorge hadn't planned on inviting her to dinner, and he was a bit aghast at his invitation himself. He wasn't quite sure what he would do if she agreed.

"Is that a good idea? You and me?" Her voice had become even more sultry than before, Alvarez was now sitting on the very edge of his chair. His feet firmly planted on the floor.

"I think it's become necessary yes. I think it's finally time."

Madam paused, her breath caught briefly in her throat, her heart beating slightly faster, "I agree, where and what time?"

"Not in town, I know a small restaurant in Bucerias, it's owned by a friend of mine, it's new, it will be quiet, we can disappear there." Alvarez was planning things as though he had premeditated the entire thing. "I will pick you up at eight?"

"No, I will meet you somewhere; and I will leave my car." She couldn't risk having the children see her leave with a man other than their father.

"Of course, I'm sorry, what about at Gigante, the grocery store?"

"Perfect, eight o'clock? I'll be there."

Alvarez hung up the phone and took a deep breath. His office suddenly seemed too small and he felt claustrophobic.

His breath came too fast, he bent over and placed his head between his knees. He wondered what on earth had gotten into him, who was speaking for him? He felt as though he hadn't had control of his own decisions. Why he had made the call and how he was going to get himself out of it?

CHAPTER 52

Madam chose a little black dress for dinner, it was an A-line with a v-neck and a fitted bodice, in a silk chiffon that fluttered and billowed in the gentle ocean breeze. She wore flip-flops and let her dark hair fall in loose curls down her back. She didn't want to appear as though she was dressing for a gala or an evening event, but she also didn't want him to get the impression that the dinner was of no importance to her. She fussed for hours over which dress to wear and had decided on the black because it made her tan look the most golden.

Madam arrived at the grocery store promptly at eight, the parking lot was barren, a cement haven full of concrete barricades and empty shopping carts. She pulled her vehicle into a stall, and searched for Jorge's vehicle. She used her driver's visor to check her lipstick, and then put her sunglasses into her purse. She watched the sun disappear into the ocean and in the blink of an eye, with a flash, it was dark, and night was upon them.

Jorge pulled up beside her, with the top down on his jeep. He smiled and winked at her; which made her feel like a young girl once again. She grabbed her purse from the seat beside her, and locked her car.

Chief Alvarez was tall, he was half-Spanish half-German, his hair was dark, his eyes as green as the Sea of Cortez. He was a physically large man, over six feet tall with broad shoulders and strong arms. His army training had instilled in him a love for fitness, he ran everyday, mostly in the mornings, which kept his body strong, virile, he was athletic. The sight of him made her knees weak. She braced herself on the side of the jeep as he opened the door for her to get in.

Their conversation on the drive to Bucerias was light, they spoke of the weather, of their work and of the upcoming election. She shared titbits of her time with her family that had visited, and of the change of schools for the children. Alvarez didn't believe that it had been good timing with the trial for them to have to move their school as well, she shrugged it off and looked out the window.

They approached a bridge on the highway and he touched her hand with his own. "Madam, listen, did you know that this is the longest bridge in the world?"

She peered at him sideways. "No, Jorge, it is not. It is not the longest bridge in the world, where on earth did you get that idea?"

He smiled from ear to ear, the sight of which filled her heart with joy. "Indeed it is, and I will tell you why, it is the longest bridge in the world because it is going to take us an hour to cross it."

"Impossible."

"No, no it's true! How long have you lived here and you don't know this?" He laughed at her. "Here we go now, ready, yes, and we are crossing; crossing and now it is one hour later than it was when we started."

She was laughing with him now. "Jorge, what are you talking about?"

"The bridge, it crosses a time zone. We have moved from pacific to mountain time, we just gained an hour, Madam."

She laughed out loud, she knew that he was in fact correct and had never thought of it in that way. He continued to hold her hand. "This means that I have one extra stolen hour with you tonight, one extra hour to enjoy your company, to hold your hand, to listen to your laughter. A few more stolen moments in time to take home to my loneliness later."

"Let's just please enjoy what we have, please don't make me feel that I have made the wrong decision in accepting your invitation for dinner tonight." She looked at him as he drove the last few minutes in silence. She thought about what he might be thinking, and she hoped that she hadn't been too harsh.

They pulled into a parking spot on the street and he got out and opened her door for her. As he did so he took her hand into his own again and looked into her dark eyes. "Please forgive me, can I kiss you now before I totally mess the evening up with my nervousness?"

Her heart skipped a beat and leapt before landing somewhere in her throat. She nodded as he leaned forward, he inhaled deeply through his nose, experiencing every bit of her scent. He allowed his mouth to gently brush hers, gently parting her lips with his tongue. Her breath quickened, he could feel it ever so softly, as his lips found hers. His was no longer able to contain his passion for her. For too long he had kept his desire bottled up, in that very moment he had unleashed years of longing. His hands found her hair, the soft cashmere curls caressing his palms, his fingers wound through the ringlets behind her ears. She pulled away. He felt obliged. "I'm sorry, Madam."

"Don't be." She had been as lost in the moment as he had.

"Are you ready for dinner?"

She shook her head no. "I'm not hungry, seem to have lost my appetite for food." Waves crashed on the beach to the west of them, the sound of the pounding surf was soothing to her.

Alvarez looked around. He saw a hotel up the road facing the beach. He closed the passenger door again and got back in the driver's seat. He started the jeep and placed the vehicle in drive.

CHAPTER 53

She woke early, it was still dark. She wondered if Lupita would be awake or maybe Her mother. She opened the door from Her bedroom into the hall, it was eerily quiet. She saw no signs of life and none of immediate danger. Strange shadows fell on the walls, creating oblong immortal images in the darkness. Her mind flew into overdrive, imagining flying dragons and castles with hundreds of soldiers dressed in silver armour. Their forlorn and weepy wives left behind as they went off to fight another battle for the King. The Princess was always kept safe in the castle, with plenty of food and luxuries, that was always Her role in the drama. She would always be cared for, Her long auburn hair brushed out daily by a wench who only did that; just brushed Her hair. Well, maybe washed it too, but the wench was always at Her beck and call.

She tiptoed down the hall not knowing if there was anyone awake yet, and unsure of the time. She reached Her brother's room, the door was open a crack so She pushed Her way in.

His room was so very different from Hers. Hers was cool and calm decorated in soft shades of blues with lace and mosquito netting over the bed, it was tranquil, and a place of rest.

His room was bold, like his personality. His draperies were black with images of Betty Boop on them, in front of the window was a large window seat with big red cushions and yellow throw pillows, he would lay on it and look out at the stars for hours if he couldn't sleep at night. Sometimes She thought maybe he saw things out there, things that other people couldn't see, or maybe he imagined them like She did with the castle and the dragons. She wasn't sure because they didn't talk about those kinds of things.

He had bunk beds with a double on the bottom and a single on top, but they were not the usual kind, the beds ran perpendicular to each other. Their mother had designed these in a way that a desk and a quiet hiding spot had been created in the back. He could escape if he wanted to.

He had an area rug on the floor that was full of roadways, and buildings. And of course a million cars and trucks; he loved to drive, or imagine that he was driving. She thought about the day that Abraham had taken them to the Go-Carts, and how happy he had been to be behind the wheel. How free he had felt, how exciting it must have been for him to have control of the small cart. She Herself had been liberated by the experience for different reasons. She knew that he also had been affected by the events of that day, and although they had done the required psychological counselling and they had talked it to death with their mother, there were still things that had not been said. Things that tormented Her.

She worried at night for Abraham. She prayed for him, and for his safety where he was. She knew from things that She had heard kids talking about at school, that he was not in a good place. The children had filled Her in on the conditions in the mexican prison where he had been sent. There were too many men for the number of cells that they had, he wouldn't have his own room, as he had had at the residence. There weren't enough beds for all of the prisoners, never enough food, the prison guards kept the cells filled with rats, and they were built partially underground; ensuring that when it rained the cells would be partially underwater.

With no place to escape from the rain, cellmates skin would fall off, erode and rot. Just thinking about it made Her feel sick.

He did not have a wench to do his hair everyday, or a nanny to help him with homework. She felt truly blessed to have the things that She had, and yet somewhat responsible that his life had been taken from him.

She understood that Abraham himself had made a series of bad choices. She had listened, as the psychologist had explained it all to Her. However, She knew him before it had happened, She knew that he had cared for Her and Her brother, the psychologist didn't, and She knew that something happened to the poor man that had driven him over the cliff, something in him had caused him to make those choices. She just didn't understand what they were.

She looked at Her brother sleeping, on the top bunk. He slept on his back, toes up. She took a moment to look around and then crept back into the hallway.

She heard a sound coming from the foyer, and stopped in Her tracks. She held Her breath for a moment and whispered out loud to her friend Mary Mack, "What Should I do, Mary Mack? I think there is someone breaking in the front door."

She was certain of it. She could hear the rattling of the door, the heavy metal tumblers turning. She ducked into the bathroom next to her brother's bedroom and hid behind the door.

The bath towels were clean and smelled of lavender, She marvelled in the concept of clean laundry and wondered how it was always managed in this house. She listened intently. The door was opening. She felt Her bladder full and pressing on Her abdomen. The need to urinate was intense. She held her breath, because She was certain that if She did that, She would either die before She was found, or they would never find Her because She was so quiet. Either way could potentially be a win for Her. She hadn't hoped to end Her days in Her brother's bathroom, but if that's the way it was to be, then She would accept it as it came.

She decided a short prayer was probably in order, it would get Her mind off of Her need to pee if nothing else.

"Lord, please get me out of this one. I promise, Father God, to never get out of bed again when I'm not supposed to. Please, Lord, help me to be a better girl. I really do try but I know that I fail you. Please help me to see the things that I am doing wrong so that I can be better, and show me where I can help others. Please bless Abraham and make sure that he is cared for and comforted, and that he has enough food. And bless Lupita and Justo because they are good people, Lord, and they would really like a baby. And watch over my brother because, well, he might need some help. I just have a feeling. And whoever is coming through that door, Lord, I pray for them too, that you will take mercy on them. Amen."

Her nightgown clung to Her tiny frame in the tight space. She felt confined, restricted and suddenly frustrated and angry. She wasn't certain where the feelings came from but they were stronger than Her fear. She peeked through the crack between the door and the door casing. Which allowed Her only a quarter of an inch of space to see who was coming into the hallway. It was still dark, and the shadows that filled the night with obscurity, made Her identification of the intruder challenging but not impossible.

She let out her breath as She watched Her father walk down the hallway towards the master bedroom. He closed the door to Her parent's room, and She released herself from Her hiding place. She quickly and quietly moved back to Her own bedroom, and snuck into Her bathroom to pee. She relieved herself and returned to Her bed.

She looked at the digital clock on the night stand, it was five forty-five in the morning. She wondered what Her father could possibly be doing anywhere at five forty-five? There were no stores open, no bars nor restaurants. She knew that there wasn't any type of business or negotiations that could possibly be happening at this hour.

Restlessness overcame her. She tossed and She turned, Her mind churning different scenarios, plotting and planning different ideas and concepts that may or may not have happened. She watched the clock's numbers change through the various fives and sixes, into seven and then She saw the sun coming up, She thought and She pondered. She could only come up with one possible explanation that was realistic and potentially feasible.

Her father must have been in an accident. He must have been lying in a hospital bed all alone and wondering why his family wasn't coming to help him. She knew the very best thing to do was tell Her mother. She would tell Her mother in the morning and then Her mommy could apologize and then it would all be okay. She just hoped that her father wasn't too angry with them. After all no one ever benefitted when he was mad.

She rolled over and finally fell back asleep.

As She fell into a deep slumber Mary Mack appeared at the window, her shiny dark chocolate hair glimmering like diamonds in the morning sunshine, she smiled at the sleeping child, straightened her black silk dress and began to sing.

"Amazing Grace, how sweet the sound,
That saved a wretch like me.
I once was lost but now am found.
Was Blind but now I see.
T'was Grace that taught my heart to fear
And grace my fears relieved.
How precious did that grace appear
The hour I first believed.

Through many dangers, toils and snares,
I have already come,
Tis Grace hath brought me safe thus far,
and Grace will lead me home.
When we've been there ten thousand years,
Bright shining as the sun,
We've no less days to sing God's praise,
than when we first begun.
Amazing Grace, how sweet the sound,
that saved a wretch like me,
I once was lost but now I am found,
was blind but now I see,
Amazing Grace, oh Amazing Grace,
that saved a wretch like me,
oh Amazing Grace, Amazing Grace."

She looked over Her. "And with all of the power that you have used, Lord, to create the heavens and the Earth, to save your people from struggle and strife, bless this child. You have chosen Her, Lord, and we walk with Her on Your command, we ask in Jesus name that She always act on Her own free will, with Your promises guiding Her. Her path is laid, we protect Her every step, Lord, despite their attempts to slay Her. You have made us warriors, Lord, we act on Your command. Thank you for Your great forgiveness of sin, for Your compassion everlasting and the Gift of Your Son. Amen." Mary Mack performed the sign of the cross over the sleeping girl and knelt briefly beside the bed for a quiet moment of her own meditation and reflection.

CHAPTER 54

In the centuries after the Romans departed Britain, there were four groups within the boundaries of what is now known as Scotland. Scotland was largely converted to Christianity from the fifth to the seventh century, which aided in the adoption of Gaelic languages and customs.

The long reign of Constantine II in the Ninth Century led to Scottish Christian conformity with the Catholic Church. Malcolm I and Malcolm II maintained reasonable relations with England during this time, until Macbeth became King by way of the sword. King Macbeth ruled for seventeen years until his stepson Malcolm relieved him of his spot on the throne.

Malcolm III had acquired the nickname Canmore, which meant Great Chief. He was proud, and boastful of his own family's empire, and was rich with food and wine when he took his second bride, Princess Margaret; who was of English Hungarian descent. Malcolm was enamoured with Margaret's beauty, her olive skin and dark curly hair were a rarity in his land, a luxury to add to the blood lines of his own fair-skinned red-headed Dunkeld Dynasty, she was just what he needed.

The English got news of the marriage and were enraged with his choice; he knew bloody well that William the Great Conqueror would be coming for him. He would be prepared for the war. Malcolm was in dire need of an heir and his loins were in dire need of his new Queen; Margaret.

Their union resulted in three children. A beautiful boy, a successor to the throne properly named Malcolm IV; the heir, a royal spare, named David, and a lovely girl, with dark curly hair like her mother's, which they named Mary. Mary was christened in the spring of 1060 to the house of Mackenzie. And was therefore duly named Mary Mack.

CHAPTER 55

She woke and was sweating, Her mosquito netting was closed and the window was open. Her drapes were pulled back allowing the sun to pour into the room, and escalate the temperature to unbearable heights. She reached for the water jug next to the bed. It was empty. She rubbed Her eyes and called for Her nanny. "Lupita, vengas por favour, please come." She felt over heated and was sleep drunk. She lay waiting.

Her thoughts returned to Her father. She had decided to speak to Her mother immediately. She felt it was important to always bring family information to the forefront. Put everyone's cards on the table. She knew Her mother would feel awful when she found out that he had been out late, and most likely hurt and laying in a hospital bed somewhere.

Lupita came through the door, her smiling face full of gratitude and pure joy. Her apron was neatly pressed, her hair tied up in a tight bun. "Good Morning, sweet princess, how did you sleep? My goodness I didn't think you would ever wake up!"

"Good morning, Lupita. I had a good sleep thank you, well, mostly."

"What do you mean well, mostly? Why is the window open again, baby? Hmm?"

"I don't know, I didn't open it."

"Well, who did then? Because it was closed when I went to

bed, and there hasn't been anyone in here since then, except for perhaps your mother. And we both know that she wouldn't open it *'too many bugs and things'* so? Hmmm? Hmmm?" She bent down and began to tickle Her. She began to giggle. "Hurry go pee, and brush your teeth please, then let's get dressed and have some breakfast. Many things to do, and today you get to go to the theatre with your mother!"

She was pleased to be getting some time with Her mother. She wasn't quite sure what She was going to say exactly. But She knew that Her mother was going to feel awful. Her mother had such a profound sense of compassion. She brushed Her teeth and hair and returned to Her room to dress. Lupita had laid out an outfit for Her to wear for the day.

"Lupita, is my father home?"

"No, baby, he left early this morning to go to Brownsville Texas. He will be back in a week I think."

"Why did he go there? Who lives in Brownsville? Do you know when he's coming back? Why did he go and not say good-bye?"

Lupita really had no idea, and really didn't want to be involved. She had heard him in the morning arguing with Madam. She knew her place and knew that it was nowhere near the middle of their business. She did find it odd that he kept such strange hours, and that he left quite often without saying good bye to the children. And then he would have periods of self-professed love where he would shout from the roof tops, of how much he loved his family. He was an odd man. He found it necessary at times to find acceptance from his peers, and yet not from his children. She found him perplexing, a complex and yet simple type of person. She did wonder though what Madam saw in him. Again it was none of her business so she kept her opinion to herself. No one liked an opinionated care giver. "I am not sure, Sweet-heart, but I do know that if you hurry up I will make you some special eggs! How does that sound?"

She made a face. "How about just some mango?"

"No, no, not enough, eggs too, mango fine yes, and avocado."

"Fine then, coffee?" She looked at Lupita sideways as they walked down the hallway towards the kitchen.

"Are you joking with me now, baby?"

"Maybe a little bit." She snickered and sat at the counter where She could watch Lupita making Her breakfast.

Her brother came into the room and sat beside Her. He liked the stools, the feeling of his feet dangling was something that he found thrilling.

"Hey, whatcha doin?"

"Just woke up, what are you doing?" She looked at him with still sleepy eyes.

"Just playing cars, hey did you hear that Dad went to Texas? Isn't that cool?"

"I dunno, why did he go there?"

"Well, I'm not totally sure but I think it has something to do with his papers or something. I heard him and Mom talking this morning. I hope he brings me something cool. Everything from Texas is big and super cool, I'm pumped. Hey, is that what you are wearing to the theatre today?"

She looked at Lupita for help, and then back at Her brother. "Yes, I was going to wear this, what are you wearing?" She silently hoped for coffee.

He shrugged his shoulders, and pushed his blond hair back from his forehead. "I guess I will wear whatever Lupita tells me to wear. I don't actually care. What time are we leaving?"

"I just woke up, I don't know."

"Geez, cranky, maybe you should go back to bed."

"I know I'm sorry I didn't sleep very good, I umm…" She thought quickly about whether or not to share her story from the night before, of seeing their father come in at five forty-five and decided against it. "I had bad dreams. I was too hot and just couldn't sleep. I even came into your room around five forty in the morning."

He found his sister amusing. "You did! What was I doing?" He was eager, fun-loving and easy to be around.

"What do you think? You were sleeping, on your back, total toes up. Sleeping like a log."

Lupita found the two of them entertaining. She longed for her own children one day. She and Justo had been married for so many years she really lost track of time sometimes. She had married at the tender age of fifteen after falling madly deeply in love with her own father's apprentice. Justo was thirteen years her senior. Their life together had been wonderful, except for the fact that they hadn't yet been blessed with a baby. Now at the age of twenty-nine she was starting to question whether or not children would ever be in their future. She had to believe that they would be, for her faith in God was dependent on it. She continued to pray that the good Lord would come through on her behalf.

CHAPTER 56

Jorge Alvarez did everything in his power to stay focused on his job. The weeks were passing by slowly, like sand through an hour glass. He was doing as Madam had requested and he hadn't called her. He had respected her wishes and he had made no attempt to contact her after their evening together at the Beach Hotel in Bucerias. They had skipped their dinner reservations, and had instead enjoyed each other rather than the bland taste of food from a restaurant.

The Police Chief found himself now in a state of mental anguish. His mind for many years was wracked with thoughts of what Madam might be like, what her hair might feel like, what her lips might taste like, what the touch of her skin would be like on his own. Now that he knew; he was tormented with knowing that she was outside of his grasp.

He had waited his entire life for a woman that would be a mate, a potential match for himself. He fell hard in love for one that was off limits, out of bounds, the forbidden fruit; he wasn't sure if the exclusion from her life made him want her more or not, but he couldn't work hard enough or drink enough to rid her of his mind. He could only hope; or assume that time would heal this. That he would soon forget her. He would move on. He would have to. Eventually.

CHAPTER 57

She waited for Her mother to return from work so that they could go to the theatre as planned. She and Her brother were totally ready, dressed, fed, and amply prepared; excited too. Madam had telephoned Lupita to inform her that she was running a few minutes behind, and to have the children waiting on the front step, they were all set when she arrived.

"Hello, my darlings, how are we this afternoon?" Madam embraced both of them at the same time, squeezing their heads together into her breast. The two children made faces at each other at such a close range.

"Good, Mommy, we've had a lovely day with Lupita." Her brother was always quick to offer positive input. "Can we stop on the way for something to eat?"

Madam looked at Lupita. "I thought you had something to eat already, Sweet-heart, I thought we would eat after. I have reservations for dinner at Café Des Artiste."

Lupita piped in, "They did eat, Madam, you know how he is though, always hungry."

"Oh of course, well, I think you will survive a couple of hours, hey? Let's go, pumpkins... off we are to the ball..." The kids giggled as they piled into the vehicle. They drove through the downtown streets from the residence to the theatre. The children babbled and chattered about their day with Lupita and trivial things that they had been arguing about since breakfast. It was then that She brought it up.

"Mommy, I didn't sleep well last night." She looked out the window of the car and into the crowded street.

"I'm sorry to hear that, Honey, what happened?"

"I'm not sure exactly, I woke up and then I got up and walked around, went into his room, looked out at the stars for a while, watched him sleeping, watched father come in at five forty-five in the morning, then went back to sleep."

"Ahh. You saw your father come in at five forty-five? And it's been bugging you all day?"

She shrugged. "A little yeah, I mean I worried all night about what he could have been doing until that time, all of the bars and restaurants are closed, so the only thing I could come up with was that he was in the hospital."

"Well, that's creative for sure, but I can assure you that he was not in the hospital, he was not injured in any way, he was just fine." Madam was angry that one of her children had seen him.

"Mommy, what was he doing?" She didn't understand.

"Yeah, Mom, why would Dad be out so late?" Her brother was even curious now, and he wondered why She hadn't discussed this with him earlier.

"Well, I think that he was probably getting ready for this trip that he had to make to Brownsville Texas."

Her brother was now really curious, and a little choked. "Why did he have to go to Texas? And why couldn't he take us with him? I would like to go to Texas. I heard from some of the boys at school that everything in Texas is bigger." He imagined, like many boys that the pick up trucks there were twice the size of normal pick ups, the breasts on women were instead of B and C cups, E and Fs and every drive-through meal from McDonald's was Super Sized. The minds of eight-year-old boys were a vast and wildly creative place.

238

"Honey, I cannot explain that to you, because I don't have the answer myself. I wish that I did, your father sometimes has to do things that are explainable only in his own world. So we are going to give him some space okay?"

The two kids looked at each other in the back seat and She rolled Her eyes. She placed Her hand on the window crank and moved it forward and back, the window tightening and loosening slightly. "Mommy, does Father love you? We never see you together like the other kids' parents. He doesn't hold your hand or kiss you or anything."

"Of course your Father loves us, Honey, we are a family, families love each other, your father just doesn't like to show his affections publicly. He likes to be very private about things. But he loves you very much."

She made a very mental note that Her question had not been answered, but avoided. She knew Her mother had deliberately dodged the query by trying to include the family unit. She didn't like the feeling of being manipulated.

They enjoyed the live theatre and drove straight to the restaurant after. Her brother was starving and ordered a plate of fresh calamari to start. The three of them sat and chatted about the theatre performance, while She stewed over the situation with their father.

She pondered which box to place Her memory in, overall She had enjoyed the time with Her mother, so it felt pink, however there were elements of red, and even orange. She decided to not file it at all. As it clearly did not fit in any box easily and if the shoe didn't fit, a girl couldn't wear it.

The next morning She woke early, the sound of feet pounding on the floor throughout the house was annoying her. She buried her head beneath the pillows and attempted to return to sleep. She looked out the window from under Her mosquito netting at the ocean off in the distance and thought of Her friend Mary Mack. She hadn't seen her for a what seemed to be quite some time. For an odd reason She felt that She needed her now.

"Mary Mack, if you can hear me, please come back…"

The hustle and bustle about the house was becoming louder, She could hear voices although She wasn't able to make out what they were saying. Male voices and females, Her mother's and Lupita's too, but others as well. She needed to pee.

She opened the door from Her room to the hallway and peeked to where the voices were coming from. She could see maybe six or seven people there. She closed the door again. And went into the bathroom. She relieved herself, washed Her hands, brushed Her teeth, brushed Her hair, washed Her face and tidied the space.

Lupita entered her bedroom. "Oh good, you are awake, good morning, lovely!"

She ran to Lupita and hugged her tight around the waist. "Good Morning, Lupita, what is going on? Why are there so many people in the house?"

Lupita was cautious to choose her words, she knew that the child would pick up on a lie, and she also was careful to protect Madam. "Sweet-heart, there are some people here to see your mother. And so I think we should get dressed for school, and then if your mother would like to tell you about it, she can, how about that?" Lupita didn't enjoy any type of conflict and she most certainly didn't like anything that put her children, or her boss in harm's way. She was on the verge of boiling on the inside and it was taking every ounce of energy that she had to remain calm.

"Did Mommy do something wrong, Lupita?" She had tears

240

in Her eyes when She asked the question.

Lupita knew that fear was the basis of the query, having seen what had happened to Abraham, and knowing what could happen to a foreigner in this country if lines were crossed. "Good heavens no, your mother has done nothing wrong, my love, the people are just here to ask her some questions about someone else. Okay? Let's get our uniform on for school please while I go and wake your brother yes?"

She nodded and got Herself dressed quickly, hoping to at the very least over hear something while She was eating Her breakfast.

CHAPTER 58

In the winter of 1060, while Queen Margaret was pregnant with Mary, Malcolm took a mistress who later gave birth to an illegitimate son Duncan. Angst and upset grew within the walls of Scotland and a horrible war broke between England and the Scots. It had been ongoing for hundreds of years, but had lay quiet under the rule of King Malcolm I, and Malcolm II. England was outraged however with the disrespect shown to the beloved Queen Margaret and so William the Great invaded the area inhabited as Scotland.

Mary Mack was a lovely child, one that was exuberant, full of zest and bubbling with laughter and energy. She chased her brother Malcolm around the castle singing songs and making rhymes. She knew nothing of the war that raged outside of the castle walls, and was ignorant of her father's transgressions. She knew that her mother, the Queen loved her very much, and that her father, King Malcolm III adored her and her rhyming games.

After months of combat, and Scotland suffering significant losses in the battlefield, Mary Mack's father made a decision to move into battle himself. He left his bride and his heir to the throne, with his beloved daughter Mary Mack in the castle with one of his knights, and orders to watch over them.

He had been away in battle for only two days when the castle fell to the hands of the English. Queen Margaret was taken hostage, and was returned to London to be used later in negotiations with King Malcolm III. The Prince Malcolm IV was beheaded, leaving no chance of a continuation of reign of power of the family. And Princess Mary Mack, a young girl with long dark curly hair, was taken into the woods, and brutally raped and then left for dead by the English soldiers that had come for her mother.

CHAPTER 59

The Federal Agents had accepted the offer of coffee and croissants, and although it was not normal procedure, they nodded approval at each other. Whoever had done the baking was using the right kind of butter. They had arrived that morning under the orders of the Federal Courts Of Mexico. Their uniforms were crisply pressed, their pistols and hand guns as shiny black as their boots. They wore sleek cowboy hats, dark tan in colour, felt that was brushed clean of any dust or marks. These men were not thrown together by chance; their uniforms were designed to intimidate.

Mexican criminal law has several interesting and distinctive features; which differ from those in other parts of North America. Within Mexico, one who is alleged to have broken the law is deemed guilty until proven innocent. We refer to this as Napoleonic or Canon Law. In Mexico the commission of fraud is a criminal offense.

Madam was overwhelmed by all of the questions that she faced. She knew that her husband's business activity was at times questionable. She was aware that some of his business partners were not individuals that she could address on the street and also she knew that some of them were involved in organized activities. What she didn't know however was the amount of involvement that her husband actually had in those activities.

"Madam, do you know this man?" A photo was held up for

her.

She shook her head no. She was relieved that Lupita had managed to feed and dress the children, and get them onto the school bus without too many questions.

""When your husband left for Brownsville yesterday, what exactly did he tell you that he was going to be doing there? Did he say if he was going alone?"

"He didn't say, we had a fight, actually, like we always do. And then he left. Like he always does."

The agent looked over at his partner, he had seen this scenario before. The husband was using Madam as a front. She actually had no idea what was going on. They could sit here all day and question her, but he didn't believe that she knew anything. She was pretty, she was smart, and she was completely in the dark. He also knew that he couldn't tell her much about the federal side of the case, but he needed her to check their joint bank accounts. He needed to know just how much cash the two of them had, if any of the money that they were looking for was in their joint accounts, by the end of the day, the Federal Courts would confiscate it all.

"Madam, we have a court order to seize any assets that your husband owns jointly with you. Now I don't want to do that; what I would like to do, because I like you, is I would like to see if your husband is hiding the money in your joint account; and then help you to decide what to do. I don't think he has the money in your account; because I think he's actually an asshole. I think he makes you work your tiny little ass off to pay all of the bills, pretends that he doesn't have any money, and I think he's hiding millions of dollars, from his own nasty business in offshore accounts. Or somewhere, I dunno where. But I think you work too hard for someone who has the kind of money that we are looking for, someone who works as hard as you, doesn't have twenty-five or thirty million sitting in the bank in Puerto Vallarta."

Madam grabbed a cigarette, she lit the Marlboro Light and dragged on it hard. Her head became full of images of her husband; his business partners, his trips; the dinners with men and the women; and late nights. She supposed that she must have always known what he did for a living, and so for a moment she thought about how she could gain an advantage, and perhaps win this battle.

Because she *knew* that that's exactly what it had always been; a battle. She could not fully co-operate with the Feds, because she knew that if she did, she too would end up in jail, as an accessory. She was aware that the people that her husband did business with, would never allow him to spend a moment behind bars, he would walk away from this a free man. That was just a sad part of this reality. And so now she wondered, if perhaps this charade was more about getting her out of the picture? A way of dealing with her...? Her mind raced quickly through different scenarios, as she thought about all of the necessary cogs for her own wheel of survival. Because as ominous and terrifying as these Feds might appear to be, the men that her husband was involved with, were much, much worse.

And then she spoke. "Of course, I would be most happy to accompany you to the bank. Let me get my purse."

Madam knew exactly to the penny, how much cash she had saved in her own account, and she knew how much was in their joint account. She had been to the bank just the day before her husband had gone to Brownsville.

She entered the bank with three Federal Officers, and every person in the bank stood still. Their presence was ominous, dangerous and alarming. One of the officers wore silver spurs on his boots that jingled when he walked, making their entry even more elaborate and theatrical than it needed to be. Madam approached a very nervous-looking bank teller who refused to make eye contact. All three of the agents followed.

"Good after noon."

She cleared her throat. "Good afternoon, Madam, how are you today?"

Madam smiled at her attempting to ease the tension between them. "Fine thank you, could you please print out for me a current statement of account for my personal account, and for my joint account with my husband."

"Yes of course, Madam, that will just take a moment."

"Thank you." Madam turned towards the agents and made small talk with them while they waited. The teller tapped on the glass. "Madam?" Madam turned towards the teller.

"Yes." She saw the papers in the hands of the young girl and was immediately relieved that this was soon to be over. "Oh thank you so much, I appreciate your help." She hadn't noticed the ashen look on the young teller's face. Madam looked at the statements. Both accounts showed balances of zero.

"That's impossible!"

The federal agent stepped forward. "Something wrong, Madam?"

"This is impossible! There's no money! My accounts have been cleaned out, I have no money!"

The teller spoke. "I can check again, Madam, please have a seat."

She was weak. "I need to speak to your boss, where is Señor de Silva? Your Manager?"

The Agent spoke next. "Madam, please, let's not jump to conclusions, and we certainly do not want to make a scene with three federal agents at our side. Please, hmmm?"

Señor de Silva came from his office and looked at the computer screen with the teller, he reprinted the statements and beckoned Madam into his office. He was not aware that the agents were with Madam and was surprised when all three of them followed her into his office.

"Madam, please take a seat."

"No, thank you, no I don't want to sit, I would like to know where all of my money is Señor de Silva?"

The bank manager was a ball of nerves with the agents in his office. "Madam, could we please have the room alone? I am uncertain why you are in the company of Federal Agents today, and I do certainly understand that it is none of my business: but I have to be frank that these men make me very nervous; and I would be more comfortable discussing your finances without them in the room."

Agent Number Two decided to speak. "Not going to happen today, dude, sorry. We also need to know what happened to Madam's money. So you either tell us, or we get a court order, which is easier for you?"

"Fine, okay then,… it's just, well,… it seems, Madam, that your husband took it. All of it." Senor de Silva seemed relieved that he had at last, finally spilled the beans.

Madam was sick to her stomach. "You are saying that my husband has taken *my* money out of my account? And our joint account? *What about that one?*"

"Yes, indeed, and your business account too, yes. All of it, Madam. When you opened your accounts with us you added him onto the accounts as an emergency signing authority, because you had no other family in the country, and so he was able to sign for the accounts to withdraw."

Madam sank into a chair, her knees buckling beneath her,

she placed her head on the desk of Señor de Silva. "How much, Señor? In total? How much did he get?"

The bank manager cleared his throat, he was now placed in a very precarious position, one which he didn't like to be in, but that his job required. "From your joint account, Madam, one hundred and eighty thousand fifty-three, United States dollars, from your personal account, thirty-three thousand dollars, and some loose change; and from your business account, six hundred and ninety-five thousand three hundred Mexican Pesos."

The three agents looked at each other, agent Two whistled. "Aye carumba, Cabrone." They knew that all of the money in those accounts had been Madams, and that it was most likely his travelling money, the Feds were looking for much larger numbers, numbers in the millions. It wouldn't make it any easier for her now; they knew that, it was a shame that she hadn't seen it coming. He had cleaned her out, he was on the run, they wondered if they could do something to get him to come back before he disappeared for good.

CHAPTER 60

She sat in the classroom at school and wondered what Her mother was doing for the day, with all of the people that had been in the kitchen when She had left for school. She silently hoped that She was okay, and that whatever questions they had were being answered and that it had nothing to do with Her family.

She endured math class, and then language arts, french and science; and then it was time for lunch. She took her lunch box and retreated to Her favourite spot beneath the weeping tree and sat quietly by Herself. She placed Her lunch items neatly in front of Her, ensuring that nothing touched. Carrots were separate from celery and clear of cucumbers. Her soup was a lovely tomato bisque with some avocado pieces to drop into it, and She had a nice piece of goat cheese and some tortilla chips. In Her water bottle was a nicely iced lemon water, with no sugar, which was refreshing but a little disappointing. One day She hoped for some sort of lovely surprise in Her lunch kit. A diet Coke, or a Penguino, which was a delicious chocolate cupcake treat with vanilla icing piped into the middle of it. She knew that once in a blue moon Lupita would break the rules, and She and Her brother would be treated to something yummy; *once in a while*. It was just never in the lunch kit. Lupita knew that it was never to be in a situation in which anyone could get caught. A treat happened after school, or on a beach day. Lupita always said that accidents didn't happen;

they were caused. And an accident wasn't about to happen on Lupita's watch. She sighed and ate Her vegetables; all neatly cut into pieces of equal size; She liked uniformity. Lupita respected that.

She watched the other girls playing tag and jumping rope and She longed for what She believed to be a normal female relationship. She had never had a friend, a best friend; one that She could count on, one that She could jump rope with, one to have sleep overs with, one to share secrets and paint toe nails. She yearned for a girlfriend, a confidant. Tears filled her eyes as She watched them play together. She wondered if they bought matching pyjamas or if they hung out at the beach together on Saturday afternoons? If their mothers called each other to arrange play dates and birthday parties. She questioned Her uniqueness and wondered why She was always alone. Why She spent so many hours with Her nanny and none with girls Her own age? She loved Lupita, but She also ached for a relationship that She could nurture and cultivate by Herself. One that would be new and could be just for her, a friendship with a real little girl like Herself.

"Mary Mack, I know you can hear me, I know you are there. I wish you would come and see me, so that I could talk to you. I have so many things to share, and so many things that I would like to tell you. And now I am just alone. With no one here, and no one to talk to, and no one to play with. I'm just alone. I'm just a freak, I'm just that weirdo in the corner that speaks all the languages and eats the weird food, and has the strange red hair. The one with the pale skin and the skinny legs." She began to cry softly as she sat under the tree. Crying was something that She rarely did when people could see. She was not a child who felt sorry for Herself. Madam was raising Her to be of strong character. Showing emotion was fine, but

She would always be brave about it. She wouldn't cry when it was not necessary. She was not to show the world that She was scared. She would show the world that She was fearless. She would smile relentlessly, She would stand up against Her enemies, face them dead on; and shout at them, "I am a force to be reckoned with, do you know who I am?"

Today though, She cried, and today She felt sad, and She felt scared. She was sad for Herself, and scared of the events from the morning that She had witnessed. Sad for Her mother, and scared for Her father; She prayed for his safety.

CHAPTER 61

Madam gathered her purse, and what was left of her dignity, and walked out of the bank penniless. She had no idea how she would pay her staff, or for the food she would need to operate the restaurant for the remainder of the week; let alone her house staff. She felt on the verge of tears, she had her cell phone in her hand and dialled a number that she called rarely but knew from memory. He answered on the first ring.

"Hello, Dad."

Madam's father was at the office, surprised but pleased as always to hear from his only daughter. "Hello, my Love, how have you been?"

"Dad, I need to come home." She was having a hard time holding back the tears that had been threatening to come all day. Hearing her Dad's voice was so calming and peaceful to her that it made her head spin. "Dad, it's bad here, I can't explain now, but we need to come home."

"How long do you need?"

"A couple of days." She took a breath, Madam relaxed slightly knowing that there was a door that she could move through of she needed it. Home was safe, she knew she would be able to take the children home, and they could sleep safely at night and not be in harm's way. She herself, could breathe knowing that her children would live another day. Her mind wandered to Abraham, she briefly wondered if that entire episode had been a set-up.

"Call me back when you know more, sweetheart." He hung up the phone on his end and looked at the calendar, he had always known that it would eventually come to this, but he had never believed, that it would take as long as it had, for his daughter to call and ask to come home.

Madam closed her flip phone and held it tightly in her hand. She looked at the agent beside her and smiled. She knew that he empathised with her but she didn't know to what extent. She would need to keep all of her cards as close to her chest as possible. They were almost back at the residence. She had another call to make. But she desperately wanted to make it in private.

As they pulled into the driveway, she solidified her own plan in her mind. Madam wanted to hear what the agents had in store for her and for her husband, and so she decided to keep quiet for the moment. She lit a cigarette, and dragged on it hard. The nicotine reached her brain in milliseconds, soothing her agitated nerves.

"Madam, we would like you to call your husband, chit chat, like nothing has happened here; we would like you to get him to come back, without letting him know that anything has transpired. We want him back so that we can take him in for questioning."

Madam dragged on her smoke again. "That would be difficult for me. I don't hide my emotions well. Idle chit chat isn't my sort of thing."

"We are going to need you to try. It will be in the best interest of everyone involved." The agent was a straight shooter, she appreciated that about him, but she wanted something from him.

She decided the best way to get what she wanted was just to ask for it. In this circumstance, she knew that the straightest line was going to be the shortest distance between two points, and she knew that within three days she and the children would be gone from Mexico. She had was nothing to lose here. "The kidnapping case that involved my children, was my husband involved in some way? Did he hire or manipulate Abraham into taking the children?"

The agents looked from one to the other, and then back at her. "Madam, we have investigated that yes."

"And?" She wanted the answer, she needed to know, she wanted to know. "Did my husband pay Abraham to kidnap my children?"

"Madam, we cannot link your husband, or the organization that he is involved with to the kidnapping. We have no proof. We believe that maybe the children were used to scare you. We think that maybe they wanted you out of Mexico. But we cannot prove anything. Everything we have is speculation, hunches, you know."

She took one last drag on her cigarette, and snubbed it out in the ashtray. "I will co-operate with you, in anyway that you need, on two conditions. First, I must have a full pardon. In no way will I ever be prosecuted for any crimes linked to my husband's activity. Not for the crime, nor as an accessory to any crime. And second, I want Abraham released from prison."

"We are not in a position to release Abraham, he was tried, and convicted Madam. His lawyers would have to appeal that conviction to have him released. It's just not that easy. You understand."

She nodded. "I do, yes. And if you want me to co-operate, you will find a way to get that man out of prison, because I happen to know that something happened to him to make him snap. He is not an evil man, he is not malicious, nor vengeful.

He did not kidnap my children because he hated me or because he was some kind of sick pedophile, I don't know what it was that that threw him over the edge, but he should not be in there. And I would like him out. And if anyone can do it, it is you. And you and I both know it."

The agent chewed on a toothpick, he looked at her and placed the toothpick into the ashtray with her cigarette butt. "Okay, we can make a few calls. Maybe see a few people. I'm going to leave Agent Maldonado with you, just to make sure that you don't do anything crazy, and we are going to head over to the courthouse. We will see you later. You call your husband please and get him back here, into Mexico, by the end of the week. Let's get things moving. Don't push it, lady, I would like to spend the weekend with my kids."

He and Agent Cabrera moved towards the front door of the residence, he looked back at her just as he was about to leave. In their line of work, they saw mostly, drug cartel, mafia bosses and high-profile illegal aliens, fraud, money laundering, people trafficking, that sort of thing. She was smart. He could see that she was planning something; he just wasn't sure what it was. He could spend time trying to figure her out, but he really just wanted her to get home. Wherever her real home might be, it surely wasn't Mexico.

CHAPTER 62

The school bus bounced and bumped its way through the side residential streets, with dust clouds billowing behind it. She was frustrated at the amount of time these mundane things took. The ride home from school and school itself seemed monotonous, as though it was a necessary chess move, but a total bore. She desperately wanted to be home, where she could be doing something important, or at the very least eavesdropping.

She sat alone, with Her backpack on the seat beside Her. She watched Her brother chatting and playing with the other children. She envied his comfort with others, his charm, his ability to interact; his chattiness.

"It won't always be like this you know."

She looked to Her right at her companion, and was pleased, but surprised to see Mary Mack sitting on the seat in front of Her.

"How do you mean? With him? With my brother?" She was thrilled to finally have her back. "Mary Mack, you're not rhyming today."

"No, indeed, I am not, there is no time for rhyme today. And frankly, I'm not in the mood. Yes your brother, too; everything will be different, everything is changing. And quickly. But don't worry I will be with you. It will be scary. But it will be okay. In the end it is all for you, and you will see clearly one day why it all had to happen. But for now it won't seem like clear, or okay. You will be very sad some days, and then you will find happiness and then you will find your calling. And the world will be right."

"I don't know if I want to do all of that. I don't like change."

Mary Mack reached for Her hand. "He knows that, that's why He makes you do it." She smiled at Her.

"Couldn't things just stay the same for now, and maybe change when I am older? What kind of change are you talking about?"

"I can't tell you that, silly, that would spoil all of the fun! I can only tell you that I will stay with you. So that you aren't too scared, and to ensure that you make all of the right decisions, and of course to protect you."

She played with the zipper on Her back pack. "You get to protect me?"

"Yes, I do."

"Like how? Protect me from what?" She was curious, and She was excited all at the same time. She wanted to know more about Mary Mack, and She wanted to know if She had the same sort of job as the old woman who had lived in the basement when she had been a little girl living in Canada.

"Yes," said Mary Mack. "Yes I am like the old woman, and yes I can read your mind. However, I am stronger than the old woman. I am a warrior. She was just a guardian."

She smiled at Mary Mack from ear to ear, she almost couldn't believe her ears, she had seen warriors on the television, and none of which had looked anything like Mary Mack herself. Zena Warrior Princess was her favourite television show. Zena wore a breast plate for protection, she was tall and incredibly strong. "Mary, really? You're a warrior? But you're so pretty? And you're so little. What can

258

you do? Do you have super powers?"

Mary Mack frowned at Her. "First of all, size has nothing to do with abilities. That is not how it works. Second, I have many powers, many of which I have shared with you already, you just chose not to listen, and sometimes you don't pay full attention. You also have many powers, or abilities… and thank you, my father thought I was pretty too. He was a King."

"Your Father was a King? Holy cow that is cool."

"Yes I suppose. Let's focus on you, please." The bus plodded on, starting and stopping, children getting off, the laughter becoming less bothersome, there were less interuptions. "Things will get chaotic but you must remember that I am always with you."

"Does my brother see you?"

"Not me no. He has the ability to sense the presence of others, but his mind is busy, he has a difficult time focusing on the present."

She felt that Mary Mack was being vague when She needed specifics.

"You will not always be able to converse with me, because of circumstance, but if you think about me I can hear you. And I can always hear your prayers." Mary Mack straightened her black silk dress.

"Mary Mack, why do you always wear the same dress?"

"I like this one. Are we good?" Their eyes met and She nodded, Mary Mack disappeared and the bus arrived at the residence. She picked up Her back pack and gave Her brother a nudge. The two of them walked up the steps together and entered the house. A state of confusion and disorder like they had never seen awaited them.

CHAPTER 63

Madam was on the telephone, and Lupita was frantically searching for something. The entire house was torn apart. The children looked at each other as they entered the kitchen as they normally would, dropped their backpacks and sat on the bar stools, waiting for refreshments and snacks from their beloved nanny.

They watched as she pulled open drawers and cupboards, digging and searching for something. She moved through the entire kitchen and then into the living room obviously on a second sweep. Her brother got up and shrugged. He nodded at Her and moved to the fridge, pulled out a jug of iced tea and poured them each a glass. He pulled ice cubes from the freezer and plopped them into each glass. He then cut up an apple and placed it on a plate between them and the two of them began to eat. As they did Her mind wandered to Her conversation with Mary Mack.

She attempted to listen to Her mother's telephone conversation at the same time, which seemed to be going something like this. "Yes... but I cannot explain why I just need to see you... Please, I know... Yes of course... I know it's difficult... I do understand... Yes I know what was said... I do know... I appreciate that of course... Things have changed... Yes... I might need your help... No I don't only call when I need you... Yes... I do feel the same way... you have to try to understand how this would look for me... Yes of course... No it is not easy for me... Because I have two other people to consider... I am not the one being selfish... I really think that we should discuss this in person... yes of course... I have missed you too... I know... I can't make any promises... because I don't know how my life is going to look tomorrow... yes, I understand if you need to walk away... eight o'clock? ... thank you." Madam replaced the receiver and looked at her two children sitting at the counter on bar stools eating a snack. Lupita was still frantically searching for something that was still of mystery to the children.

"Hello, Lovelies!" She embraced the two of them and kissed them both on the top of their heads.

"Hey, Mom, you forgot to tidy up today." Her brother made a joke to lighten the mood.

"Ha ha! Yes, well, Lupita is helping me to look for your passports and visas, it seems that they have disappeared. Have either of you seen them?"

The two children looked at each other, they knew that their mother hid important documents, like passports and immigration papers. But they didn't know where. She spoke first. "I haven't seen them, Mom, since we went to Disneyland."

Her brother spoke next. "Me neither, I haven't seen them, what do you think happened to them?" Just as he finished his sentence a Federal Agent emerged from the bathroom. Both children froze. The spurs on his boots jingled as he moved across the floor towards them. His tan pants were still crisp, with a seam pressed straight down the front of the leg, which had held despite the humidity. He had long since removed his hat, but had a ring around his short dark hair where the hat had been sitting earlier in the day. He smiled as he took the third bar stool next to the children.

"Hola, how are you doing?" He attempted to be friendly, but his ominous presence instilled nothing but fear. The children reacted out of respect.

'Hello, Sir, How are you?" Her brother was more comfortable than She was with these types of things.

"It's been a crazy sort of day, listen how do you feel about ice cream? Would you like to go for an ice cream with your nanny?" Both of the children looked at each other and then looked at Lupita. All three of them knew that they were being cleared from the room. "Sure. We can go for an ice cream." Lupita was quick to answer. "A break would be good for me anyway."

The Agent looked at Madam after the three had moved through the door and down the steps. "We need to call your husband again, Madam, sooner or later he's going to answer."

She nodded. "Sure."

"Do you know what you are going to say?"

"I think so yes."

CHAPTER 64

Juan dressed appropriately for the occasion in khaki shorts, sneakers and an old blue T-shirt from the island of Maui that said Maui Surf Runner. The T-shirt was worn and faded, with small holes in the arm pit.

He felt oddly out of sorts in these types of clothing but alas he agreed that he should not draw undue attention to himself on this trip. His hair was pulled back into a neat loose pony tail, his beard left loose, hanging surf-style in front of his T-shirt, unkempt and mangy-looking. His hands were dirty, and calloused like those of someone who had been working long hard hours. He wrapped an old bandana around his forehead, and grabbed an old knapsack filled with junk for his added pleasure.

Brownsville is located on the southern most tip of Texas on the northern bank of the Rio Grande. It's not a particularly pretty town, but its popularity soared with the NAFTA agreement introduced in 1994, due to its location, bordering Matamoras Mexico. The close proximity of Brownsville to Matamoras enables the transport of goods to and fro. Brownsville has one of the highest poverty rates of any urban center in the United States. Drug wars, and violent crimes were becoming more and more prevelant with the trafficking of weapons, drugs and humans occurring daily. The Brownsville, Matamoras border crossing serves as one of the largest points of entry into the United States for goods smuggled illegally.

Juan was fully prepared for his adventure and was prepped and informed of what lay ahead. He would be in and out. His package would be placed, and he would deliver the goods as planned. Without being seen or heard, as usual.

He moved swiftly through the crowded street, towards the area which appeared to him to be heavily guarded. He placed his hand on his knapsack, ensuring that he had the package in place. He continued to walk towards the area at the border crossing where all of the people were lined up. Those who were on foot waited in long line-ups, for what looked like an entire day to cross into the United States. Juan didn't have that much time. He glanced at the Timex watch that he had put on his wrist, he estimated that he had no more than three hours to make the crossing and contact his mark.

He walked past the line-up of waiting individuals towards the gates that designated the boundary between the United States and Mexico. He ignored the occasional grunts and "Hey, Mother Fucker, who do you think you are? You think you are just moving to the front of the line, mother fucker?"

He didn't *think* he was moving to the front of the line, he *knew* that he was moving to the front of the line. The difference between himself and the poor shit that had actually asked him who he thought he was, was that Juan *was* moving to the front of the line. Well,… that was one of the things that was different. The other things that were different were not visible to the naked eye, and were not likely to be discussed by Juan or any other warrior of God.

He found himself feeling sorry for these people, in many ways. But he didn't have the time, nor the agenda for it today. And so he trudged on. Ignoring the grunts, ignoring the "hey, Mother Fuckers," and just moving ahead. He was here after all to complete something, something that was sensitive and necessary.

Juan approached the immigration gate and stopped. The officer behind the glass waved him towards the window. "Next, siguiente, next please."

Juan approached the window. "Your Passport please, Sir."

Juan placed his paperwork on the countertop. In actuality he had never looked at it. It had been provided to him in his debriefing, he trusted that everything was in order. "Thank you, Sir, what is the nature of your visit to our country?"

"Personal, I will be visiting a friend."

"I see, and for how long will you be staying in Brownsville, Sir?"

"Oh, just for the day today, then I will be returning, with my friend. For certain tonight, we will be returning to Mexico."

"Is your friend American, Sir? Or Mexican national?"

"Canadian actually, lovely guy. You would like him I'm sure." Juan smiled at the agent behind the glass who stamped his passport.

"Thank you, Sir, have a nice day. Please be aware of your daily exemptions if you plan on returning to Mexico today."

"Thank you so much, and you too, have a lovely day, God Bless you." Juan grabbed his paperwork and moved through the gates and into the United States. He looked again at his watch and mentally noted the time it would take him to make it to the location to which his mark would be found, and the amount of time it would take them to make the return. He had to pick up the pace if he was to make the connection without being noticed.

Juan Maria de Salvatierra was uncomfortable in his shorts and T-shirt, he wasn't accustomed to such restricting fabrics. He found them tight on his limbs, he felt constrained, somewhat controlled and he didn't like it. He much preferred his own robes. The freedom of movement that came from them was comforting to him. He liked the air flow that was possible because of the open concept, he favoured the soft linen fabric that had been washed a million times. He felt free, he felt liberated. These Khakis were just not his thing.

He walked the streets of Brownsville towards his destination swiftly. He had memorized the most direct route, and was walking at a pace that could win him a place on any Olympic team. His method of movement was not traditional, dodging in and out of crowds, avoiding strollers and old ladies with walkers. He didn't wait for cross lights and couldn't be bothered to step to the right, easing the right of way to on comers. He couldn't risk his clock running out, his time was limited and his plan was in motion.

The bar was dark on the front, painted concrete and brick walls flanked the edge of the bank next door a sharp contrast to the dimly lit saloon. The neon light in the front said 'open' but the lack of customers inside suggested otherwise. Juan pulled on the door and moved through it, as though he was stepping back in time. Peanut shells and dust covered the old hardwood flooring. Last night's beer spills and whisky had dried into crusty puddles of hard sticky memories on the floor. Each one just a faded dried-up puddle, of last night's laughter and sloppy sexual advancements.

Juan looked around the room for his mark, and saw him sitting with a woman at a booth in the back of the bar near the door to the restrooms. The woman appeared to be much younger than Juan had expected.

Juan stopped at the bar and took a moment to regroup. He had been anticipating a female somewhat closer in age to Madam. This one was young, teetering on adulthood. His memory was now photographic, a benefit to his level of security. He scanned through the documents that he had seen in his debriefing. Flashing them through his mind, for quick reference. He pulled at his khakis, readjusting them once again, longing for his more comfortable robes.

He took his knapsack from his back and placed it into his hand; and moved towards the table where they sat, laughing, and drinking margaritas.

"Good Afternoon, may I join you?" He interrupted their conversation without hesitation, and slid into the booth across from his mark and beside the young girlfriend.

Madam's husband looked at Juan. "Do I know you?"

Juan took the margarita from the paper bar coaster in front of the young woman now seated next to him, that read "Brownsville or Bust". "I don't believe you have had the pleasure yet no." Juan reached his hand across the table. "Name's Bruce, Bruce Banner."

Madam's husband looked at Juan and raised his eyebrows. He fancied himself intelligent, but had no formal secondary education. His high school had been completed by bribing teachers and paying off other students for written assignments. "Sounds familiar but I just can't place you."

Juan smiled. "Well, I'm quite sure we haven't met, I have a tendency to become sort of green with envy, and I am a bit of a Hulk of a guy, but I've been told that I have quite a temper, so let's just get down to business and make sure that no one here pisses me off okay?"

CHAPTER 65

She watched Her mother buzz around the residence, She watched the Federal Agents come and go and She tried to listen to phone conversations. She wasn't certain if Her mother had heard from Her father, but She hadn't spoken to him in days. Her last sighting of him had been in the hallway in the middle of the night, and She hadn't had a conversation with him since before then. She wondered when She might see him again.

She attempted to stay as focused as possible on Her school work, Her mother had made arrangements for both She and Her brother to work from home until things settled down. She wasn't sure why exactly, but She was content to make anyone happy that supported not going to school. She didn't enjoy it much, and although the new school was an improvement over the last one, She still didn't fit in. The other children treated Her like an outsider, Her hair was different, Her skin was a different colour, Her accent was different. She was different.

Lupita continued to be as loving and as comforting as always, but now the poor woman was making lunch and sometimes dinner for the Federal Agents as well as for the family. The house maid was busy cleaning and re-organizing the house after Madam and Lupita had torn it apart looking for the passports. She hadn't heard much more about that and decided that the best thing to do was ask. And so as soon as Her mother returned to the residence, She was going to ask her if she had found them.

She grabbed a book, and began to read, She could think of no better way to pass the time than to escape into something that had been cleverly executed to deceive and please the mind. While She read she could also listen to what was going on, but not appear to be eavesdropping.

One of the federal agents kept talking about a prosecutor, and about fleeing the country. She couldn't make out what it was exactly that he was saying because he spoke in partial sentences. She also overheard two of the agents discussing Her mother and her financial situation; the funds that had been pinched from her accounts would never be recovered, and now that they knew that he had mortgaged her home as well, he probably would never return. Why would he?...

"If I were him I would run, run like the wind. She has a right to want to cut his fucking nuts off, that's a lot of money he took from her."

The second officer was sipping on a coffee that Lupita had prepared for them. "Yep, yep it is. How do you think she made so much money anyway? Just from her restaurant you think?"

"I don't know. Maybe she had money to begin with. Maybe she has a sugar daddy on the side. Maybe she is what everybody says, and she's just a really hard-working smart lady. I can't find anyone in town with anything bad to say about her. Although there are some women who say she's made of stone, could be jealousy though, and stone is what? Just durable right? Tough, it can weather the storm, and lasts forever? The husband?, He's a different story."

Still sipping his coffee, the second agent commented, "Yeah, same thing I found. She goes to Church, she is kind to her employees, pays her taxes, tips at the salon. Never late on payments at the dance studio or the school, and she pays everything. Him, he owes money to just about every guy in town, and people hate him. Talks too much, always has a piece on the side, always borrowing money, lies like the sidewalk. Typical asshole."

"You talk to the nanny? She sees everything I bet. Or the kids, are we allowed to talk to the kids?"

"The nanny? what's the point? She's not talking. Loyal. She won't say a word about anything unless Madam gives her the thumbs up. Fucking waste of our time. The kids…" He paused before he continued. "I don't think the guy knows his kids. Or maybe the kids don't know their father. Whichever, I think if you ask the boy what his father does, he would be hard-pressed to answer."

"And the little one, what do you think? How old is she?"

"I think she's maybe six or seven, just a little thing too, tiny I mean. Look at her." He nudged his head towards where she was sitting with her book up. She was careful to turn the pages so that they wouldn't know that She was listening. "Smart too, probably like her mother. Can't talk to Her, too young and there's no way that She knows anything anyway."

She carefully placed Her open book on Her knee and swallowed hard. Her mouth was sticky dry. Her tongue felt tight at the back of her throat like She had never had anything to drink. She wanted one, She was parched, but she wanted to talk more than She wanted a beverage.

"I have seen lots of things."

Both agents looked at each other and then at Her, sitting quietly in the room next to where they were sitting. They had assumed that no one was listening. They were sadly mistaken though as what She had to share was pivotal in their investigation.

The coffee table in front of Her had a stack of magazines,

and a vase which was filled with roses, red roses. "See those roses in the vase? My father sent them to my mother. He sends her flowers when he is angry. They came this morning. That means that he knows that she has been bad. He knows that she has done something wrong. She gets the flowers and then she will suffer later. He doesn't always treat her nice. No one knows this. You mustn't tell."

The agents got up from the kitchen bar, and moved into the living room area where She sat. "What else can you tell us? How do you know about the flowers?"

She sighed. "The flowers were delivered this morning, first thing. That means that he's known, that she did something wrong since yesterday, perhaps longer. I could tell you what ever you need to know. If it will help my mother."

"Okay so the flowers come, which is a signal that he is on to her? Does he send a card?" The agents were taking notes.

"He doesn't need to send a card. It's between the two of them. She knows what it means."

The second of the two agents, scratched his head. "Where do you think your father is now?"

"I think that my father is exactly where my mother told you that he is. This is not about you, or the prosecutor, whatever his name is. This is about my father and what his next move is going to be. Trust me, he isn't dumb like you think, he just doesn't care."

"So he's in Brownsville then? In Texas?"

"If that is what Mommy told you then yes, that is where he is. She doesn't lie, to anyone, ever. She says that it's just easier to tell the truth because a lie always ends badly. The truth is sometimes difficult, but at least everyone knows what it is, there's no hidden surprise. Lies are just not so. And besides God is always watching, He knows."

"Okay, so he's in Texas. What else do you know about your father? Can you tell us anything about his work? Or the people that he sees?"

"Well, you see, my father never talks about his work. And he doesn't have a place of work, like Mommy does. Like she has the restaurant, you know? So no I can't tell you a lot about his work, I can tell you the names of some men that call here. Sometimes I answer the phone when there is no one else around. I always write their names down, on paper, and their numbers. I would never forget, but I don't like to get into trouble. So if you write the message down, you know, then you don't even have to see the person, you can just leave the message for them. Like beside the bed or something. And then the person that you are leaving the message for can get it later. You understand?"

Both Agents were in shock. "You have names?"

She nodded and closed Her book. "Oh, yes, and I have a bit of a photographic memory, since the drowning incident, so I can tell you all of their phone numbers too. I never forget anything. Mommy says I'm like an elephant that way. Never forget."

"What drowning incident is that?" Neither one of the Agents had heard about a near-drowning incident. There was nothing in the file.

"Oh yes, well, it was rather unfortunate. I, well, we, my brother and I were at the beach with the nanny, not this nanny, no, not Lupita, I know you are going to ask, so I just thought I would answer that right away. And she wasn't watching me well enough. That's what Mommy said in the end. After it all happened. I wandered off into the water and then woosh, under I went. Seems kind of silly to be talking about that now."

The agents looked at each other again, and then at Her.

"And what happened to that nanny? After the incident? Obviously you were okay? You are here with us now, can you tell us a bit about what happened?"

"Well, after the incident Mommy had to tell her that she should probably find another job, and so she packed her things and then she left. But she never even said good bye to me. Which made me kind of upset actually, yeah, I was sad about that. So what happened? Well, I was in the water for too long, and under the water. And then I was lucky because a man that the nanny had been talking to, he was a stranger, like I had never seen him before; he pulled me out. And he gave me CPR and then an ambulance came and, well, the rest is kind of an old story."

"So let me get this straight, the nanny, she didn't do anything to help you?"

"Mmm no." She shook her head, and it appeared as though She was thinking, processing. "I'm not sure if she could swim, or maybe she didn't see me go into the water. I couldn't be certain. But most definitely she did not help me, no."

"And was there police involved? Do you remember, Sweet-heart? How long ago was this?"

"Well, yes there was police, lots of them, that's when we all met the Police Chief, his name is Chief Alvarez. He's really nice, it happened before Abraham kidnapped us, so maybe two years ago or more maybe I can't remember, but Mommy will know."

The second agent looked at the first as he spoke and opened his flip phone. "Get on the phone with Chief Alvarez and let's find out if there was a life insurance policy on the girl please. And if so I want to know who the beneficiary is, or was."

"Yep, I'm on it, boss." He moved out of the room to make a call.

"So let's talk about these names and phone numbers that you have been writing down."

She smiled up at him, hopeful that She was helping, and relieved that She had told the truth. She was sure that Her mother would be pleased with Her. And if not, well, She was pleased with Herself. She felt like She was doing the right thing. She didn't know why, but it felt good. And so She sat with him, and She shared the names, and the phone numbers of the businessmen who She had spoken to on the telephone. She filed this experience in her green box, it was a good experience; She felt She had grown. It was beneficial.

CHAPTER 66

Juan had completed his mission, he had finished the margarita that he stole from the girlfriend because he felt that she probably didn't need it anyway; and had set into motion the end game for his mark. At least it would be the last chapter in this book for the sorry-assed conman that deserved nothing less than what was coming his way. Juan didn't care either way what happened, but he knew that his own efforts today had been for the greater good. He had been well briefed and was cognizant of possible outcomes should he not complete his mission. Failure was not an option, not for Juan. She must be relocated, She must be extracted. Her plan was now in full motion. He marvelled at the power and might of God. He also questioned as he often did, why He had given the human free will. In the absence of such a condition, these types of interventions would not be necessary. But alas they were, and expertly executed free will enhanced God's plan. Interventions, on the other hand were pivotal and often seemed as though the human had simply had a change of heart, or had simply lost interest in their own desire. The Lord's warriors did the work on His behalf. The safety of Her depended on it, the future for the species depended on Her.

Juan revelled in the idea that for all of His effort and involvement, it often may not appear as though the help that had been requested by man was dispatched. All of the players in this particular game would feel as though they were being squeezed hard, and that the Lord had forsaken them. He chuckled to himself. "If they only knew, forgive them, Father, for they know not what they do."

Now Juan would sit back and watch the events as they unfolded. Give or take a few hours, he knew that calamity would occur the next day.

CHAPTER 67

Chief Alvarez's cell phone rang at two fifteen in the morning. He was startled, and took a moment to collect his thoughts. He had gone to meet Madam and had ended up being angry and disappointed that Madam had needed to cancel on him. He had been glad that she had called earlier in the day, and was anxious to see her. He had looked forward to their meeting at eight earlier that evening and so when she had called to cancel, he was disappointed, and angry with her. The phone sat on the nightstand next to the bed, its ring vibrated the handset close to the edge of the table, threatening to push over the edge and onto the hard tile floor.

Jorge rolled over and grabbed it, flipped up the cover and rubbed his eyes. The room was dark except for a beam of moonlight that penetrated through a split in the draperies, a result of his pure exhaustion.

"Bueno, hello, Alvarez." He was expecting the voice of his dispatcher, or one of his senior officers. At this time of night he would be needed only for an appearance at a murder scene. Any activity with drug cartel they usually saved for office hours in order to get better television and media coverage.

"Jorge." Madam's voice called to him.

"Darling? What is it?"

"He's on his way back, I thought I could get out of here before he got back into Mexico. But now? There's just no way. I don't know what to do now, and these Feds are on me like white on rice."

"I don't know what that means Madam, white on rice?"

"I mean I don't get to be alone, I think they believe that I am going to alert him to their investigation. I don't get even five minutes by myself. They monitor my phone calls and my appointments. Everything I'm doing they watch. The only reason I can call you now is because the agent has fallen asleep on the couch."

"Okay, first let's take a deep breath. Why do you have to leave? Why don't you stay in Mexico? You can take the children and go to my house in Vera Cruz for a while. Disappear. I will come with you. I need some time off anyway."

She took a breath and thought of the two of them together with her two children. It was an odd image, a mirage of sorts. An illusion obscured by so many obstacles, and impossibilities that she couldn't imagine how it could ever solidify. "It sounds lovely. I've never been to Vera Cruz."

"I grew up near there, my parents still live there, they look after my house for me. It's quite peaceful, very different from here, but I think you would love it. The surfing is fantastic; diving too. The kids would love the water. And the food is to die for, lots of fresh seafood and fish."

"It sounds great, I just don't want to promise anything at two in the morning, when my head is clouded with all of this stuff. I just wish the world would stop spinning. I can't believe some of the stuff that is happening, Jorge."

"I know. I understand."

"You do?"

"Of course. You must be really stressed. You have a lot on your plate."

"I think that's an under statement."

"To be fair, you could have avoided a lot of it."

"What do you mean by that? How could I have avoided any of this? Exactly? I'm not sure how you could think that this is my fault or any part of it could be my fault."

"I didn't say that it's your fault, I said that you could have avoided it. Two very different things. I know that it's not nice to hear, but someone has to say it. Look, you are brilliant, you have done so much for this city, for your children, and you have such a bright future. He has been taking advantage of you for too long and you have chosen to look the other way."

"How can you say that to me right now? I have been working my ass off for years and as of yesterday I am penniless. You get it? Jorge? I have nothing left. There is no money, so if you were thinking that I was going to be helping you out financially, forget about it. The Feds don't think that I will ever see my money again. It's gone. I might get a little if I can find a buyer for the restaurant, but from what they found today, it looks like he has borrowed against that too. And the house, which I paid for, he has taken out a mortgage against it. I don't know how he pulled it off, because I thought that I was being careful, everything is in my name. But he has managed to borrow against everything that I own. Everything that I have worked for, for so long, he has taken from me. And on top of all of that, he has involved himself with some pretty bad people doing some pretty illegal shit. So how am I at fault?"

Jorge threw back the sheets on the bed and stood to his feet, he was angry that she had taken this position, but empathetic to her situation. "First, I was never interested in your money. I don't care if you have two pesos or twenty million dollars. It never mattered to me. I do understand how bad this is, and I am sorry that you never understood how bad it was, that you are now caught in the middle of this terrible humiliating fiasco, and I am sorry that you never saw the person that you were married to earlier. Plenty of people did, and I am quite sure that there were plenty of people that tried to tell you. That doesn't help you today, and doesn't change the fact that you need to do something drastic. Me being involved is not going to be of any help what so ever. I can't be in the middle of this, the feds are starting to poke around. There's a lot of questions being asked, which is making me uncomfortable. So let's just take a break. You need to focus on yourself and your kids right now. And you need to co-operate with the feds on every level."

"So that's how this is going to be? And what are we taking a break from? A one-night fling? Jorge, we spent one crazy evening together, that's it. So what was that exactly? What are we taking a break from? What do you think this is?"

Jorge was angry and very hurt by her tone. "You called me, remember. What did you think this was?"

Madam took a breath, she looked out the window of her bedroom towards the ocean, a tear rolled down her cheek which she quickly wiped away with her free hand. "I made a mistake." She pressed 'end' and dropped her exhausted body onto the bed. Disappointment and despair overcame her. Her heart breaking in two, she vowed to save her children and herself, and to never let anything like this happen to her again.

CHAPTER 68

She was dreaming of bluebirds singing merrily and of rolling cotton fields as far as the eye could see. She ran through them, her skirt flowing behind, Her hair was long, loose and bouncing in the wind as She moved briskly. The birds sang to Her, a special song, written just for Her. She couldn't be certain though if they were in the field with Her. She stopped running, She held still, waiting, listening. She could hear a choking sound, the sound of breath catching, someone gasping. A dark cold feeling of wickedness surrounded Her. She stood ever so still in one spot in the cotton field where she had just been running, Her barefeet cool. The sun suddenly disappeared behind the clouds, leaving nothing but a charcoal sky. A cool gust of wind blew past Her, a soft and subtle voice cried out, "Help me, please, help me."

The wind continued to blow Her out of the cotton field, and into a lush green meadow. The meadow bed, surrounded by fir and spruce trees, was covered in a blanket of yellow day lilies and grass the colour of emeralds. It was fragrant, fresh and revitalizing; the air still cool and damp, She felt chilled. She wanted to pull Her sweater around Herself tighter, but she was wearing nothing on but Her nightgown. She thought it odd, that She would be out in the meadow without a sweater. Her mother would never allow it. She decided to lie down for a moment amongst the flowers and rest. She suddenly felt overwhelmed with fatigue.

She knelt down to place her hand on the green grass and it suddenly transformed to the white linen sheets that She normally slept on. She could smell the lavender on them, the fresh scent of cleanliness; crisp and inviting. She could hear Lupita in the kitchen making breakfast, her voice as she softly sang, the cling clang of the cups and saucers, sounds of the coffee pot brewing the perfect cup of java. She wanted desperately to get up but her legs felt so heavy. She thought perhaps She would take just a moment more to relax when the room suddenly filled with birds. Pelicans with gnashing beaks, and wild pigeons fluttered around Her head, squawking and flapping their wings. As though in an imprisoned frenzy they swarmed around Her. Distress embraced Her. She could hear the voice again, "Please, dear God, please help me."

She cocked Her head to the left, so as to hear more clearly. She was certain that She could hear choking, like someone was choking to death but her legs were so heavy and She was just so sleepy, and the birds were just everywhere in Her room. She didn't like birds. She lay still until the water surrounded Her completely. It felt warm, it was soothing and she began to feel more relaxed. There was a musician playing the harp; a piece of music that she had heard many times before, and She could see a man off in the distance. He seemed to be quite far from where She lay. She lifted Herself up on Her elbows so that she could call out to him; but no sound came. Still She could hear the choking. She looked to the left and to the right, there was no one around, it was just Her in the pool of blood. She was startled when She realized that the water was not water, but was the ruby-red liquid that everyone knew too well, thicker and heavier than water. She wanted to get Herself up but Her legs were as weighty as cement. Like two concrete pillars, securing Her place in an eternal blood bath. She was soaked in it. Her nightgown drenched, her hands and feet dripping. He was closer now. Oh! She was relieved that he was moving closer. She felt elated, excited that He was moving towards Her. She could see Him smiling, His outstretched hand reaching to Her. His hair was long, and he was beautiful. He moved right up to where She was laying in the water. "Hello."

"Hello." She was honoured to be in His presence.

"Do you know who I am?"

"Yes, of course, you are Jesus." His presence was calming, soothing and exuded tranquility. His face void of scars or markings, his eyes icy blue and clear like the ocean.

"Yes, you must get up now. Your mother needs you. Go, lie with her and I will do the rest."

She rose from where She was laying in Her bed and moved down the hallway to Her mother's bedroom. She placed Her hand on the doorknob and turned it slightly as She pushed. She could hear Her mother choking. Her breath laboured. She lay down next to her, placing Her head on Her mother's shoulder. Her hands lay softly on her mothers chest. Immediately her mother caught her breath. She opened her eyes to look at her young daughter. She took a moment to slow the inhale of air, and the deep exhale of appreciated breath.

"What are you doing here, honey?"

"I came for you."

Her mother took a few breaths, her heartbeat slowing, her pulse decreasing slightly, a mild sweat building on her torso. "How did you know? How did you know to come?"

"Jesus woke me. He said you needed me. That I just needed to be with you, he said he would do the rest."

Her mother took a few intense breaths, and swallowed deeply, her throat was tight, it had been restricted and dry she needed more air. She stroked the head of her young girl.

"Thank you. It felt like someone was choking me to death. I couldn't catch my breath. And I had the weirdest dream."

She responded, "I was having a dream too, and Jesus came, I could hear a noise in my dream like someone was choking, and he said that you needed me. He told me to come to you, to lie with you. He is here too, Mommy."

Madam pulled the sheet up to her chin. "Oh dear, well, thank you, thank you, my sweet, and thank you, Jesus." She swallowed hard as she held the small figure beside her.

"He says you're welcome. And He says He loves you. He says you think no one will ever will, but He does now and forever more. Night, Mommy." She cuddled with Her mother, she felt warm and soft. She smelled of roses and sweet vanilla. She placed the moment in her Pink Box. Her happy feel good box. Tucked away in her safe place, where She could use it later, or just look at it if She wanted to.

Madam lay quietly with her child in her arms. The youngster slept soundly while she prayed in gratitude. A million thanks, and just as many offerings to help others, she prayed earnestly. Eventually sleep overcame her weary body and she rested.

CHAPTER 69

It was before dawn that he returned to the residence. He snuck onto the property unnoticed. There were no feds, no policemen, no one watching the property. The house was dark, the doors locked tight. He slid his key into the lock and opened the door. It creaked as it swung open, the vast expanse of the living area empty. Void of laughter, or song, his heart was heavy, but he knew what he had to do.

He moved to the doorway of the master bedroom, which was slightly ajar. He peeked in, having a quick look at the sleeping bodies of his wife and daughter. He turned and moved down the hallway to his son's room, opened the door and moved into the room which was tidy, and organized. Hot wheels cars were neatly lined up on the carpet, his blocks stacked and set aside, out of the way. The boy slept soundly, his blond hair hot, and damp with sweat.

He turned around and walked back to the living area. He threw himself down on the couch and pulled a blanket up over his chilled and tired body. He was disappointed and alarmed at how quickly things had unravelled. His thoughts drifted to the stranger who had approached him in the bar in Brownsville. He had followed the instructions that had been given, because frankly he was scared not to. His plan had been to disappear at this point, he had enough money stashed away to last many lifetimes, but now he had no choice but to return here. In the end it would be better anyway. He just wasn't sure what to do with the knapsack.

CHAPTER 70

She woke before her mother. She carefully pushed back the covers and got out of the bed. The marble floors felt cool on her tiny feet as she tiptoed to the doorway. She snuck through the door once she had opened it, surprised at how hungry she felt. She hoped that Lupita was already awake and ready to make some tasty breakfast.

She moved out of the hallway and into the living area, and was shocked to see her father on the couch where the federal agent had been sleeping for days. She moved closer, careful not to wake him from his slumber. She looked around the room for signs of another adult and saw none. She had begun to step back when he opened his eyes wide.

She gasped, alarmed by his presence and by how alert he was. He grabbed her wrist. "How's my baby?"

She took another breath, unsure of how much he knew about Her deception. She realized that what She had done in telling the agents was the right thing to do, but nonetheless it was in deceit of her relationship with him that She did so. "Fine, Daddy."

"Why were you sleeping with your mother?"

"Oh, I had a bad dream, that's all." She looked around for an escape but saw nothing. Her heart was pounding in her chest, She felt the need to pee. "Daddy, I need to use the bathroom."

"Hang on there, didn't you miss your dad? It feels like I've been gone forever. Come sit with me here." He looked different to Her, he was ragged, he hadn't shaved in days, his clothes were wrinkled.

"Daddy, it's just that I have to go pee. I'll be right back." She ran to Her room and closed the door. She went into the bathroom and sat on the toilet.

"Mary Mack, if you are here, help me out please. I really need you." She finished and washed her hands. She was reluctant to return to the living room, and so decided to get herself dressed while She waited for Lupita to rise.

Within a few minutes She could hear her mother up, and in her own bathroom. Her father needed to be dealt with. She knew that her mother would take care of things, She was relieved to know that Her mother would deal with it. Her mother always dealt with things. She liked that about her. Her mother wasn't afraid.

As She pulled some shorts and a T-shirt on She could hear her mother's bedroom door open, and then her footsteps as she walked down the hallway towards the living room. She wanted to shout out to her "He's in there waiting for you, go back and lock the bedroom door." But instead She kept quiet, kneeling on the floor, close to the door so that She would be able to hear what they were saying.

She heard him stand, push back the sofa a little bit. He threw something on the coffee table, his cell phone maybe. "Madam, I am back."

"Well, look what the cat's dragged in." She was surprised to see him. Madam had really thought he would disappear this time. Maybe to an island somewhere in the South Pacific, somewhere in the vicinity of Tonga or Niue, a speck in the ocean, uninhabited, uncivilized. A place where he could essentially vanish and cease to hurt people, cease to hurt her, cease to impact the lives of her children.

"Did you think I wouldn't come back?"

"Let's just say that there is a part of me that may have been hopeful. What are you doing here?"

"This is my home, I decided to come back, to be where I am most comfortable, to see my children and my wife. Why are you so surprised to see me? Hmm? Have you been up to something that you shouldn't have been?" He looked at her sceptical, his eyebrows were raised slightly, his lips quivered slightly as he spoke; she wondered what he knew.

"What have I been up to? That is an interesting question. Well, let's see, I have been to the bank, I had to have a meeting with the bank manager, I tried to make a simple withdrawal, but couldn't, it seemed that all of the money in my personal and business accounts and of course, our joint account, had been transferred out, or withdrawn. Then I had a meeting with my attorney, about a possible share sale of my restaurant to an investor, and it seemed that my business has been mortgaged to the hilt. So then we looked into the house, this exact one, that we are standing in; and found out that this property too, has been mortgaged by you. And you have not been making any of your payments... Tsk tsk."

"All lies, none of that is true. It's a simple misunderstanding. I had to make some adjustments in order to get my business off the ground, you understand. But it was never my intent to hurt you in any way." He waited for her to respond.

"Bullshit. You're a liar." She turned to walk away from him and he grabbed her. He pulled her back by the arm to where he was standing.

He reached down and into the knapsack, pulled out a black-and-white photograph of her, with Chief Alvarez. He was startled, but thrust it at her regardless. "And just what do you think of this? You bitch? How long has this been going on? How long have you been hanging with the chief of police? Hey? Did you really think I wouldn't find out? Did you think it was okay to just fuck him because he's a big important man in town? Hmmm?"

"Kiss my ass, you hypocrite. How dare you ask me anything about my personal life. You and I both know we had an arrangement, it was simple, and it was just fine until you stole my money. Now that your little espionage is out in the open you think you can make a case out of my affairs?"

He pushed his hands through his hair, inhaling deeply. "The arrangement was that I could do what I wanted and you would not embarrass me. This is what? Love? You are in love with the police chief? Hey? You are a joke, you're pathetic."

"Oh, so you thought that I would just sit back and do nothing while you run around with a new whore every week? Our deal was not that I wouldn't embarrass you, but that I wouldn't make your escapades public. But I will. I will make it very, very public. I don't care any more who knows. Why don't we call your boss right now? I bet he would love to hear from me again? He was the one that wanted you to behave right? I should have let him kill you back then, years ago when you screwed up, you fucking coward."

"Go ahead, call him! How do you think that made me feel? My fucking boss too? I have to listen to him rave about you? Madam this and Madam that; you make me sick. Everyone thinks you're so fucking spectacular, but I know the truth. You're just plain, madam underneath everything. Under the dresses and the fancy talk. You're just the same plain jane, scared and uninteresting, boring girl I salvaged from the rubble. You are just a piece of shit."

She pulled her arm out of his grip and moved towards the

kitchen, he threw his cell phone at her and missed, but it smashed into a hundred and one little pieces as it connected harshly with the wall. She turned and looked at him. "I cannot endure another week, nor another month, or year. This is not going to get better, we cannot fix this. I cannot be around you."

She returned to the bedroom, sat on the bed for a moment and then picked up her cell phone. She flipped open the lid and dialled the all-too familiar number.

"Dad, it's time, we need to come home."

"Honey, where are you?" Her father was at his office, his suit jacket hanging neatly on a hook behind the door, his tie sharp, eccentric and fashionable. His desk organized for the day, his pen and paper ready. He placed his reading glasses on the bridge of his nose and listened.

"Still here, at the house; but we need out, I can't talk long, Dad, the kids' passports are here but their visas are missing. I have looked everywhere."

"Just leave, so what if they can't go back, who cares now?"

"No, Dad, listen; immigration won't let them leave without surrendering their visas. So I could leave but they would have to stay. I can't let that happen. I don't know what to do. He must have destroyed the visas. Or something, I think he knew that I was on the verge of leaving him. The Feds are everywhere I go, I don't get two minutes alone, I can't just walk over to the immigration building, the Feds might figure out that I am planning an escape. They can't know that I'm leaving the country. "

"No of course not. I will take care of it. Listen, it's eight thirty here, so early for you? Seven thirty?"

She wiped her nose. Something about talking to her Dad brought the emotions to the surface. "Yeah, the sun is just coming up."

"Okay, I will call you when I have everything arranged, it might take me a couple of hours. I will get the visas done. When I call it will be quick. Be ready. I will book you on Continental airlines. For three only; not four. Chat soon."

"I love you, Dad, just in case." She smiled at the sound of his voice.

"It's going to be fine. We will get you home. Wait for my call. And I love you too, Princess."

She hung up and moved into the bathroom and turned on the shower. She dropped her nightgown on the floor and looked at herself in the mirror as she waited for the water to heat up. She noticed something on her neck and moved closer to the mirror. She tilted her head back slightly and pulled her hair to the side. On her neck were bruises deep and dark in the shape of two hands on either side of her throat as though someone had been choking her.

CHAPTER 71

Juan watched the residence from across the street, he was becoming more comfortable in the khakis and T-shirt, and had decided that perhaps he would try to wear them more often. It was abnormal for a gentleman of his age to adorn such casual clothing, but the feeling was growing on him, and he had to admit that he liked fitting in to the crowd a little bit better.

Lights were coming on inside, and so he knew that it was go time. He was prepared now to sit and to wait, and do nothing until further instructions came. He wished that he had brought a book to read. He had heard that the Holy Bible had been rewritten and he thought it might be an endeavour that he would greatly enjoy.

He sat and he watched, and he waited.

CHAPTER 72

She sat behind the door of her bedroom, holding hands with Mary Mack. She had heard the entire conversation and although She found it engaging to listen to adults, this was more than She had been prepared for.

Mary caressed her hands and whispered in her ear. "Don't worry, it will all be just fine. Everything is happening according to plan."

"I'm scared, Mary Mack. Mommy has never used those words before and her voice was so angry." Her tears came fast and fluid. She held onto her friend tightly, She was uncomfortable in situations that were uncertain, She didn't like change, and She didn't particularly like that Mary Mack could only be around when there was no one else there.

"She's not angry with you though, don't worry about that. She loves you very much. And, your Dad loves you too, he just doesn't know how to express it the same way. One day you will experience things very differently, like I said, change is coming. None of this is your fault. You must remember that always."

The two girls sat together in silence, waiting for Lupita to wake. Waiting for change to come. She hoped that it would come quickly. She prayed that Mary Mack would stay with her.

CHAPTER 73

He had been told by the stranger only to reach into the knapsack when he felt desperate. When he felt that he really needed help. He had done exactly that and he had pulled out a photograph of his wife with the police chief. He was also told not to look inside of the knapsack when he wasn't in a desperate situation, but he really needed to see what was inside. He really wanted to see what was there because it was heavy. He sat on the sofa alone. The children were in their rooms, Madam was in the bathroom, he could hear the shower running. He held the bag in his hands and felt the weight of it on his thighs. He imagined that it had to weigh close to fifty pounds. And yet it was quite small. He ran his fingers over the zipper on the front, and debated his need to open it. He could rationalize a feeling of desperation if need be. With his fingers on the zipper pull, he rewound his conversation with the stranger in his mind, looking for clues as to whether or not there was a rational explanation for what he had pulled from the bag. The stranger's tone had had seriousness to it. He played it again. And again, over and over in his mind, and even though he had been specifically told not to open the bag, he couldn't help himself.

He placed his hand firmly on the zipper and pulled it back, the flap falling open, the contents of the bag exposed. He sat in awe as he looked inside. He reached his hand into the opening, his heart beating a little faster. He could hear the sound of the shower running down the hall and the sound of cars passing by on the street below the residence.

He had put the black-and-white photograph of Madam and the Police Chief back inside the bag, he knew that he had; he was certain of it. And yet the bag that was so heavy, that he had estimated weighed close to fifty pounds, was completely empty. Not even the photograph that he had returned to the bag himself was in it. He was quite taken back, and quite disappointed now that he had actually opened it. Shame over came him. He was incapable of following instruction. He was everything that she said and more. He was pathetic. Even he himself knew it.

CHAPTER 74

Juan moved down the street towards the corner store. Grief filled his heart. He was always so hopeful that humans would follow instructions; that men would learn to listen to advice, and actually act on it. Now things would unfold very differently. He was saddened by the potential of what may happen. No one knew, not even Juan what the plan would now be. Each player made choices, as in a game of chess, and the next move was although calculated ahead of time; executed dependent on each player's choice.

He entered the store and after greeting the shopkeeper, took one of the small wicker baskets and placed a few mangos in it. He moved to the counter and set down his fruit, making eye contact with the lady who had struggled all her life. Rosa had never suffered any significant tragedy, but daily tasks and a mundane life were difficult for her. Her husband was a womanizing heavy drinker, her children were in and out of trouble with the law. Her corner store, provided the necessities of life but never more than the very minimum. She longed for a beautiful dress, or a nice new pair of sandals. She only dreamt of having her hair done at a salon, or of having her nails painted with pretty colours. She found peace in the people that came into her store, the smiles they brought her, the stories of grandeur, the tales of triumph and gratitude. She found sanity in her small area, and she found love in the faces of those who crossed her path each day.

Juan's gaze was profoundly severe, his eyes penetrating through the iris of each of her lenses and to her very soul. He saw the sadness, and he also saw the greatness in her. He reached into his pocket for pesos to pay her for the mangos. When he pulled his hand from the pocket of his shorts, he had nothing more than an american one-hundred-dollar bill. Her eyes grew wide.

"I'm so very sorry, Sir, but the mangos come to only ten pesos. That's less than one dollar. Do you have change? I don't think that I can change that bill, it's just far too large."

"I'm so very sorry, Ma'am, I don't have anything smaller, but I would very much like to buy these mangos. They look very lovely, I'm betting that you grow them on your own trees? How about if I give you the hundred, and you keep the change? You can do with it, what you please, maybe get something for yourself."

She shook her head. "I couldn't possibly, that's too much. I wouldn't be able to ever repay you."

Juan picked up the fruit, still in the basket. "Tell you what, if you have a wonderful day; then you have already repaid me. I'm sure you will find something excellent to do with that hundred, do some good in this world." He turned and started to the door. As he did he heard her folding the bill and placing it in the front pocket of her dress, which was in need of repair. He turned back to her and smiled. "Adios."

She held up her hand and called back at him. "Gracias, have a great day, God bless you."

Juan's sad heart began to feel right again as he approached the residence. *If she only knew.* He walked up the driveway towards the long steps into the entrance of the residence and noted all of the beautiful landscaping that had been done. He thought it really quite spectacular; especially for a property so central; in the heart of the central core most homes were surrounded by concrete and void of any signs of natural life.

As he stood at the wooden front door, he took a moment to gather his thoughts. He pondered the risk of Madam recognizing him and quickly discarded the idea. With his change of clothing, and his hair in a ponytail the chances were minimal, and he was willing to take the risk.

He knocked using the large brass ring plated to the centre of the door.

He could hear foot steps moving in the direction of the front entry.

"I'm almost there, hang on to your hat." Lupita was shuffling as fast as she could through the foyer to the front door. It was constructed one solid piece of wood, it was heavy and took effort to open it.

Lupita swung the door open using both hands, and met him face to face. "Good Morning.

Juan was startled by the woman's beauty. She looked so much younger than her years. And her heart was filled with joy. It showed abundantly on her face. "Good Morning, Senora, I am selling mangos this morning, and I wondered if the lady of the house might be interested in sampling some of these great fruit."

"You're selling mangos? Here? At the door? Normally I go to the market for these, you seem familiar to me. Your face seems familiar."

"We have never met. It would be impossible. I'm not from around here."

Lupita thought about the complexity of the situation in the house that morning; and wondered if inviting a stranger in for a mango sampling was a good idea. "Please come in, Madam will be out in a moment, I will let her know that you are here.

Don't leave the foyer please. Visitors do not come into the main area of the house."

"Of course." Juan waited for her to move around the corner and then he walked into the living area. He knew that he was trudging dangerously, that he had overstepped his mission. If he messed things up, he didn't know what would happen. He could hear little-girl giggles from behind a door down the hallway. And he could hear the sound of a little boy playing behind another. On the sofa in the middle of the room he could see him sitting. The knapsack in his lap.

"Morning." Juan cleared his throat.

He turned and saw him standing across the room. Madam's husband didn't get up from the sofa. "You are really fast, man."

"Yeah, I warned you. That's how we work." Juan rocked on his heels. His hands clasped together.

"I just couldn't help myself. I had to do it."

"You could have helped yourself, but you made a choice not to. You are weak, and you are a liar. You used the knapsack not in the way that you were instructed to do. You used it to harm another. It was given to you as a tool to help you. Your instincts however provoked a very negative consequence."

"The fucking knapsack is empty." He tossed the bag towards where Juan was standing.

"Yes, that bag is empty, and you were told not to ever look inside. You didn't listen."

"I never listen, *to anything*." He remained still, sitting in the same place on the sofa, he turned his head back towards the window. Gazing out at the ocean.

"Well, that is really a shame. You were given so many talents, and had such promise. And you blew it all. That however is not the issue today. Listen, we don't have much time, before she comes back." Juan tossed the bag back at him. "You can have one more shot. One more chance with the bag. Like I said before, the bag responds to the will of your heart. So if your intentions are driven by malice what you pull from the bag will have a negative impact. Get it? Figure it out, you dumb ass."

Lupita's heels clicked on the marble floor as she came down the long hallway. She caught Juan's gaze and said, "Madam will be right with you. Sir, I remember asking you to remain in the foyer. Please…" She guided him back to where he should wait. The foyer was a large square room with a small fountain in the centre of it. There were plants flanking one side; Peace Lilies, Palms and Anthuriums, windows and the grand wooden door on the other.

When she returned to the living area Lupita apologized to the husband of her boss who was sitting alone on the sofa. "My apologies, Sir, for the interruption."

He waved her off. "It's fine, don't worry about it. He's just someone I met yesterday."

Lupita stopped in her tracks. "No, I don't think so, he's not from around here. He's just a farmer selling his fruit. I think you must be mistaken."

"Nope, no mistake, and believe me, Lupita, you're right, he is not from around here. Not from fucking anywhere around here."

Madam entered the room then, the energy in the air was heavy with anguish and disappointment. "Morning, Lupita."

"Madam, there is a gentleman waiting in the foyer for you, he has some fruit to sell. I know you don't normally do that sort of thing, but he had really kind eyes, and I just couldn't say no."

Madam touched the shoulder of the nanny as she moved

towards the foyer. "It's fine, Lupita, thank you."

She moved down the hall and turned the corner to the foyer; she found an empty room. The door was closed and locked, on the floor a wicker basket with six fully ripened mangos.

CHAPTER 75

She decided with Mary Mack's assistance, that it was time to emerge from Her room. She was hungry and She had heard Lupita's voice so She knew that breakfast would be happening soon.

She cracked open the door and saw that Her father was still sitting in the living room, on the sofa, and had barely moved. She walked down the hallway towards Her brother's room without being noticed, and tapped softly on the door. She didn't want to draw attention to the fact that She was in fact moving about the house.

He cracked open the door. "Yes."

She whispered, "Let me in." She found him frustrating at times. But they were still siblings.

"What's the password?" He found amusement in games. He enjoyed that others became frustrated with his antics.

"I don't know what the password is but if you don't open the door I will tell everyone that you still sleep with a teddy bear." She pushed on the door just as he stepped back which allowed the door to swing freely, and Her to fall flat on her belly. She smacked Her elbow on the marble floor and winced. "Jerk."

He laughed, and wished that he would have had a camera to catch the look on Her face as the door let go, swinging open with all of Her weight behind it. "What's going on?"

"What's going on? Are you kidding me? Did you sleep

through World War Three?"

He shrugged. "I don't know what you are talking about."

"Okay, well, Dad and Mother had a huge fight, and Mother used swears. So she is really, really mad. I'm scared, it sounds like something big is happening but I don't know what it is."

"So what? What are you worried about?" He looked at Her nonchalantly.

"What am I worried about? I'm worried about a lot of things, and I am worried about what is happening to our family, aren't you? Doesn't it concern you that those federal agents have been here all week?" She poked him in the chest.

"Not really, look, why worry? Does it make it better? We can't do anything anyway. So relax, you know what this is? This is about faith. And if you have faith then you can just chill and know that everything is going to be okay. God never lets the birds go without food so why would he let any harm come to us? I feel like we are being cared for. I know that sounds dumb. But I think we are okay. It's going to be fine."

She wondered if he knew about Mary Mack. She was certain that he did not, and yet his words possessed the same assurances that she had been given by Mary. "Okay look Dad is here, we should go say hello."

"Yeah, I'm hungry anyway. Let's see what Lupita plans to cook up for breakfast.

The two children moved into the living room and threw themselves onto the sofa, one with their father and She on the other sofa. Her brother put his feet onto the coffee table and gave his Dad a hug. "Hey, Dad, how was your trip?"

"Fine, thanks for asking. It's nice that someone cares." He looked for his wife and made eye contact.

Her brother looked at the knapsack on his lap and touched it. "Hey, Dad, cool bag."

"Thanks, it's new." He pulled the bag away from the touch of his boy.

"Really? It doesn't look new, it looks really old." The boy was grabbing at the bag from across his father's chest.

"It's new to me. Leave it please." He took his free hand and forced the boy back onto the sofa. His movement was abrupt, and aggressive.

She spoke up. "Where are you going, Mommy?"

Madam was dressed and was putting shoes on. "I have to go to the restaurant for a few minutes and then I have a short meeting. Would you two like to come with me?" It was a rhetorical question. They would be fed breakfast and dressed, ready to go when she was ready. Lupita was already making food for them and coffee for Madam. "Lupita, I will need a moment with you please before I go to the restaurant."

Lupita adored her employer, but she too felt the winds of change. She had seen everything that had happened in the past thirty-six hours and although Madam hadn't shared all of the details, she knew that the story was much larger than any of them knew. Even the federal agents who seemed to have disappeared were in the dark about a lot of it. She fixed the breakfast for the children and silently prayed for safety, and for closure.

CHAPTER 76

Madam took the children and went to the restaurant. She posted a notice on the front door, stating that the business was temporarily closed for minor renovations. She left cheques for all of her employees, which with the past two days' revenues would just barely clear her business account.

The three of them then walked two blocks, to the offices of her attorney, where they climbed the long steps to the upper floor of the building, announced their arrival to the receptionist, sat in the lobby and waited. He finally emerged and motioned to her to come in to his office. He sat behind the desk, his hands neatly folded on top of a pile of paperwork.

"Madam, nice to see you. Sorry about the circumstances. I have all of the documents prepared as we discussed. I will take care of all of the incidentals that occur following your departure. I have everything here that you asked for, and I will ensure that everything is properly executed."

Madam held back her emotions, all the years of hard work, of labour and love that she had poured into her business to just hand the keys over to the bank and run. She felt terrible for her employees who would never see this change coming, and many of them would be angry with her. All of them would be out of work, and many of them had families of their own to care for, children to feed, she felt a sense of obligation, of responsibility and she felt horribly overwhelmed.

"Thank you, Jose, for doing all of this on such short notice.

I appreciate everything that you have taken the time to do for me."

Her attorney himself was having a hard time with his emotions and struggled to hold back tears. "When you leave, what will be left that we have not accounted for?"

"Just my car, which I own outright, you can sell that to clear up any taxes or bills that come up after I am gone. I will leave cash for the residence employees, which now, is just Lupita and the house maid. But I will pay them today and explain that I am leaving on an extended vacation. The house papers are here? In the pile?" She gestured at the pile of papers on his desk in front of him. The ones that she had been dreading coming to sign.

"Yes, today is Friday, so the bank should receive these on Monday, Tuesday at the very latest. As I explained to you yesterday, he hasn't paid the mortgage on the residence for months, it is already six months behind. The bank will be grateful that you are voluntarily handing back the deed to the property. And as far as the restaurant is concerned, he never made a payment. They will probably move in right away and sell off the equipment to cover off part of the loan, or perhaps they will sell it as is. Maybe to an investor who wants to purchase an operational, successful business." He noticed her discomfort. "I'm sorry."

"It's okay, it's not your fault, but it was mine, the restuaruant, the house, Jose, it was all mine, it was never the bank's to begin with. And it certainly wasn't his."

He frowned, and empathized with her situation. "I know, it's very difficult I am sure, and it is unfortunate that this has happened to you. I cannot at this time comment on how he managed to get all of this done, but he did. You are doing the right thing here. A couple of more months and the bank would take the house anyway. It will come back to haunt him, he will pay someday."

From deep within her soul Madam spoke. "Vengeance shall be mine, so sayeth the Lord." She signed the paperwork and stood. She now felt prepared to fully face the music. Her instincts told her that she wasn't going into this battle alone. She felt angry; but she felt strong. She was ready for change.

They left the offices of the attorney and moved down the street towards where they had parked the car. Both kids climbed into the backseat and buckled themselves in to their seatbelts.

She opened her flip phone and called the lead federal agent that was assigned to her. He answered on the first ring.

"Bueno, hello, Officer Mendez."

"Good Morning, Officer Mendez, Madam here."

"Madam, hello. I was just about to call you. We have had some new information come to light that I must discuss with you, and also we believe that you might be in serious danger. I am assigning extra officers to you and the children. They should be at the residence by noon."

Madam took a breath. "Thank you, I appreciate that. Do we need to meet in person or can we discuss on the phone? I am just near my restaurant, I have kind of a busy morning and I am not certain that I can get away until later."

"Madam, the gravity of what we have uncovered in the past twelve hours is staggering. I don't believe that we should discuss on the phone, but I do understand that you have a business to run. Look, it's nearly ten now, could we meet at your residence at say, noon? Would that give you enough time? I will escort my team to you then and brief everyone on site."

She manoeuvred her vehicle through traffic like a seasoned

taxi driver, she looked at her watch. Two hours. "I hope so yes. Thank you, Officer Mendez, Good Bye."

With Mendez and his team set in play she moved to her next call. She quickly dialled the number while sitting at a stop light. She had missed a call from her father while in the meeting with Jose, the attorney.

"Dad?"

"Hi, Honey, everything is ready, Continental Airlines twelve forty is your flight time. So just over two hours, two and a half to be exact; does that give you enough time?"

She swallowed hard. "Yes that's perfect. The visas, Dad?"

"Taken care of, you will need to be at the airport within ninety minutes, someone will meet you there; honey, just get yourself to the airport. You will have a layover in Houston, about three hours. It's the best I could do on such short notice."

"That's fine, Dad, thank you." She was crying. The children were looking at each other, wondering what was going on.

"See you tonight, baby."

"Dad, if this doesn't go well, I love you, and tell Mom that I love her too please."

Her father held on to the edge of his desk, he pushed his glasses up with his left hand and wiped his eyes. "It will be fine, you will be home soon."

She hung up and pulled the car over to the side of the road. She placed it into park and then turned around to face the children in the backseat.

"Look, I know this is crazy, but it's about to get crazier. So I need you guys to hang on tight okay. We are going to go on a little trip, for a while. To see Grandma and Grandpa. But you can't tell anyone okay, not even Lupita. You can talk to each other but that's it. When we get back to the house, things are going to be a little nutty, so I just need you to be strong, and know that I have your back. Okay? We are in this together." She lifted her fist and held it forward, towards them; waiting for one of them to fist pound her.

Her brother asked the question, that both of them had been waiting to ask for days. "What about Dad? Are we just leaving him here? I don't get it?"

She held onto the steering wheel with her left hand and reached her right towards him. He took her hand in his and stroked the back of it. She smiled, thinking what an odd gesture for such a young soul. "Well, your Dad has some things here that need to be taken care of. Those agents that have been around have been investigating a bunch of stuff and your Dad is going to help them with that. He can't leave until all of that is handled."

She looked at Her mother. "Are you and Daddy getting a divorce?"

Madam wasn't prepared for the question entirely, but didn't want to avoid it either. So she did her best. "We are going to have some time apart to see if things get better between us. But I can't say either way whether or not we will get a divorce. It's too early to tell."

She knew that her mother was lying, or at least not being fully truthful with them. She could smell it. Like one can smell bacon cooking or fresh cookies when they are in the oven, She could smell a lie. It was a fairly new thing for Her. She couldn't remember for how long She could smell such things, but She knew that She didn't like it. It made Her uncomfortable, it made Her anxious and it made Her upset.

"You don't have to lie, Mommy. We know the truth, I spent some time with the agents the other day, and I answered all of their questions."

Her mother was shocked that the agents had taken the time to speak with the children, especially without her knowledge. "What exactly did they ask you about?"

"Well, lots of things really, but they were very interested in Abraham, and remember that day that I nearly drowned, the day we met Police Chief Alvarez? They had lots of questions about that day too. I answered all of their questions the very best that I could."

Her mother looked at Her brother. "What about you, buddy? Did they ask you lots too?"

He shook his head. "Not as much, they asked more about Dad's travel schedule and when he comes and goes, stuff like that."

Her eyes got big. "Oh and I also told them all of the names of the men that call Daddy at home, well, the ones that called when I answered the phone. I was able to give them all of the phone numbers for them as well. I never really forget anything. Remember you said that, Mom?" She looked up at her mother for approval. Her mother nodded at Her and tried to smile.

Madam turned forward in her seat and looked out the window. This was getting really big now. Now even she was scared. If she had given them all of the names then it was possible that all of them knew about the investigation, which meant that her husband would too, which also meant that they would do whatever it took to cover up the mess. She figured that was what Agent Mendez was talking about when he said the "gravity of what we have uncovered is staggering."

She put the car into first gear, let the clutch out, and eased forward. Not one hundred percent certain what would happen next. She needed to return to the residence to pick up the passports, and to give Lupita her paycheque. She also needed to grab a couple of things. Her gut was telling her not to bother, but she couldn't travel without the passports. She wished now that she had grabbed them in the morning. She also really needed a cigarette.

The car raced up the hill towards the residence. She decided to stop at the corner store for some Marlboros. She pulled the car up front and she grabbed her purse and got out. She smiled at the kids as she walked into the store.

"Good Afternoon, Madam, how are you?"

She smiled at her neighbour. "I'm good, how have you been?"

"Really well thank you, Raul is doing better." She had shared the secrets of her marriage with Madam one afternoon when she had been seriously upset. Madam had come in for cigarettes and had listened, and had never repeated anything. She thought of Madam as a friend even though they didn't spend a lot of time together, and they didn't see each other very often.

"That's great, Rosa, I'm so glad for you. I hope that he can keep things on an even keel. It will be better for everyone, especially you and the children."

She agreed with Madam, and couldn't help but feel grateful for the support. "Indeed, what can I get for you today? Marlboros?"

"Yes thank you, you know me too well." Madam reached into her purse to look for her wallet. She felt around and found nothing. Her cosmetic bag, sunglass case, keys for the car, some Kleenex. No wallet. "Oh my, I seem to have misplaced my wallet." The pressure of everything came to a head, and Madam crumbled. Tears started to pour down her cheeks, in seconds she was sobbing.

"Madam, what is it? What can I do to help?" The

shopkeeper was genuinely concerned for Madam's well-being. She knew of the kidnapping and some of the other tragedies. She felt for her. Wanted to support her in any way that she could.

"I have no money for the cigarettes. I'm sorry, Rosa. And now I don't know what I am going to do. I need my wallet, so that I can pay you and get a cab to the airport."

"You're leaving?"

"Yes, well, extended vacation of sorts. Except that I can't lie to you, yes I am leaving, I have to. I won't be coming back." Her voice was strained, her face showed her stress.

"Children too? And what about your husband? Is he leaving too?" Rosa was curious.

"No, he will be staying. For a very long time I think. I will take the kids with me yes."

Rosa reached into the pocket of her dress. In her pocket was still the one-hundred-dollar bill that she had been given earlier that morning. "Take this. This should get you to where it's safe. To the airport and it should help with whatever else you need." She slid the bill across the counter towards Madam.

"I can't take that from you, there's no way. You must have been saving this for something special."

"Actually I have only had it for a short time and the person that gave it to me told me to put it to good use. This feels like it's good. Go, be safe. And try to keep in touch."

The two women held each other's gaze, and then Madam picked up the cigarettes, shoved them and the hundred into her purse, thanked her friend, and dashed out the door and back to her car. The shopkeeper thought about the purse she might have bought, or the shoes. Maybe the dress, and then she thought of her friend, that she would likely never see again. She wondered why she was leaving so abruptly, but she knew that there had to be a reason, and a good one. She was happy to have helped her. And she felt good knowing that she had done something positive today. Rosa had done something to make a difference. She could die tonight knowing that the world might just be a better place after all.

From where Juan sat alone on the beach, holding Madam's wallet in his lap; he watched the interaction between the two women. He was pleased with Rosa's decision to hand over the hundred, and he made a mental note to have her taken care of. He would ensure that her actions were compensated for.

"God Bless you, Rosa." He smiled and held his hands in prayer.

CHAPTER 77

She sat in Her room and waited while Her mother was preparing for their departure. She looked over all of Her dolls, and Her favourite dresses and wondered which ones She would be able to take with Her, and which ones would have to be sacrificed. She had Her favourite doll, which could not be left behind. She was a Cabbage Patch doll with a pink lacy top and bottoms. She had red hair and freckles to match Her own.

She thought about pulling out a bag that She could pack, but Her mother had asked Her just to sit and wait. She didn't want to do anything to upset anyone. So She sat, with Her book, and Her doll and Her closet doors open. Her dresses hanging beautifully inside, Her shoes and accessories all neatly lined up in rows.

She was too upset to read, so She decided to sit and pray. There was never any harm in praying, and She always felt relaxed after.

"Dear Lord, thank you for today, for the sun and for the moon that lights our way at night, thank you for the abundance that You provide, and the grace You give us to recognize that it comes from You and not from our own hands. Thank you for my Mother, and for my Father, and I ask that You bless them, Lord, in their ways and in their travels. I pray today for a safe voyage, and a comfortable place to land. I would also like to ask that whatever it is, Lord, that is brewing for my Father, that you be easy on him, and forgive him, Father. His ignorance should not yield him a victim in this case, but if he is truly guilty of all of the things that they may say, then again I ask that you take it easy on him. He is my only daddy, and even if the world doesn't love him, *I do*. For this and all things I pray in Jesus name, Amen."

She sat and patiently waited, Her mind wandering. Her thoughts often drifted to her birth, the difficulty, the strain and the delays. The pure anguish of waiting, wondering if She would survive that leg of Her journey. In the minutes after She was born, She lay in the bassinette, brown eyes open, alert and making eye contact with the nurses, the doctors and Her loved ones. She knew their voices, She recognized those who had spoken to Her while She was in the womb, of that there was no question. She lay naked and watched people move around Her, her tiny head turning from side to side, Her eyes following each person as it became busier in the room. Her hands reached up towards Her face and she placed Her fingers into her mouth, her tiny nails catching on her lip. She surprised Herself with their sharp edges. She listened as those who had come and who spoke about Her in wonder and awe.

Her mother was clearly there with Her, and Her grandmother, there were doctors and nurses. Her mind searched the memory for the face of Her father. He was not there. Not in Her memory. She searched again. Her mind raced through the visions in her databanks like running through a film reel on fast forward, and found nothing. She had an audio of his voice before She had made Her great debut, but as she lay in the bassinette, he was absent.

She focused on Her father's face, trying to see him, trying to find him. Knowing that he must have been there. He had to have been there. She meditated and zoomed in on him. Searching desperately to find him.

She saw him, his face, but not in the delivery room at the hospital where She had been born. She saw him with a man, in dark clothing, a suit, with a necktie. They were having a conversation. She wasn't able to hear what was being said, but she could feel the energy between them. Her father was nervous, he was suppressing anger and resentment; but he continued to smile and laugh. The other man, who wore the dark suit was suspicious and alarmed, he also laughed but he was hiding feelings of doubt. He didn't believe what Her father was telling him.

The two men exchanged something, her father handed the man a duffle bag. And the man gave him a navy blue school bag in return. She recognized the bag, She could see the emblem of Her current school on it.

Her body felt as though it was floating. Like an untethered balloon She was hovering above the two men. But the two of them were not aware of Her being there. She tried desperately to listen to the conversation, but could hear nothing but the sound of Her own breathing. Her breath softly caressing the air as She exhaled. She continued to watch, as Her father turned to leave the second man, She saw on his shoulder the knapsack. The very knapsack that She had seen just that morning while She sat on the sofa with Her father.

She opened Her eyes quickly. She was startled by the vision and by the realization that it was not one of Her typical memories. Inhaling deeply in a swift gasp she shouted, "Mary Mack, what is happening to me? *That was not a memory. It could not have been*. I have only seen that knapsack once. Mary! Mary Mack!"

The tiny six-year-old girl, with auburn hair and fair skin sat shaking on Her bed, beneath Her was the urine-soaked quilt that had kept the evening chill at bay while She normally slept. Her assigned warrior watched Her without being seen, and then moved on.

CHAPTER 78

The front door of the residence opened, and Her father entered the house. His footsteps were loud and hurried as he moved into the living area.

"Madam!" He bellowed, his voice heated. "Madam!"

Her mother had expected more time to prepare. She came out of the bedroom and greeted him. "Hello."

She opened Her bedroom door slightly and peeked into the living room. She strained to hear the exchange of conversation.

Her father had something in his hands, She opened the door farther, enabling Her to get a better look. He turned his back towards Her just then and She could see the knapsack on his left shoulder. It appeared to be very heavy, as though it was loaded with rubble; rocks or bricks.

"Madam, I have found some shit on you that I just can't live with."

"What kind of "shit" would you be talking about? You're lying."

"No, I am not." He turned ninety degrees to the left, she could see from where She hid behind the door, the navy blue school bag in his left hand. Instinct told Her to close the door, something else deep within Her however kept Her standing there, in Her wet shorts and panties.

"I'm leaving, I'm leaving you. Do you understand?" Madam was calm, her voice at an even tone, not soothing, but not in any way threatening.

He bellowed, "You know, I don't even care any more, I'm

so sick of you and your needs. Go fuck yourself, bitch. But you go alone. I told you before, and I will tell you again. You are not taking my children anywhere. I have taken care of that. So grab your shit and get the fuck out. You leave alone, and penniless."

She held her cards, without wanting to reveal her next move to him she said, "I will have you served with divorce papers as soon as possible. Make sure that I can find you."

"I won't sign them, I will never give you what you want. You want to fuck that policeman, go ahead, you want to leave me, go for it. But I wont *ever*, *ever* as long as I live, give you a divorce. I will keep you prisoner without having to actually deal with your nagging nasty shit every day."

She snickered at him. "Fine, whatever, I don't care. I just want out. You cleaned out my bank accounts, and mortgaged my house and my business, you have ruined me; I have nothing left. I need some money. I know you have all of mine, and Lord knows what else that you have stolen or skimmed from people, I want you to give me some before I go."

He glared at her. "Not a chance, you can go, and you can take what you can carry, but you will never get a cent out of me, you fucking cunt." His voice roared, loud and aggressive. His fist was raised to strike her but their son ran out of his room reaching his arms towards his mother.

"No, Dad." He lunged forward and grabbed the vase full of flowers from the coffee table, and with all of the roses still in it, threw it across the room. The sound of the glass shattering shook all of them. The surprise slowed things down for a brief second, and then all of them took a breath.

With one swift blow, Her father struck Her brother across the cheek; his strength and the force of the swing knocking him to the floor. The boy landed on his back, his head crashing against the cool Spanish marble.

She ran from where She had been hiding in the bedroom. She bent down to where Her brother lay on the floor, and touched his chest with Her hands. "Are you okay?"

The boy sat up, and shook his head. "No… Yes, Mommy?"

Madam reached down for her son, and checked the back of his head for visible signs of injury. He was tough, built also from stone perhaps, he had the strength of an ox and the constitution of a great fighter. He took his mother's hand and stood. "That is the last time." Madam raged. Both children sat on the floor beside her, their eyes wide with fright.

She looked at Her father from where she knelt. In his left hand he still held the navy school bag. She wanted to reach for it, but something held Her back. She was frozen, unable to move. She watched his face from where She was, the lines and creases seemed more etched to Her than ever before. Perhaps she hadn't noticed them, or perhaps he too was just so tired. He appeared old, and weathered.

"You can take what you can carry. I will never give you what you want. Ever, I can promise you that, I wish I never would have married you. You've been nothing but a pain in my ass from day one. If you leave you are not coming back, ever."

With that Madam pivoted on her heel and picked Her up, allowing her daughter to sit on her hip; grabbed her purse from the table and took the hand of her still wobbly boy. The three of them moved towards the front door, while Her father stood screaming profanities at Her mother. "Walk out and we are done! You hear me? Finished! There is no coming back from this, Madam." The rant continued from behind them as they ran down the front steps of the residence with nothing but Madam's purse and what little amount of dignity they still had left.

CHAPTER 79

Madam hailed a taxi, and the three of them piled into the backseat together. "To the Airport please." She hugged both of her children. "I am so sorry that you had to see that. And I am sorry that he hit you. Are you okay, honey?"

The youngster rubbed the back of his head. "I think he almost broke my head this time. But I'm fine ya, Mom."

She looked up at Her mother. "Mommy, do you know what he had in the bag?"

"Which bag, Sweetie?" Madam hadn't noticed a bag in all of the commotion.

"He had a navy bag from our school, in his hand. What was in it?" She was surprised that Her mother hadn't noticed the bag, as it was to Her significant.

Madam thought for a moment, going over the scene, trying to remember the bag. "I'm not sure why."

"He didn't have that bag this morning, only the old stinky knapsack." She replayed the entire morning over in Her mind, the conversation She had seen with the man in the dark suit, the argument, the vase crashing to the floor, Her brother being hit and knocked down.

"'scuse me, lady?" Their driver was looking at Madam in the rear-view mirror.

"Yes, I'm sorry?" Madam responded.

"There is an SUV, big one, *muy grande*, black one, lady, see? Following us from your house. Should I stop? Did you forget something?"

Madam turned around to look. A large black SUV was racing up behind them. "No, don't stop, we didn't forget anything, we just need to get to the airport."

"Okay, lady, everyting okay wit you? I mean I don't want no trouble, just a fare, that's all I needed today."

"That's my husband. We are leaving him, going back home. Yes everything is going to be fine."

"Did he hit the boy, lady? Is that what happened?"

Madam nodded, with tears in her eyes she answered him. "That and many other things. I have to make a quick phone call, I don't mean to be rude."

The heavyset driver nodded at her in acknowledgement. "Course, I'm sorry, didn't mean to pry."

"Please don't apologize, there is no need." Madam took out her phone and dialled the number for Agent Mendez. He answered on the first ring. "Mendez."

"Agent Mendez, it's Madam... I am in a cab, with both of my children, travelling north on Juarez. My husband is in his black SUV chasing us."

"Madam? What is going on? I am en route to your residence."

"We seemed to get into an argument. I am in a cab, he is behind us."

"Cross street, Madam? Please."

"Allende."

"We are close, Madam. Tell your driver to stay on Juarez, we will catch you. What is your destination, Madam?"

Madam pressed end. She then dialled again, this time Jorge Alvarez answered. "Jorge, I am on my way to the airport, I can't stay. I hope you can understand."

"Where are you going, Madam? I will find you."

"I can't say, Jorge, I will call when it's safe."

Jorge closed his eyes and placed his head into his free hand. "I'm sorry, Madam."

"Me too." She pressed end again, terminated her fleeting moment with the Police chief; turned her phone off and threw it in her purse. She was sorry, in more ways than she was able to express. She was sorry for so many things. She was sorry that her children had been exposed to such a life, she was sorry that she had chosen not to see it. She was sorry that she had stayed as long as she did. And she was sorry that she was now leaving a country, where she had worked and laboured so hard, with nothing but her own life and her two children as salvage.

CHAPTER 80

She watched out the back window of the cab, the Black SUV chasing them through the streets. She wanted to believe that Her father was sad that they were leaving, but Her instinct told Her otherwise. The hair on Her arms stood up as She watched him manoeuvre the vehicle around others and wanted to wave to him. Like She would if She were leaving on the school bus, or if he was just coming home from a business trip. She felt gloomy on the inside, Her heart was heavy, like she was carrying around that knapsack that Her father refused to leave behind or let Her see inside. She still found his behaviour strange, his movements and meetings. She kept reflecting on the vision with the man in the suit, and the exchange of bags. She continued to wonder what was in the navy school bag, and what Her father was doing with it.

The cab driver pulled into the airport entrance, slamming on the brakes of his beat-up Toyota Corolla as he reached the departures' doors. "Lady, here we are. The airport."

Madam smiled at him, she was reluctant, to speak, but needed to. She took the hundred from her purse and held it towards him. "This is all that I have."

He looked at her in the rear-view mirror, a smirk on his face. "You kidding me, Lady? That's all you got? I don't have change for a hundred."

Madam was on the verge of tears again. "It's all I have. I am so sorry but I don't have any pesos. This is the best that I can do today."

The cabbie looked in the mirror again, he could see the SUV and the Federal Vehicles approaching. "Lady, just go. Forget about it. Go. I dunno who those guys coming are, but they been on our tail since we left your house. You need to go. Go. Be safe. Hurry."

Madam grabbed her purse and the hands of the two children. She had heard the term "Be Safe" twice today, she assumed it was a sign. She opened the door of the cab and escaped the tin box. She paused before she closed the door, looked at the driver and said, "Thank you." She noted the number of his cab, 3447; turned and ran into the building.

Madam could see the Continental Airlines check-in counter, in front of it was a cluster of people. She instantly worried about lining up and the probability of a clean exit. She hadn't told Agent Mendez of her planned departure, and she was now certain that her husband had not believed she would actually leave him.

The two children ran as quickly as they could falling slightly behind her. Madam could hear commotion happening, she chose to ignore it and forged onward. She focused on the check-in counter. She was able to see the face of the Canadian Consular, Sarah Ryner, and the head of immigration Señor Felipe Calderone standing at the counter for the airline. She ran to them.

"Madam." Sarah Ryner spoke first. "Your Father called me regarding paperwork for the children. I have brought Señor Calderone with me to exercise the signatures."

Madam looked behind her and saw her husband running towards them, he had his knapsack over his shoulder, and in his hand the navy blue school bag. Behind him just coming through the doors to the airport were the Federal Agents,

Mendez leading them.

"Thank you, Sarah, I cannot thank you enough."

Sarah Ryner looked at Madam empathetically. "I spoke with your father in length this morning, Madam, I am so sorry for all that you have gone through. On behalf of the Canadian Government, I would like to wish you safe travels, and please if there is anything that we can do, please do not hesitate to let us know. Your father is a very special man, he obviously loves you very much."

"Yes he is, and yes he does." Madam was grateful for the acknowledgement.

Señor Calderone spoke. "Madam, for Mexico, we too wish you safe travels home to Canada, these papers are everything that you will need to clear Mexican customs with the children. Please pass through security with me now. I will accompany you. Come now please."

The head of immigration for the state of Jalisco, walked with Madam and the two children behind the glass partition, to where they would need to clear security before boarding their flight. The children could still see their father as he approached the area, screaming and crying. Behind him the Federal Agents were on top of him. A crowd of people had gathered, all of them watching the episode as it unfolded.

Her brother broke free of Madam's grip and ran towards the glass. He could see and hear his father without physically touching him. The agents were now attempting to manipulate him onto the ground. Three of them using force to bend his arms and legs at the joints. His knees buckled and he went crashing down onto the tile floor. His face smashing into the glass his cheeks and lips distorting his appearance.

"DAD!" He screeched! "Mom, what are they doing to Dad?!"

Her father managed to get one hand free and reached into the knapsack that Juan had provided him the day before, he felt pressured and he knew that this was one time that he could use some help. He reached deep into the bag but without checking his own intentions, he pulled from the empty bag a Colt Pocket Hammerless Pistol, which filled his hand and startled his opponents. Time slowed to a crawl. Everyone's movements became magnified.

She screamed. "Daddy has a gun!"

Her father's eyes met Hers. Sorrow filled Her heart as She saw a broken man in front of Her. On the floor, he was desperate and needy, wanting change but ignorant of how to accomplish it; She saw into his soul, the pain, the history, the anguish. She saw his transgressions and his path of destruction, his lies and deceit. She felt his desire for women and his hunger for money, his lust for power and his hatred for Her own mother.

The Agents drew their own weapons. "Stop! Don't hurt him," She shouted. "Please don't hurt my Daddy!" He looked up at Her and saw the tears rolling down Her cheeks, Her hand still in Madam's. Her brother stood just inches in front of him. His blond hair falling on his forehead, his palm pressed against the transparent barrier between them. A single pane of bullet proof glass was all that physically separated them, their worlds however would never again meet.

The Agents handcuffed Her father, and stood him to his feet, the children watched as he was marched away from them. She could see only a red box in her mind, red for anger, red for sorrow.

Madam stood shaking, looking at the empty knapsack on the floor. Her plane tickets, passports and immigration papers in hand; a senior immigration official beside her.

Juan Maria de Salvatierria pushed a tooth pick into his teeth and turned away. He smiled at Mary Mack who stood beside Her. Mary nodded at Juan, and straightened the front of her black silk dress, silver buttons all down her back. She hoped the flight to Canada wasn't too long. She was never particularly comfortable on commercial flights. This one however would be her pleasure.

Made in the USA
Charleston, SC
29 January 2017